THE
SLEEPING
GIRLS

BOOKS BY RITA HERRON

THE
SLEEPING
GIRLS

RITA HERRON

bookouture

Published by Bookouture in 2024

An imprint of Storyfire Ltd.
Carmelite House
50 Victoria Embankment
London EC4Y 0DZ

www.bookouture.com

ISBN: 978-1-83790-671-0
eBook ISBN: 978-1-83790-670-3

He poses them as if they were sleeping...

PROLOGUE
HAYES STATE PRISON

All Darnell, AKA Digger, Woodruff wanted was to leave this hellhole in prison and go home. But even if he was released, that would be a mistake.

His stepfather and little brother hated him. And who could blame them? He'd murdered his little sister.

He stared at his shaking hands as he sat on the narrow prison cot. Hands that reminded him of what he'd done.

Last night, he'd had the nightmare again. Only it hadn't been a nightmare because it was real.

He'd been sleepwalking that night. It had been happening all his life. As a child, he'd end up in bed with his parents or outside in the treehouse or down the street peeing in some neighbor's driveway. One time, he'd been digging a small hole in the backyard. Another, he'd been standing on a ledge about to jump off.

Anna Marie's face haunted him. His little sister.

He'd been sixteen at the time of his arrest. Locked away like a monster.

Sixteen and scrawny and a perfect target for the prison gangs. He'd been beaten. Shanked. Raped.

Footsteps sounded as a guard approached. And he shut out the memories.

"Let's go, Digger," the guard said as he unlocked his cell. The metal-on-metal turning of the key grated on his last nerve. The guard, a two-fifty-plus man with a mean streak in his eyes, patted his baton and motioned for him to get up.

Digger dragged himself from his cot and shuffled to the door, half-expecting to be hauled to one of the no-camera zone rooms where the guards took you to supposedly teach you a lesson. The lesson was to bend over and do whatever the hell they wanted. He'd tried fighting at first until they'd beaten the fight out of him.

"Might be your lucky day," the bastard said as he jerked Digger's hands behind him and cuffed him. "Some pretty lady done come to your rescue."

Digger frowned at that. The only lady he'd seen since he'd been moved here was a woman named Caitlin O'Connor who had a true crime podcast associated with the Innocence Project. It was run by a do-gooder organization of lawyers and investigators who actually wanted to find the truth and free inmates who'd been falsely convicted. She'd taken it upon herself to look into his case and had questioned him half a dozen times already, forcing him to relive the night he killed Anna Marie.

Not that he had any hope she'd succeed.

Digger was, after all, the seed of some evil loser from Red Clay Mountain who'd screwed his mother and left her high and dry, barefoot and pregnant. His stepfather, Gil, had swept in to save her and her bastard child—*him*—but he never let Digger forget for a second that he was pure dirt.

Shouts and jeers from the other prisoners boomeranged off the concrete walls as he was escorted down the hallways and led to the visiting room.

The guard opened a locked heavy metal door and shoved

him inside, standing close to him with his baton ready, in case Digger decided to pull a stunt and run.

"Sit," the guard instructed as he pushed him into a chair bolted to the floor.

Digger sat. Legs spread out. Cuffed hands on the table. Wondering where the hell all this was going.

It was probably the public defender telling him that, yet again, his parole hearing was declined. No, the guard had said it was a woman.

A minute later, Caitlin O'Connor stepped inside.

A man in a three-piece suit followed.

She waited until they sat, and the guard stepped outside. "Hello, Darnell," she said. "This is Ethan Baldwin, the attorney who's been working with me."

Darnell simply stared at them. Waiting for the bad news to drop.

Instead, Ms. O'Connor smiled. "You're being released on parole, Darnell."

He swallowed hard. "What?"

She squeezed his hand. "We're working to get you a new trial. But for now, you can go home."

Home? He didn't have a home anymore. Even if he went back, no one wanted him there.

ONE

RED CLAY MOUNTAIN

Three weeks later

Some men were not meant to be fathers. Some women were not meant to be mothers.

And some children were the victims of this.

The blood that ran through their veins was troubled. As was his.

The night sounds brought the demons. The whine of the wind. Leaves crackling. Storm raging.

Just like it had that night fifteen years ago. He'd relived the memory every day since. Now it played through his mind in vivid clarity.

The window was open. A storm striking the mountains just as a storm raged inside him. She'd turned fifteen today. The age where she was somewhere between a woman and a child. Wanting to watch R-rated movies. Yet still sleeping with her teddy bear at night.

She was the picture of innocence.

Yet now that innocence was gone.

Her angelic face stared up at him with trusting eyes. He

loved her so much. Couldn't get her out of his mind. Was consumed by his feelings.

But she had to die.

Shock glazed her eyes as he approached her bed. Then fear. She looked as if she was going to scream.

He didn't give her time. He snagged the heart-shaped pillow from her bed and lurched toward her. In one sudden movement, he pressed the pillow over her face, straddled her slender body and pinned her to the bed.

She kicked and clawed at him. Cried out for help. But he pressed harder on the pillow, drowning out the sound. Her fingernails dug into his arms. A muffled sob escaped her. Then a strangled sound.

Perspiration beaded on his upper lip. He pressed more firmly on the pillow and snuffed out her life. Her body jerked and spasmed. Seconds ticked by. A minute. Two. He lost count.

Another minute that felt like an eternity, then she gasped. Took her final breath. Her body went still.

Tonight, as he watched the young girls through the bedroom window, his hunger mounted. The three of them were what they called besties. They shared secrets. Dreams.

Dreams they would never get to fulfill.

Dreams that would end just as Anna Marie's had.

A car pulled up, lights blaring, and he ducked into the shadows of the woods. Dammit, her parents were home. He couldn't take her tonight.

But soon he would. Until then, he'd keep watching and waiting. And when the perfect moment came, he'd kiss her goodbye.

TWO

BLUFF COUNTY HOSPITAL

Cord was gone.

Detective Ellie Reeves searched blindly in the dark, shouting his name. One minute, she was running through the woods, tripping over brush and sticks, the next she was trapped in a cold basement with him. Gas was coming through the vent.

She clawed at the door to escape. Tried to yell out for help.

Monsters lurked all around her. Beady eyes bore into her. The wind howled like a mad animal.

She and Cord... He'd come to rescue her. But he was hurt. Unconscious.

Not breathing.

She jerked awake and glanced at the clock. Seven a.m. It was early but her irrational fear took hold. She'd been worried about him, but never had this feeling before. She had to check on Cord in the hospital before heading to work.

Forcing a calming breath, she threw her feet over the edge of the bed.

The wood floor felt cold beneath her feet.

She rushed to the closet. Threw off her pajamas and dragged on jeans and a T-shirt.

Tugging her hair into a ponytail, she grabbed her phone and weapon from her nightstand then snagged her keys. Seconds later, she stepped outside into the early morning light and climbed in her Jeep.

Rain from the night before made the roads slick as she drove toward the hospital.

"You can't leave me, Cord," she whispered. "You can't."

Ten minutes later, she swung the Jeep into the parking lot, cut the engine then jumped out and rushed to the entrance. Nurses and other staff were bustling through the halls. Breakfast carts clattered. The scent of antiseptic and cleaning chemicals suffused her, making her nauseous. Machines beeped and whirred as she passed patient rooms.

By the time she reached Cord's, she'd finally calmed her nerves.

She peeked through the open door and saw Lola Parks, the owner of the Corner Café, sitting by his bed, spoon-feeding him eggs. Cord pushed her hand away as well as the plate.

Lola's back was to Ellie, and Ellie hesitated. Didn't Lola realize how much Cord hated to be hovered over?

Although she and Cord—Ranger McClain—had shared a night together years ago, they'd settled into a friendship since. He was the best tracker on the Search and Rescue (SAR) team with FEMA, and had been working with her and Special Agent Fox on a task force to solve crimes in the mountains. The Appalachian Trail, with over 2,200 miles of untamed forest, wildlife and isolated areas, had become a hotbed of crime. And a place for criminals to hide.

As if Lola sensed Ellie's presence, she pivoted, her gaze locking with Ellie's through the window in the door. Lola stiffened, eyes narrowing and pinning Ellie to the spot.

Ellie opened the door and stepped inside. "He's awake?" she said softly.

"He woke up last night and has been alert off and on for

hours." Her voice was as tight as her forced smile. "He asked for you this morning."

Ellie swallowed hard at Lola's angry look. Almost losing Cord to death had stirred feelings she hadn't even realized she had.

But she couldn't act upon them. Cord was having a baby with Lola.

THREE

Cord McClain's cheeks burned as Ellie stepped inside the hospital room. He felt like he'd slept for a year, but had woken last night and this morning felt almost normal. He'd also remembered that Lola was pregnant.

Had heard her crying and begging him to come back to her and her baby. *Their* baby.

His fingers curled into the sheets and he clenched them into a fist. He hated being confined to a bed like a damn weakling. He was a doer, not a sitter. A man who rescued and saved others, not a guy who needed waiting on by a team of nurses. Or by anybody. And he certainly didn't want pity. Or Lola hovering over him like a mother hen.

What was he going to do?

His heart skipped a beat as Ellie approached and Lola stepped into the hall. Ellie looked tired and worried and so damn beautiful that she stole his breath. Except for her stubbornness, he liked everything about her.

Hell, he even liked the stubbornness.

Her sandy-blond ponytail swung when she walked. Her soft blue eyes were soulful, loving and tough at the same time.

And he admired her fierce determination, even when she threw herself under the bus to save someone else.

"Hi," she said softly as she rested her hand on the bedrail.

Dammit, he felt grungy and needed a shower and a shave bad.

"How are you feeling?" Ellie asked.

He rubbed a hand over his beard stubble. "Like I want out of here."

She laughed softly. She hated hospitals as much as he did. "What does your doctor say?"

"Another day stuck here," Cord said. "You were put through the ringer, El. How are *you* feeling?"

Ellie absentmindedly rubbed her arm. She'd dislocated her shoulder during a fight with a killer and it still throbbed at times. "It's been three weeks now, so I'm good. Especially now I got rid of that sling. How the hell was I supposed to shoot a gun with that thing on?"

He was the one who laughed this time.

But as his laugh died, tension stretched between them, an awkwardness that was new and unsettling. Cord wasn't good at small talk, and he didn't know how to fill the silence.

Or whether to say what was on his mind.

"Thanks for rescuing my butt," he finally said.

Ellie shrugged. "Back at you."

Cord gave a quick nod. They made a good team. He didn't want to lose that. But how could he declare his feelings knowing he was going to be a father? That still hadn't sunk in.

Ellie shot a look at the door, a reminder Lola was in the hall.

"El, I wanted to tell you—"

"I know you and Lola are having a baby," Ellie said, cutting him off. "Congratulations."

His tongue felt thick in his throat. He still couldn't believe it.

He didn't know how to be a father. He'd never known his own. His foster father had been cruel and demented.

Cord made a sarcastic sound. "I don't deserve a child." Not after what had happened years ago.

"That's not true, Cord. You'll be a great father," Ellie said with a smile.

Memories clogged his mind. He started to argue that point, but the door opened and Lola stepped into the room, eyes darting to Ellie with a menacing glare, then honing in on Cord. A smile curved her mouth as she pressed a hand over the small baby bump and crossed to him.

Ellie lifted her hand in a wave. "Get better, Cord."

Cord clutched the sheets between his fingers, his heart in his throat as she slipped out the door and closed it behind her. A sinking feeling overcame him, a feeling that he'd lost Ellie.

But how could you lose someone you'd never had?

FOUR

WHISPERING PINES

One week later—Friday night

The wind whispered through the tall pines, the quarter moon barely noticeable with the storm clouds that darkened the night sky. Fallen leaves crunched beneath his boots as he moved closer to Kelsey Tiller's house.

He'd been watching her for days now. Knew she was popular at school. That she played the piano. He'd stood outside her house and heard her practicing. She obviously had an ear for music. Too bad she wouldn't live to reach her potential.

He also knew she had a crush on a kicker named Mitch Drummond and that he snuck into her room at night. She left the window of her bedroom unlocked for Mitch to get in.

Her parents had no idea.

They were too caught up in their own lives and affairs to take notice. Instead, they practiced deceit and betrayal.

The girl was already starting to follow in their footsteps.

The wind grew stronger, hurling dead leaves across the ground. The rocking chairs creaked from the force of the wind as if ghosts occupied them. Inside, the house was dark and quiet. The mother had turned in and the father had left earlier, carrying an overnight bag with him.

But tonight, things were different. Kelsey had climbed out of the window and she and Mitch had gone into the woods. He followed, staying in the shadows of the trees and watching. Kelsey was crying. Started screaming. The boy was arguing with her about something. Their voices got lost in the wind but something was definitely wrong.

Seconds later, she took off running. Mitch called her name and chased after her. More shouting.

"Leave me alone!" Kelsey screamed.

Finally, the boy jogged back the other way.

He smiled, stretched then went after the girl. Here in the woods, she was finally alone. It was the perfect time to take her.

FIVE

CROOKED CREEK POLICE STATION

Saturday

Early morning sunlight tried to fight its way through storm clouds as Ellie drove toward the police station.

A myriad of emotions as gloomy as the dark sky raged in her heart. Should she tell Cord how she felt?

If she did, it was bound to cause problems.

Was she that selfish?

Cord and Lola's baby deserved to have the love of both their parents. Would there be wedding bells for them in the future?

She shouldn't care. Dammit. But she did.

She shut off her thoughts. Couldn't dwell on what might have been. Ellie Reeves lived in reality, not daydreams.

Signs advertising Octoberfest adorned the town along with fall decorations. The mountains were a rainbow of green, red, yellow and orange, drawing tourists to enjoy the fall foliage. At the edge of town, Clarence Stancil had already created his popular corn maze by his pumpkin patch where he offered hayrides. In town, there would be tents with arts and crafts, food trucks, a farmer's market boasting local products that included jams, jellies, cheeses, fruits and vegetables, candles and soaps, and a stage erected for various musical guests. Other signs advertised that it was "Homecoming Week" for the high school, always a big event in a small town.

The rival schools of Crooked Creek and Stony Gap always made for an exciting homecoming game. The dance was the highlight of the season, with mothers and daughters bonding over finding the perfect dress, teens' flirting and young love sprouting.

Not that she'd known young love or homecoming dances, which had disappointed her adoptive mother, Vera, to no end. Instead, she'd loved maps and hiking with her father.

Her phone buzzed on her hip. She snagged it, saw it was her boss and connected the call.

"Captain?"

"We may have a missing teen. Kelsey Tiller, age fifteen. Parents called in hysterical. I'll text you the address."

Ellie heaved a breath, checked the address and turned the Jeep around. "On my way, Captain."

A rainy mist began to fall as if the mountains were already crying for the missing teen. The wet roads and fog forced her to a crawl as she wound around the curves and hills leading to Whispering Pines, a neighborhood catering to the middle class. The name of the area originated from the fact that when the wind blew through the tall trees it sounded as if the trees were actually whispering among themselves, keeping the secrets of those that traveled along the trail.

Deer and other wildlife roamed freely though the surrounding woods. Ellie's tires chugged over the narrow drive to a gorgeous white farmhouse set on a hill with an immaculately groomed yard. Pansies and black-eyed Susans added color to the greenery and bird feeders gave the impression the family enjoyed nature.

By the time she parked, Deputy Eastwood had pulled up

behind her, Deputy Landrum in the passenger seat. Shondra's expression was grim as she climbed from the vehicle and surveyed the exterior of the house.

Deputy Landrum looked rough around the edges, his dirty-blond hair spiked and mussed, dark circles beneath his eyes as if he hadn't slept. He was a computer whiz which was advantageous to the team, but Ellie didn't know much about his personal life. Maybe he was coming down with something? Or he'd been partying the night before?

She didn't care what he did on his own time, as long as he did his job.

"Missing fifteen-year-old," she told them as they stepped onto the path to the porch. "Hopefully she just snuck out for the night."

"I ran a background on the Tillers on the way," Landrum said. "They seem like a solid family. Mother is on the school PTA board, also volunteers for Meals on Wheels. Family belongs to a nondenominational church. Father works in pharmaceuticals. Financials solid. No record on either of them."

"Thanks," Ellie said. With an adult and no evidence of suspicious circumstances, police might wait thirty-four to seventy-two hours before considering a person missing. But with juveniles, they acted immediately in case they were dealing with a runaway or a kidnapping.

Either one would mean Kelsey Tiller was in danger.

SIX

WHISPERING PINES

A couple of neighbors stood on their porches in the sleepy little community, curious as Ellie and the deputies headed toward the wraparound porch.

Flowers and bird feeders painted a warm, homey feel, and a pond and garden to the right of the house gave the impression of a picture-perfect home. Yet the mountains and woods backed the property, the tall ridges and overhangs daunting. So many miles of untamed forest in the Appalachian Mountains. So many places to hide.

The way the house was situated on the property, a predator could sneak up behind the house and enter without being seen. Recluses, hillbillies and criminals had sought refuge out in the thick forests before, and Ellie tried not to think of the number of bodies they'd found during previous cases.

Although, with a girl missing, it was hard not to imagine the worst.

"Deputy Landrum," Ellie said. "Look around the property for signs someone was outside last night or if there was an intruder."

Dread knotted her stomach as she knocked on the door,

which stood ajar. She and Shondra entered the house and heard
voices from the living room, which was visible from the foyer. A
dark-haired man in gray slacks and a dress shirt was pacing and
looked frazzled, his shoes clicking on the white oak floor. A
woman in leggings and an oversized shirt stood facing him, her
hands thumbing through her short brown bob, her cheeks tear-
stained.

"Where were you last night, Tim?" the woman screamed.

"Where were *you*, Jean?" the man shouted.

"Here in bed," the woman cried. "I had a headache and fell
asleep."

"Without setting the security system," the man said, his
nostrils flaring.

"Because I thought you were coming home," she yelled.
"But you were out all night with some floozy while our daughter
disappeared."

"And we both know your headache was vodka-induced," he
bit out.

Ellie cleared her throat. "Excuse me, please. You're the
Tillers?"

The couple jerked their heads toward her then the man
nodded. "Tim and Jean."

"I'm Detective Ellie Reeves and this is Deputy Shondra
Eastwood. I know you're worried, but I need you to tell me
what happened."

Mrs. Tiller dabbed at her eyes with a tissue. "This morning
I went to wake Kelsey for breakfast. She usually sleeps in on
Saturdays, but we had plans to go dress shopping for Home-
coming today."

"Was she in bed when you went to sleep last night?" Ellie
asked.

Mrs. Tiller shook her head. "No, but she was in her room
for the night, looking at her phone, probably texting her friends.

They were all excited about Homecoming and planning what stores they wanted to go to."

"Did anything in her room look out of the ordinary?" Ellie asked.

"No, not really. I checked her bathroom and she wasn't there either. I ran all over the house looking for her. And I called her phone a half dozen times but it went straight to voicemail."

Ellie didn't like the direction this was going. "You said she was excited about Homecoming. Who was she going with?"

"Her girlfriends," Mrs. Tiller said. "Girls do that these days, you know."

Ellie arched a brow. "Was there a boyfriend or special girl-friend in the picture?"

"No." Mr. Tiller halted his anxious pacing, his tone emphatic. "Our daughter was not into boys."

Ellie wasn't sure she believed that. Socializing and dating were everything to teenagers. But if Kelsey had a boyfriend or if she was into girls, she obviously hadn't shared that with her parents.

Deputy Eastwood covered a cough with her hand. "May I get a glass of water?"

"Sure, glasses are in the cupboard to the right of the sink," Mrs. Tiller said.

Ellie and Shondra exchanged a look, and Ellie knew it was an excuse to poke around in the kitchen.

"Go on, Mrs. Tiller," Ellie said.

"Jean, please call me Jean."

"All right," Ellie said. "Let's talk about Kelsey. Was she worried about something? Having problems with a teacher or friend?"

"No, no. She played piano and was on the Honor Roll," Jean continued, her leg bouncing up and down nervously.

"Tell me about yesterday and last night," Ellie said.

Jean glanced at her husband, who glared back at her, then twined her fingers together. "Everything seemed fine. She had orchestra practice yesterday as usual. She plays the piano and flute. She came home talking about the piece they'd chosen to play for the halftime show." She jumped up from the couch, hurriedly crossed to the bookcase and returned with a framed photograph of Kelsey and two other girls.

"That's Ruby and June, her best friends."

In the photograph, the girls looked happy, close. Kelsey was a slender blond with green eyes and a timid smile. "Your daughter is beautiful," Ellie said. "She was looking forward to the band performance?"

Jean nodded. "The kids had persuaded the band leader to let them play a more contemporary piece this year. That was a big win since he's used the same music for the last three years."

"Was she upset about anything else? Had a falling out with one of her friends?"

"No, nothing like that," Jean said, her voice rising. "I told you she was excited. Happy. Well adjusted."

Mr. Tiller whirled on her. "Now why aren't you out there looking for her?"

"I am going to do that. But it helps to know Kelsey's mind-set. If she was upset or had a disagreement with a friend, she might have snuck out to see them."

Mr. Tiller's eyes snapped with fire just as his tone did. "She would never sneak out. Never, you hear me. So don't come in here bashing my daughter."

Ellie reined in her irritation. "I'm not doing that, sir, but in order to find Kelsey I need to know everything about her."

"She's trying to help," Jean said to her husband. "When I realized Kelsey was gone this morning, I called all her friends. None of them have heard from her since last night."

Ellie kept an open mind. If Kelsey had snuck out to meet someone, her friends might cover for her.

"I'd like to see Kelsey's room now." Then she'd talk to the friends.

Mr. Tiller had lapsed into silence, his scowl dark and unreadable as if he was barely holding on to his emotions.

Was he holding something back?

SEVEN

"Deputy Eastwood, please stay with Mr. Tiller while I look in Kelsey's room," Ellie said when Shondra returned from the kitchen.

"Of course," Shondra said softly.

Mr. Tiller's eyes pierced Ellie. "Shouldn't you be doing something more like combing the streets?"

"We will do that, sir. Deputy Eastwood is going to issue a missing persons report. While I'm upstairs, I need you to give my deputy a recent photograph of Kelsey so we can circulate it on the news."

He nodded, seemingly relieved to have something to do, and began to search his phone.

Ellie glanced at the kitchen table as Jean led her toward the hall, cataloging details as she went. A box of cereal, milk and orange juice containers sat on the table, confirming that Jean had been preparing breakfast for her daughter.

Kelsey's room was the first one on the right. Ellie gloved up, surveying it before entering. It was a typical teen's room with posters of a popular boy band on the wall, photographs of the orchestra and one of the band at the University of Georgia.

Textbooks and a neon green girl's backpack sat on the small desk in the corner, and shelves held several stuffed animals, family photos and a framed Honor Roll certificate as well as a reward for leadership in the orchestra.

The purple comforter hung haphazardly off the foot of the bed, but she saw no clothes scattered on the floor or chair, indicating Kelsey was either neat herself or her mother picked up after her.

"Do you see anything out of the ordinary?" Ellie asked Jean.

Jean's breathing rattled out. "Kelsey usually makes her bed neatly. She's a little on the OCD side."

That explained the color-coded clothing hanging in the closet and the order in the room. But the bedding was rumpled.

"Do you see her phone or computer?"

Mrs. Tiller glanced around, then hurried to Kelsey's backpack. A second later, she removed a laptop. "It's here."

"What about her phone?"

Jean searched Kelsey's desk while Ellie checked the bed. She pulled back the covers, dug into the sheets then checked beneath the mattress and the floor. Nothing.

"She probably has her phone with her," Mrs. Tiller said. "It's always glued to her hands."

"We'll need her number to see if we can track her phone," Ellie said.

Her concern mounted as she crossed the room. When she reached the window, she noted it was unlocked and slightly ajar.

"Is this window usually locked at night?" Ellie asked.

Jean looked down at the window. "Usually, yes."

Ellie peered closer. "No sign the lock was picked which suggests Kelsey may have unlocked it herself."

Confusion marred the mother's face. "I don't understand."

"It means she may have opened it to let someone inside or to climb out. Are you sure she hasn't snuck out before?"

The woman's eyes widened in stunned surprise at the suggestion. "No, Kelsey's a good girl. Besides, I told you we had plans to shop for homecoming dresses today and she wouldn't miss that."

"Check her closet, ma'am," Ellie said. "Make sure her clothes are there, and if she has a suitcase, that it is as well." Although, if the girl had run away for some reason, most likely she would have taken her backpack and computer and they were right here.

Panic streaked the woman's eyes, but she raced to the closet and Ellie heard hangers being shifted, drawers opening.

Jean lifted a small purple rolling suitcase. "Her bag is here. And I don't think any of her clothes are missing." Jean ran her fingers through her hair. "If she did go out on her own, she'll come back, right?"

Various possibilities ticked through Ellie's mind. "Hopefully so. But I'd still like to put a trace on her phone as well as yours and your husband's, in case Kelsey tries to call."

Jean's face paled to a milky white as the implications sank in.

EIGHT

Ellie returned to the living room, Kelsey's laptop in hand. Jean followed on her heels, her fear palpable as she called Kelsey's cell phone again.

"Kelsey, if you get this message, please call me right away. Dad and I are worried sick about you." She inhaled sharply. "If you left to meet up with someone, you aren't in trouble, but I n... need to know you're okay... Please, please call h... home."

Kelsey's father looked more harried than before, his face ruddy with emotions.

Deputy Landrum had come inside and stood by the doorway with Shondra. Ellie explained about the unlocked window. "Kelsey's cell phone is missing. Did you find it or see anything suspicious outside?"

"No. We didn't find a phone either," Shondra said.

Ellie addressed Deputy Landrum. "Kelsey's window was unlocked. Check the area around it and look for footprints in case she climbed out or someone else was here. Deputy Eastwood, start canvassing the neighbors. Landrum can help after he finishes with the window. I'll request a team to search the woods," Ellie continued. If Kelsey ran away, she had a reason.

And if she was meeting someone, she had secrets.

The deputies headed to the door, and Ellie called for the search team then turned to the couple. "Please think, Jean, did you hear anything during the night? A voice? Footsteps?"

The woman shook her head. "No, nothing. Well, except the thunder and rain."

Rain could have washed away any footprints left outside and drowned out the sound of an intruder.

"Dammit, Jean, did you have to get drunk last night?" the father said bitterly.

"I've been stressed," Mrs. Tiller said. "And I only had one vodka tonic."

Mr. Tiller made a sound of disbelief.

Ellie ignored the tension between the couple. "Let's focus on Kelsey right now. You mentioned she was on her phone when you went to bed."

Mrs. Tiller fidgeted. "Yes, I heard her whispering when I checked on her before I turned in."

"Do you know who she was talking to?"

Mrs. Tiller exhaled. "I told you, her girlfriends."

"Did Kelsey have problems with any of her teachers?" Ellie asked again.

"No, we told you she was a great student," Mr. Tiller said defensively.

"I understand this is difficult, but please try to stay calm, sir, so we can sort through this," Ellie said. "In order to do that, I need a list of Kelsey's friends and their contact information."

Jean nodded, then retrieved a notepad from the end table, consulted her phone and jotted down the information.

Ellie turned her attention toward the father. "Where were you last night, Mr. Tiller?"

His jaw tightened, and he glanced at his wife for a second then looked down at his hands. "I had a dinner meeting in Atlanta and stayed overnight in a hotel."

The wife spoke with a bite to her tone. "Yeah, with a hooker."

"I was not with a hooker," Mr. Tiller snapped.

Ellie threw up a hand to silence the argument. "Tell me about your job."

"I'm in pharmaceutical sales," he replied. "Yesterday I met with staff at Emory Hospital, then my colleague and I went to a late dinner and had drinks with two of the docs."

Atlanta was only an hour away. "What time did you get to the hotel?"

"I checked in about five before the meeting then we got back to the hotel around midnight."

"You weren't alone?" Ellie asked.

He shifted. "No."

Jean set her phone in her lap. "You bastard," she cried.

Ellie cleared her throat. "I'm going to need the name and number of the hotel as well as whoever you were with to verify your story."

"Yeah, who is she, Tim?" Mrs. Tiller shouted.

He pulled his phone and walked to the desk in the kitchen. A minute later, he returned and handed a slip of paper with the information on it to Ellie.

"What time did you get home this morning?" Ellie asked him.

"About eight." His voice broke. "The minute I opened the door, I heard my wife screaming." He pinched the bridge of his nose, fear overcoming him.

Ellie gave him a minute to purge his emotions, then another to compose himself. "Go on."

"I ran inside and... saw Jean crying and frantically running through the house looking for Kelsey."

"And then?" Ellie coaxed.

"Then I ran outside and started searching while Jean called Kelsey's friends." He took a breath. "I'm sorry, Jean. I should have been here and then maybe this wouldn't have happened."

"Yes, you should have been here," she said coldly. "When we find her, I want a divorce."

"That's rich," Mr. Tiller snapped. "When I brought it up before, you refused and said we would make the marriage work."

Ellie sucked in a breath, thinking. "If you two discussed a divorce, is it possible Kelsey overheard you and was upset about it?"

The couple traded horrified looks of denial. But now she'd planted that seed, doubt and fear darkened their expressions.

NINE

SOMEWHERE ON THE AT

Digger had been out of prison four weeks now. He'd bought a junker car with the little bit of money he'd made in prison and had driven straight toward the mountains. The sharp peaks and ridges stretched ahead, pines, aspens, oaks and cypresses that were both beautiful and ominous at the same time. As a kid, he and his brother had explored the woods, waded in the creek and fished, all things he'd been robbed of while in the pen.

Inhaling fresh air after all this time was a gift he'd never take for granted again. Which meant he had to follow the rules. Be on his best behavior. Stay away from trouble.

His car hit a pothole, tires skidding toward the embankment. He quickly righted it and barely avoided hitting the mountain wall.

He had to report to his parole officer regularly and couldn't leave the state without permission, but after what he'd tolerated in prison, that was nothing. Caitlin was trying to arrange a job for him, another requirement of his release.

He didn't mind what that job was, but almost preferred manual labor. Anything was better than the monotony of sitting on his ass in a cell.

I won't stop until I prove your innocence and clear your name, Caitlin had promised.

He didn't hold out much hope for that, but at least he could close his eyes at night without bracing himself for an attack.

He knew that he shouldn't go home, but for some morbid reason he couldn't not go back. The place was like a magnet drawing him there. Maybe he was a glutton for punishment.

Or maybe he thought being on Red Clay Mountain would trigger details of the night Anna Marie died, details that would help him understand why he killed his sister.

But looking at the endless miles of forest and ramshackle houses along the highway brought the demons knocking at the door to Digger's mind. Tap, tap, tap. They'd stormed him while he tried to sleep just as the thunder clouds and lightning stormed the mountain. They'd sent him running, hiding, lost in the shadows of the woods until dawn. The early morning sunlight had burned his eyeballs, dragging him from hell to the real world.

One he hadn't been part of for a long time. One where he didn't belong.

He gripped the steering wheel with sweaty hands as he drove around the switchbacks. He'd craved the taste of freedom ever since those cell bars had slammed shut on him.

Although he'd occasionally imagined being exonerated and learning he hadn't actually killed his sister, a sense of hopelessness weighed him down.

Even if he was innocent, it wouldn't bring Anna Marie back. He'd lost years of his life, but she'd lost hers entirely.

He tried to imagine what she'd look like now. As a teen, she'd been gangly and awkward, freckles still dotting her nose, and braces straightening her teeth. She'd been obsessed with basketball and cooking shows and had dreams of becoming a chef.

Then her life was snuffed out, dreams stolen.

He deserved to rot away. Every night when he closed his damn eyes, that first year he'd been caged, he saw himself with that pillow in his hands and knew he deserved to be there.

His lungs tightened, straining for air as he made a sharp turn onto a gravel road. The shackles and chains might be off now, but in his mind he could still hear them clanking as he parked at the cheap motel. The neon sign Last Chance Motel mocked him.

As he went inside to rent a room, he struggled to act normal, not like a felon. Hard to do when he felt as if the word *Guilty* was permanently tattooed on his forehead.

TEN

WHISPERING PINES

At the sound of a knock, Ellie answered the door at the Tillers' and was surprised to see Cord standing with his SAR dog, Benji, and his partner, Milo.

"Have you been cleared to return to work?" Ellie asked.

"Yeah. I can't sit around and do nothing," Cord said. "Especially if I'm needed."

"I told him I could get someone else," Milo said.

"The team is scattered with two other calls," Cord muttered. "Just tell us where you want us."

Ellie explained about Kelsey's disappearance. "I need y'all to search the woods," Ellie said. "My deputies are canvassing the neighbors to see if they saw or heard anything."

"Can we get a piece of clothing or something belonging to the girl for Benji?" Cord asked.

Ellie nodded, then hurried to ask the Tillers. Jean pulled Kelsey's hoody from the hook on the wall and Ellie carried it to Cord. They traded an understanding look.

Every minute Kelsey was missing decreased the chances of them finding her, much less finding her alive.

Cord, Benji and Milo set off to search and Ellie stepped into the kitchen and called the hotel where Mr. Tiller had allegedly stayed the night before. She spoke to the desk clerk, Carl. "Was a man named Tim Tiller registered at your hotel last night?"

"Yes, he checked in about five, left for a while then returned about midnight."

"Was he alone?"

A hesitant pause. "It's against policy for employees to discuss our clientele's personal lives."

"I understand that, Carl, but I'm investigating the disappearance of Mr. Tiller's fifteen-year-old daughter. It's important I confirm his whereabouts last night and this morning."

The man cleared his throat. "Oh... I'm sorry to hear about his daughter."

"Was Mr. Tiller alone when he returned to the hotel?"

Another hesitant pause, then he answered, "No, he was with a woman."

Ellie gritted her teeth. "Did he leave the room during the night?"

"I really can't say what happened after they got on the elevator."

Still, Mr. Tiller had admitted he was with a woman. "What time did he check out?"

Ellie heard keys tapping and realized he was checking. "He paid his bill online. That would have been at six-thirty a.m. this morning."

"Did you see him leave the hotel?"

"No, but hold on a minute." Computer keys tapped again. "He retrieved his car from valet at six-forty-five."

With Atlanta an hour away, he could have been back home around eight.

"Does Mr. Tiller stay at your hotel often?" Ellie asked.

"About once a month, always on business."

Or so he said. "Have you seen him with this same woman before?"

"What does that have to do with his daughter's disappearance?"

"In a missing child case, it's important we know everything we can about the family, including their routine, acquaintances, financial problems, business contacts, and the couple's relationship with each other as well as others." She took a breath. "Have you seen him with this woman before?"

He sighed. "Maybe a couple of times."

"Did he mention his family to you?"

"No, we weren't friends, Detective. I simply handled his registration."

"Thank you, Carl. If you think of anything that might be helpful, please give me a call."

He agreed and she ended the call, then phoned the woman Tiller claimed to have spent the night with. She answered on the third ring.

"Valerie Bowman. How can I help you?"

"Ms. Bowman, this is Detective Ellie Reeves with the Crooked Creek Police Department," Ellie said. "I'm calling regarding a missing persons investigation. Can you tell me your whereabouts last night and early this morning?"

A long awkward pause. "What are you talking about? Who's missing?"

Ellie spoke firmly, "Just please answer the question."

"In Atlanta at a business meeting. Now—"

"With a man named Tim Tiller?"

"Well... yes. We had dinner to discuss a new drug about to enter the market. Why? Did something happen to Tim?"

"Did you spend the night with him in his hotel room?"

Ellie heard a noise and realized the woman had closed a door, probably to keep whoever she was with from overhearing her conversation. "Yes, but I don't want that to get out. It's only happened a couple of times. I... was going to call it off."

"Did he leave the room during the night?"

"No. I left about six this morning and returned to my room. Some of my colleagues were there and we didn't want them to see us together."

"Was he alone when you left?"

"He was getting in the shower," she said, her tone impatient. "Now tell me, did something happen to him?"

Ellie's fingers tightened around the phone. If Valerie was telling the truth, she'd just given Kelsey's father an alibi.

"Is Tim okay?" Valerie's voice grew shrill.

"Yes, Mr. Tiller is fine. But his fifteen-year-old daughter disappeared sometime in the night."

She gasped. "Oh, my goodness. Poor Tim..."

Poor Kelsey, Ellie thought. "How would you describe his relationship with his daughter?"

Valerie's voice trembled, "Fine as far as I know. He said she was a sweet girl and she played piano. But... truthfully we didn't talk about family much, except he said his wife was drinking a lot lately, and that he thought she was having an affair with their accountant."

Jean had failed to mention that. What other secrets were this family keeping?

ELEVEN

Ellie contemplated that revelation as she returned to the living room. "Jean, may I speak to you in the kitchen?"

Kelsey's mother looked up with red swollen eyes then stood on wobbly legs and crossed to the kitchen. She sank into one of the wooden chairs at the round table. "What's going on? Did someone take my little girl?"

"I don't know yet," Ellie said. "But you mentioned your husband was sleeping around. Were you also having an affair?"

Jean twisted the tissue in her hand. "Why do you ask that?"

"As I mentioned, I need to know everything about your family. Were you seeing someone else?"

Jean's face turned scarlet. She glanced at the living room where her husband was pacing anxiously, then lowered her voice. "I just did it to get back at him for cheating on me."

Ellie arched a brow. "Then your husband knows about your affair?"

Jean shrugged. "I... he figured it out."

"How did he react?"

She bit down on her lower lip. "He was angry. Thinks it's

okay for men to run around but if the wife does it, she's a tramp."

Ellie refrained from commenting on that. "Tell me what happened."

She nodded. "That's when he said he wanted a divorce. What a double standard, huh?"

Ellie ignored the question. "And you argued?"

"I told him we should work on the marriage because a divorce would destroy Kelsey," she continued.

"Who did you have an affair with?" Ellie asked. "Your accountant?"

"Do I have to tell you that? He's married, too, and I don't want to get him in trouble."

"Jean, if you want me to find Kelsey, you have to cooperate. Fully."

"Of course I want you to find her," she said sharply.

"Then answer the question. Who were you sleeping with?"

Tension stretched for a full minute. "The gym teacher at Kelsey's school," she said softly. "But it's over."

"What is his name, ma'am?"

"Buck Ward," she answered. "But kids call him Coach because he coaches the track team."

"How did you two get together?"

"He stopped me one day when I picked up Kelsey from school. He noticed she was a fast sprinter and wanted her to join the track team." She shrugged and then flushed uncomfortably. "We got to talking and one thing led to another."

"Did Kelsey know about the two of you?"

"I don't see how she would have found out," Mrs. Tiller said. "We were very discreet."

Still, secrets and lies had a way of coming out. And blowing up in people's faces.

"You said Coach Ward showed special interest in Kelsey?"

She fidgeted with the tissue again, ripping it. "In her

running, yes. But I can assure you he had nothing to do with Kelsey's disappearance," she said emphatically. "He liked her."

Maybe too much? "You said your affair is over?"

She tapped her foot nervously. "I broke it off two days ago over lunch."

That timing could be significant. "How did he take it?"

"He agreed. He didn't want to hurt his kids either or create a scandal at school so we both decided it was for the best."

"I need his contact information."

"But—"

"Jean, I meant it when I said I need your full cooperation. If Kelsey learned about your affair, she may have gone to talk to the coach. Or if she heard you and Tim discussing a divorce, she may have confided in another adult."

Shock flared in the woman's eyes. "All right." She snagged a sticky note from the counter, then scribbled down the coach's number. "Please be discreet though," she whispered. "I don't want to mess up his life or his job."

Ellie didn't comment. She needed to find out if the breakup was as amicable as Jean Tiller claimed.

Another possibility taunted her. If the coach didn't want the breakup, perhaps he thought getting Kelsey out of the picture would mean they could be together. Or maybe he was interested in something more with Kelsey than running ...

TWELVE

A knock sounded on the kitchen door, and Ellie let Deputies Landrum and Eastwood inside. Sergeant Williams from ERT was behind them.

"We aren't sure what we're dealing with yet," Ellie told him. "A runaway or kidnapping. Process the doors and windows and Kelsey's room upstairs. I need to know if there are prints belonging to someone besides Kelsey or her parents."

"Right on it," the sergeant said. He spoke to the techs and they divided up. The tech took the exterior and, with Ellie's direction, Williams headed toward Kelsey's room.

Then Ellie turned to Shondra and Landrum. "What did the neighbors have to say?"

Shondra tapped the pocket notepad she always carried with her. "The couple across the street are in their eighties. Both have poor vision and hearing. Said they saw the family coming and going all the time but they didn't know anything." She sighed. "Two doors down, the eight-year-old girl said Kelsey was sweet to her and she liked her."

Ellie smiled.

"The neighbor on the left overheard the couple arguing but

never saw signs of physical altercations. No records of a domestic call. But apparently Kelsey was left alone a lot at night."

Deputy Landrum checked the notes on his phone. "Two other neighbors work full-time and had nothing to add. But the old man on the left is a night owl. He saw a boy sneaking around the house after lights were off downstairs a couple of different times. He was there last night."

Ellie arched a brow. "The Tillers said Kelsey wasn't into boys."

Landrum made a low sound in his throat. "Probably didn't know."

Maybe not. "What's the kid's name?"

"Man didn't know, just that he had brown hair and always wore a black Georgia Bulldog hoodie."

Ellie nodded grimly. She had to find him. He might have been the last person to see Kelsey.

THIRTEEN

WALNUT GROVE

The sound of sixteen-year-old Mitch Drummond's phone jarred him from a deep sleep. He muttered a curse and buried his face in his pillow. Geez, it was nine o'clock on a Saturday morning. No school. No football practice. It was his day to sleep in and hang with his buddies.

The *Star Wars* ring tone sounded again, and he realized it was Justin. Why so early?

Irritated, he snatched the phone. "What the hell? Do you know what time it is?" he growled.

"Yeah, dude, but you gotta know. An Amber Alert has been issued for Kelsey Tiller. Apparently she's missing."

Mitch jackknifed to a sitting position, his heart pounding like a drum roll. "What are you talking about? Missing?"

"My mom saw her picture on the news."

Mitch grabbed his laptop from his desk and quickly googled the local news channel. The headline *LOCAL GIRL KELSEY TILLER GOES MISSING* was the top story.

> *Amber Alert has been issued for fifteen-year-old Kelsey Tiller.*
> *She was reported missing by her mother in Whispering*

Pines this morning. If anyone has information on the where-abouts of this teenager, please call the Crooked Creek Police Department.

"Crap," Mitch muttered.

"Police will probably be asking questions. Delete any texts between you and her and you and the team," Justin said.

Sweat exploded on Mitch's forehead. Justin was right. If the police saw the texts, it wouldn't look good for him or the others.

FOURTEEN

Ellie was anxious to talk to Kelsey's girlfriends and find the boy. But first she had to finish up with the parents. "Mr. and Mrs. Tiller, is there anyone who'd want to hurt you by taking your daughter? How about your work, sir? Any problems with a coworker? Did you owe anyone money?"

Mr. Tiller ran a hand through his short hair. "No. My financials are solid."

"How solid? Do you have a substantial portfolio?"

"No, nothing like that. Just a few thousand in savings." He pulled a hand down his chin. "Are you suggesting someone kidnapped Kelsey for ransom?"

Ellie breathed in. "Just covering all the bases. You said you were in pharmaceutical sales. Were there problems with any of the drugs you handled? A lawsuit or something like that?"

"No," he said, his voice defensive. "Nothing."

"Keep your phone charged and turned on in case you receive a call." Ellie explained about the neighbor seeing a boy visiting. The couple both looked shocked.

"That can't be right," Mr. Tiller said.

"If she had a boyfriend, why wouldn't she tell us?" Mrs. Tiller asked.

Ellie shrugged. "Perhaps it was nothing," Ellie said. "But I'm going to talk to him."

"I'm going with you," Mr. Tiller said.

Ellie shook her head. "No, sir, stay here in case Kelsey comes home. And let me do my job. I'll also talk to Kelsey's friends. Deputy Eastwood will stay with you."

Ellie and Shondra exchanged a silent look. Considering that both parents had had an affair, she still hadn't dismissed the idea that one of them might know more about their daughter's disappearance than they'd let on. Or that the husband of Mr. Tiller's lover or the coach's wife might have discovered the affair and decided to punish the family. Hurting the daughter would be a strange attempt at revenge, but people had killed for less.

She stepped outside and saw Cord walking back toward the house along with Deputy Landrum, both grim-faced.

"I found a phone in the woods," Cord said then handed it to her. "It's been smashed."

Ellie's stomach twisted at the broken screen. The neon purple case bore the initials KT. "That means Kelsey was in the woods sometime during the night or early this morning."

"There were also flattened brush and weeds, indicating footsteps, surrounding where I found it," Cord said darkly. "Looks like there was an altercation."

Fear clogged Ellie's throat. "Organize a search team and have them comb the woods, Cord." She gestured to the deputy. "Landrum, take the phone and Kelsey's computer to the station and look at her communications and social media."

He nodded and accepted the computer while Cord phoned for a SAR team.

Dread seized Ellie as she stepped back into the house to tell the parents. They looked up, surprised to see her back so soon.

"Ranger McClain found your daughter's cell phone in the woods," Ellie said.

"What?" Jean gasped. "Why would it be there?"

"I was hoping you could tell me."

Tears filled Jean's eyes as she realized this was not good news. "You find that boy, Detective. If he had something to do with this, make him talk."

Anger reddened the father's face and he stood, hands fisted by his sides. "I want to talk to him myself."

Ellie stopped him with her hand as he tried to pass her. "No, sir, like I said, you and your wife are going to stay here in case Kelsey comes home. Just let me do my job."

She just prayed that when she found the girl, she was alive.

FIFTEEN

SOMEWHERE BETWEEN ATLANTA AND CROOKED CREEK

He missed Ellie. Dammit.

Special Agent Derrick Fox left the impressive Atlanta skyline behind as he drove north toward the Appalachian Mountains. After the last three weeks of staying in the city with its noise, traffic and clogged air, he couldn't wait to return to the quaint small town of Crooked Creek, the scenic trails and waterfalls, the endless miles of untamed forest and the fresh country air.

Traffic was thicker this morning with folks driving to see the fall foliage and visit the apple houses where apples were harvested, and jams, jellies, apple butter and other apple products were sold to tourists.

Red, gold and yellow leaves dotted the rising peaks, the trees shivering in the crisp wind.

He'd spent the last three weeks at the trial of the woman he and Ellie had arrested in conjunction with the case of the Southside Slasher. Numerous women had been murdered over the last decade in a conspiracy case that had them stumped at first. But with Ellie's perseverance and the help of the task force he spearheaded for the governor, they'd finally uncovered the truth and now the perpetrators who'd orchestrated the crimes were locked away for life.

He was glad to close the book on that one.

But he'd heard the news report this morning. A teen girl had gone missing in Crooked Creek. Ellie hadn't called him in yet, but he was headed there anyway. Although his personal relationship with Ellie was as rocky as the cobbled paths on the AT, he refused to let personal issues interfere with the task force.

Using his voice control, he instructed his Bluetooth system to call Ellie's number. She answered on the third ring.

"Derrick?"

"I saw the news. Has the girl been found yet?"

"No," Ellie replied. "At this point, we aren't sure if we're dealing with a runaway or an abduction. I'm at the parents' house now and plan to question Kelsey's friends and a possible boyfriend who may have seen her last night. Cord found her phone in the woods and Landrum is searching her computer."

Derrick's fingers tightened around the steering wheel at the mention of Ranger Cord McClain. He'd been friends with Ellie for ages. And Derrick had to admit he'd earned his trust. McClain was a damn good tracker and had helped on numerous cases.

Though Derrick and Ellie had gotten close, there was something between Ellie and the ranger that stood in the way of him and Ellie moving forward.

He put that thought out of his mind. They had a case. That was all that mattered right now.

"The trial ended. I'm almost back to Crooked Creek. How can I help?"

Ellie explained about the parents' affairs. "The woman Mr. Tiller was seeing gave him an alibi. The wife slept with the track coach at Kelsey's school. Maybe you can pay him a visit."

"Sure. Just text me his name and address."

"Done."

He hung up, his lungs straining for air. Just hearing Ellie's voice stirred feelings he shouldn't have.

Feelings he didn't know what the hell to do with.

SIXTEEN

BACKWATER'S EDGE

Ellie was grateful for Derrick's return. He was smart, savvy and had resources she didn't. They made a good team and she didn't want to lose that. Ever.

She tasked Deputy Eastwood with contacting the high school principal and counselor for their insight into any problems Kelsey might have had at school then headed to Backwater's Edge where Ruby Pruitt, one of Kelsey's besties, lived with her mother, Billy Jean.

The midday sun struggled to break through the rain clouds and failed, casting the run-down mobile home park in grays. The area looked bleak compared to the well-manicured properties in Whispering Pines.

Weeds choked the overgrown yards, some areas patchy as if Mother Nature was trying to wipe out any greenery. Fall leaves were already turning brown and had gathered in thick piles adding to the sense of decay in the tiny neighborhood.

Ruby's home was a single-wide that had once been beige, but the color had faded and mud and dirt streaked the exterior. Three cinder block steps led to the front door, which bore scratch marks as if a dog or other animal had tried to claw its way inside.

As she walked up to the door, she noted a scrawny man in overalls watching from across the graveled parking lot where he was yanking at his dog's leash to keep him out of the dumpster, which desperately needed emptying.

She knocked on the door, a gust of wind bringing the stench of the garbage. A minute later, the curtain was pushed aside and she saw the face of a young girl staring wide-eyed at her through big square glasses.

Ellie knocked again. "It's the police, please open up."

She tapped her foot while she waited, then the door screeched open. The girl looked terrified as she thumbed her glasses up her nose. They were too big for her face, Ellie thought. The girl's red hair was pulled back in a ponytail, her blue eyes filled with a wariness that tore at Ellie's heart strings.

"I'm Detective Ellie Reeves," Ellie said, revealing her badge. "Are you Ruby Pruitt?"

The girl nodded.

"Is your mother here?" Ellie asked.

Ruby's mouth drew into a frown. "She's sleeping."

Ellie mentally noted the time. It was nearly noon now.

"Is she in trouble?" Ruby asked.

Ellie shook her head, wondering why that would be Ruby's first thought. "No, but I need to talk to you about your friend Kelsey, and I can't do that without your parent being present. Is your father here?"

Ruby gripped the door edge as if she didn't want Ellie to see inside. "I don't have a father," she said bluntly.

"Then go wake your mother, please."

The girl's wariness intensified but she closed the door and disappeared. Ellie had the odd sense that Ruby was hiding something.

When she pushed open the door, she understood. The

house was filthy. Obviously a hoarding situation, there were old, dusty magazines, boxes of junk, dirty dishes and laundry piled everywhere in sight. The picture was not a pretty one, rousing her sympathy for Ruby even more.

Ellie stepped inside, almost tripping over a bag of trash. A good five minutes later, she heard shuffling and Ruby appeared again, her head downcast. A thin woman in an old housecoat was behind her, scraggly brown hair tangled around her face. Ellie guessed her age to be forties although her pale complexion and sallow skin made her look older.

She staggered slightly, the scent of booze wafting off her as she looked at Ellie with bloodshot eyes.

"What do you want?" she mumbled as she tapped a pack of nonfilter Camels in her hand.

"I'm sorry to report that one of Ruby's friends, Kelsey Tiller, is missing."

Ruby hugged her arms around her waist, but the mother's only reaction was to light up her cigarette and shuffle to the kitchen table. She pushed some crusty dishes away and propped her chin on her hand.

"What's that got to do with me?"

Her lack of concern irritated Ellie although she realized the woman was hungover.

"I need to ask Ruby some questions."

Mrs. Pruitt waved a dismissive hand toward her daughter. "You know where Kelsey is, Rubes?"

Ruby shook her head.

Ellie offered the teen a compassionate smile. "I just came from talking to Kelsey's parents, Ruby. They said you're good friends with Kelsey."

Ruby nodded, her teeth worrying her bottom lip.

"When was the last time you talked to her?" Ellie asked.

"Last night. We texted," Ruby said.

"What were you texting about?"

"Homecoming," Ruby said. "We were supposed to go shopping today for dresses. Kelsey's mom was taking us. But she called this morning..." Her voice cracked with emotions.

Ellie gave her a moment. "I know, Kelsey's parents are really worried. Do you have any idea where she is?"

Ruby shook her head and wiped at a tear.

"Do you think Kelsey would run away?" Ellie asked. "Because if she did, you can tell me. She's not in trouble and you won't be either."

"She wouldn't run away," Ruby said.

"Okay. One of Kelsey's neighbors saw a boy sneaking over to Kelsey's," Ellie said, watching the girl carefully. "Did she have a boyfriend?"

Ruby chewed her thumbnail. "Her daddy wouldn't let her date," Ruby said, sidestepping the question.

Ellie arched a brow. "But there was a boy she liked?"

Ruby's chin quivered as she gave a tiny nod.

"I need you to tell me his name, honey," Ellie said gently.

An indecisive sigh escaped the girl.

"Fuck, girl," her mother snapped. "If you know it, tell her so I can go back to bed."

Ruby's cheeks flamed as red as her hair.

Ellie gritted her teeth. She wanted to hug the girl. "You're not in any trouble, Ruby. I just need to talk to him, to know if he saw her last night."

She wiped at her eyes, which had filled with tears when her mother yelled at her.

"Ruby, please, I know you care about Kelsey," Ellie said. "This boy might know something that will help us find your friend. You want to do that, don't you?"

Another pale-faced nod. "His name is Mitch," she said, her voice strained. "Mitch Drummond."

SEVENTEEN
DEER CROSSING

Derrick's gut tightened. He hated missing children cases. They always roused memories of when his own sister disappeared. The years of not knowing, the sleepless nights, the torture over the what-ifs that could have happened to her.

Finally, he and his mother had closure. Only it wasn't the outcome they'd prayed for. She was dead. Her body found in these mountains.

He hoped Kelsey's case turned out differently.

Derrick entered the small neighborhood of Deer Crossing where Coach Ward lived, an area named so for the abundance of deer roaming the woods and venturing into yards.

He slowed as he approached the modest ranch home, a doe and her fawn grazing at the edge of the property. It was a beautiful sight, peaceful compared to the hectic streets of Atlanta. As he parked, he noted a man he assumed was the coach tossing a football to a teenage boy. The man had dark brown hair and looked like a gym rat while the boy was gangly and hadn't yet grown into his body. Still, their faces looked so much alike that Derrick knew they were father and son.

The image of the two of them together sent a twinge of

longing for Derrick's godchildren and made him hope that the coach wasn't involved in Kelsey Tiller's disappearance. He hated breaking up a family.

Worse though, he hated that someone would hurt or abduct a young girl, so he cut the engine and slid from the car. The man turned and spotted him as Derrick walked up the drive. He told the boy he'd be back, then joined Derrick in the driveway.

"Coach Buck Ward?" Derrick said.

"Yes," the man answered.

"Special Agent Derrick Fox with the FBI." Derrick flashed his credentials. "I need to talk to you about Kelsey Tiller."

The coach scrubbed a hand over his beard stubble. "I heard she's missing. That's awful."

His son yelled his name, and the coach looked over at him. "Go inside and take a break while I talk to this agent. We'll pick practice up later."

The boy grumbled and dragged his feet but did as he was told.

Derrick cleared his throat. "Yes, well, Detective Reeves spoke with Kelsey's mother and she said you wanted Kelsey to run track for you."

A vein bulged in his neck. "Yes, Kelsey was athletic."

"Were you upset that she declined?"

A wariness slid over his face. "I was disappointed, but not upset. She was well rounded and at this age, kids can't do every activity. At some point, they have to choose and she chose the band."

"Mrs. Tiller mentioned that you two had an affair," Derrick said, catching the coach off guard.

He lowered his voice. "That was very brief. And I'd rather my wife didn't know."

"I'm sure you would," Derrick said. "But I need you to tell me about the affair."

"It only happened a couple of times," he said. "Jean was

upset when I ran into her at a coffee shop. I just meant to comfort her but one thing led to another. My wife and I had a rough patch before that, but soon Jean and I realized it was a mistake, that we didn't want to hurt our families. So we broke it off a couple of days ago."

"You weren't angry that she broke things off?"

The coach's eyes narrowed. "No, it was a mutual decision. I love my wife and son and didn't want to mess that up."

He sounded so sincere that Derrick wanted to believe him. "Did Kelsey ever say or do anything to indicate she knew about the affair?"

A muscle jumped in his cheek. "No. And if you're thinking I was mad about the breakup or that I'd hurt Kelsey, you're way off base."

"Do you know of anyone who *would* hurt her?" Derrick asked.

Coach Ward shook his head. "No, everyone liked her." A frown tugged at his eyes. "Although there were some rumors about some popular girls bullying her and her friends."

"Who was behind that?"

He shrugged. "I don't know. But you should ask her friends. Ruby Pruitt and June Larson."

Derrick made a mental note to follow up with the bullying angle. Bullying, especially cyberbullying, was a growing problem and had been associated with teen suicide.

EIGHTEEN

SOMEWHERE ON THE AT

He traced his finger over the photo of the girls. Kelsey Tiller. Ruby Pruitt. June Larson.

The young teens had such firm bodies. Small breasts on the verge of bursting into voluptuous bosoms. Caught on camera without their knowledge, they exuded a raw innocence that made them even more beautiful and alluring.

Kelsey looked so much like the girl from his teens. Her buttery-blond hair had been as soft as corn silk, her lips pale with just a touch of strawberry-flavored lip gloss. She smelled of rose water and her skin was porcelain, uncontaminated by the hordes of makeup that some of the girls layered on like pancake batter.

Kelsey reminded him of the girl in so many ways. Not just her looks but her friendly demeanor to everyone she came in contact with. She was smart, studied hard, loved to play the piano.

Yes, his first love had been so special. Until he found out the truth about her... Hell, he'd loved her even then.

But she was off limits to him in the special way he wanted.

He stretched out his fingers and saw the pillow in his hands.

Saw Kelsey lying so still, her eyes staring at him in terror. Heard a low whimper as he moved toward her.

"Sorry, darling," he whispered. "But it's time to go to sleep." He swallowed against the guilt as he shoved the pillow over her face. Sometimes sacrifices had to be made.

"Bye, bye, Kelsey."

NINETEEN

BACKWATER'S EDGE

Ruby Pruitt tucked her phone in her pocket, her stomach jumping with nerves as the conversation with the detective echoed in her head. Shame burned her cheeks. She hadn't wanted the lady to come in, to see how she and her mother lived.

Backwater's Edge was on the poorer side of Red Clay Mountain, which made for teasing from other students who looked down on the kids in the trailer park and clapboard houses that were barely standing after the last tornado. Blue tarps covered holes in the roofs and downed trees still hadn't been cleared from several yards. The creek running along the properties was black with debris and muck and if the rain continued as they were predicting, it would probably flood.

Rumors about areas near landfills and chemical plants leaking bad chemicals into the water floated around the town. Sometimes she thought Backwater Creek was filled with them.

"What was that about Kelsey? Do you know where she is?" her mother asked as she lit another cigarette, inhaled and blew a smoke ring. The nasty smoke swirled around Ruby, suffocating and clogging the air.

Despite the drizzling rain, Ruby cracked a window to let in some fresh air, anything to escape the insufferable smoke that stunk up the house and her mother's hair and clothing and made it hard to breathe. She'd begged her to quit dozens of times but got backhanded for it so she'd learned to keep her mouth shut.

"No," Ruby said.

Her mother cut her a sharp look and flipped ashes into the empty Mountain Dew can on the table. "Don't lie to me, girl. Are you and the others up to something?"

"No, Mom," Ruby said although the lie burned in her throat. Somehow, things had gotten out of control. She had to delete all the texts between her and the others. And Kelsey... Where was she?

"Maybe Kelsey just got tired of hearing her parents argue and went for a walk to get away from them."

Nerves clawed at her. She didn't think that was what had happened at all. Kelsey was one of the most level-headed kids in the school. That, and the fact that she didn't look down on her, had drawn Ruby to her.

Ruby tried to ignore the dirty windows and shutters hanging sideways. She wished she didn't feel so embarrassed about the trailer park. But she was ashamed of it and her mother's smoking and drinking and her job at The Hungry Wolf, where the booze flowed freely and she suspected her mother did more than serve drinks.

Her mother shoved the chair back from the table. "Well, since Jean isn't taking y'all shopping today, you can clean up this pigsty while I take a nap. I pulled the late shift last night and again tonight."

Ruby wanted to protest but didn't bother. They needed the extra shifts her mother pulled to make ends meet. She just hoped she was wrong about how her mother earned it.

Her mother hurried to her bedroom and Ruby turned to the kitchen to wash the stacks of dirty dishes.

As she dumped them and scraped the burned ends of the bacon, her phone dinged.

Anxiety tightened her shoulders as she glanced at it and saw texts flowing.

June: *Why do you think Kelsey isn't answering?*

Ruby's thumbs flew over the keys on her phone.

Ruby: *I don't know but a lady cop was here asking questions.*

June: *What did you tell her?*

Ruby: *That I didn't know anything. But she knew Kelsey had a boyfriend and asked his name, so I told her about Mitch.*

June: *What about the pictures?*

Ruby: *No way. My mama would have a cow.*

June: *Come over and stay with me.*

Ruby: *She'll ground me forever if I leave the house. Maybe tomorrow.*

A thumbs-up emoji pinged back and she set down the phone and hurried to clean up. The house was always a mess with cigarette ashes filling the ash trays, junk and laundry strewn around. Kelsey and June were the only teens she'd ever allowed inside.

Yet as she cleaned, the photo that had been posted the night before taunted her. She'd immediately called the others on a group call. Panicked, the texts had started flying.

June: *Grandma will have a heart attack.*

Kelsey: *I bet Bianca did this. Maybe we can fix it.*

Ruby: *No, once it's on the internet it's there forever.*

Ruby pushed her hair from her face with the back of her forearm. Kelsey was usually the solid one. She had confidence. She straddled the line between the popular girls and Ruby and June. She could fit anywhere.

But she'd chosen them.

Except... lately something was bothering her. She'd acted jittery. On edge. Had been secretive.

When they'd asked her what was wrong, she'd said, "Nothing," and changed the subject.

And now Kelsey was missing. Where in the world was she?

TWENTY

LAST CHANCE MOTEL

Digger stared at the news, sweat beading on his neck.

"This is Angelica Gomez from Channel Five News with this breaking story. Fifteen-year-old Kelsey Tiller has disappeared from her home in Whispering Pines early this morning. At this point, police are considering it a missing persons case. Search parties are combing the area surrounding her house, but we need your help, folks." A photograph of the teenager appeared on screen, the reporter continuing, "If you have any information regarding her whereabouts or her disappearance, please call the police."

Déjà vu struck him. This girl Kelsey was the same age as his sister when she died. Had the same heart-shaped face, same shoulder-length sandy-blond hair, same pretty eyes. Digger's stomach knotted. Holy hell, the police might make the connection to him.

He flexed his hands and grimaced at the dirt that had settled beneath his fingernails. Last night was as foggy as the night Anna Marie died.

It was a bad idea going home, but he couldn't help himself. He climbed in the jalopy and headed toward his old homestead.

He didn't know if it was still standing, or if his stepfather had sold it. A little research and he'd discovered his brother lived in Crooked Creek. Ironic, but he was a cop. A cop who'd never bothered to visit him. Bitterness ate at his insides.

His stepfather worked construction with Red Clay Mountain Builders. He'd helped build the new Red Clay Mountain High School. They'd broken ground the year Anna Marie died and had planned to open the following fall.

Both his half brother and stepfather had believed he was a killer. Had looked at him with hatred and contempt.

Digger's pulse pounded. First, he'd go to the old house. See if it was still standing, decaying with the memory of the violence that had happened there. If the walls still echoed with the shrill cry of his sister's scream as she struggled to survive.

With his own sob of horror when he realized that he'd killed her.

TWENTY-ONE

WALNUT GROVE

Pansies, hydrangeas and sunflowers dotted the landscape with color and walnut trees lined the street along Walnut Avenue as Ellie found Mitch Drummond's house. It didn't escape her that his neighborhood bordered Whispering Pines where the missing girl had disappeared.

The traditional Colonial was set in a nice neighborhood that sported tennis courts, a clubhouse and pool. The stiff peaks and ridges in the distance were a sea of red, orange and yellow, and despite the rain clouds the area seemed brighter than most on Red Clay Mountain, as if the more affluent side of town was lit by hope instead of bound by poverty.

Money didn't make for better people though. And you never knew what went on behind closed doors.

Thankfully the rain had died down and she rang the doorbell, noting a black Mercedes in the neighbor's driveway and a silver Beamer in the Drummonds'. A dark-haired woman dressed in a tennis outfit and expensive designer tennis shoes opened the door, diamonds glittering from her ear lobes.

"Mrs. Drummond?"

"Yes."

Ellie flashed her badge and identified herself. "I don't know if you've heard but Kelsey Tiller, a girl from your son's school, is missing. May I come in? I need to speak to him."

The woman's brown eyes narrowed. "Why do you want to see Mitch?"

Ellie stiffened at her condescending tone. "I'm speaking to students and teachers at the school. Please, it won't take long."

Mrs. Drummond's frown deepened but she allowed Ellie to enter. "Wait here. I'll get him."

She disappeared down the hall and five minutes later, footsteps echoed on the polished wood floor. A tall man dressed in a khakis and a white button-down collared shirt appeared instead of Mitch, his jaw hard.

"Detective Reeves, I'm Baxter Drummond, Mitch's father. My wife said you're here about a missing girl."

"Yes, Kelsey Tiller. She goes to school with your son. Her parents are frantic."

His shoulders straightened. "How do you think my son can help you?"

"I'm just gathering information at the moment. Interviewing students at the school to see if Kelsey might have been upset about something, or if they saw someone bothering her."

He gave a clipped nod, then guided her into a formal living room. Sleek modern furniture and a baby grand piano gave the impression of sophistication.

A minute later, the teenage boy appeared with his mother. His hair looked mussed as if he'd just crawled from bed and he wore workout shorts and a black UGA hoodie.

"Mitch, this is Detective Ellie Reeves," Mr. Drummond said. "This morning a girl at your school disappeared. It's been all over the news."

Mitch's brows pinched together in confusion. "I know. The Amber Alert popped up on my phone."

"Did you know Kelsey Tiller?" Ellie asked.

Mitch twisted his mouth to the side as if debating how to respond.

"Mitch?" his mother said. "Did you know her?"

"I... uh, know who she is. But she doesn't hang out in my crowd."

"And what crowd is that?" Ellie asked, fighting annoyance. She knew exactly how high school cliques worked. And that he was lying.

"My son is the star quarterback," Mr. Drummond interjected as if that explained everything.

Ellie bit her tongue to keep from commenting. "I see. But you knew Kelsey, didn't you, Mitch?" Ellie pressed.

The parents exchanged concerned looks and Mitch's eyes cut to the floor.

"Not really," he muttered.

Ellie crossed her arms. "That's interesting. Because one of Kelsey's neighbors claim they saw a boy sneak into Kelsey's bedroom window a couple of times. And I was told Kelsey liked you, Mitch."

Mrs. Drummond frowned and Mr. Drummond stepped in front of his son, his hand lifted in a gesture for his son to remain quiet. "Don't say anything else, Mitch. Not until I call my lawyer."

"Is that what you want, Mitch? Don't you want to help us find Kelsey?" Ellie asked.

Mitch started to speak, but his father cut him off. "Not yet, son."

Ellie silently cursed. "Then call your attorney," Ellie said. "I'll wait here until he arrives. Every minute Kelsey is missing is another minute she could be in danger."

TWENTY-TWO

The fact that Mitch's father immediately requested an attorney raised suspicions in Ellie's mind. He ushered his son and wife into his study for a private chat, leaving Ellie in the living room wondering what the hell was going on.

She texted Deputy Landrum to ask him to run a background on the family, specifically to dig around and see if Mitch had been in trouble with the law before. Of course, if he had, his father could have arranged to have any charges erased from his record. He struck her as *that* kind of man.

While she waited, she surveyed the room. Abstract paintings and a collection of glass figurines added to the sophistication of the room. Built-in bookcases flanked the marble fireplace, where she noted books, a collection of Van Gogh's painted eggs, along with several framed photographs of Mitch in football gear and Mitch receiving athletic awards including MVP for last year's season.

Her phone buzzed. Deputy Landrum. Hoping he had news, she pressed Connect.

"Ellie, this may be nothing, but I found something interesting on Kelsey's computer."

Her pulse jumped. "Go on."

"Her social media is filled with photos of her and the girls you mentioned along with numerous ones of the band and their performances. She also posted pics of her piano recital last year along with the tag line #*Juilliard Here I Come!*"

"She had big dreams," Ellie said. "All that fits with the way her parents described her. Not a girl who'd run away."

Landrum continued, "There's something else. On her phone, I also found a photo of Kelsey with her girlfriends, their hands joined as if in a show of solidarity. It was labeled *The Virgin Pact*. It was also posted on social media."

Ellie exhaled. "Interesting."

The deputy made a low sound in his throat. "There's another post on social media. I'm forwarding it to you now."

The doorbell rang and Ellie heard footsteps before Mr. Drummond answered the door. A hefty man in a three-piece suit entered, his bald head shiny beneath the crystal chandelier. Mitch's father steered him into his study.

A ding indicated the text from the deputy had come through, and Ellie's stomach plummeted as she realized what she was looking at.

#*ChallengeWhoCanBreaktheVirginPact?*#*Only8weeksuntil-Christmas!*

Below the hashtags were avatars of three girls labeled Kelsey, Ruby and June. A string of comic-book type balloons below the girls' names held the phrasing: *HoHoHo*.

TWENTY-THREE

Anger churned through Ellie. Kids could be so cruel. If the girls were being bullied and this post had something to do with Kelsey's disappearance, why hadn't Ruby mentioned it?

"Find out who posted this. It could be connected to Kelsey's disappearance."

"On it," Landrum agreed.

"I'll text Agent Fox and tell him to coordinate with you and to get warrants for the friends' phones. Maybe we can recover any deleted texts from them."

She ended the call, then sent Derrick the text. A minute later Mitch returned with his parents and the attorney.

Mr. Drummond introduced him as Walton Jenner and gestured for everyone to sit.

"Detective Reeves, I understand you want to question my client, Mitch Drummond."

Ellie raised a brow. "If you think he needs an attorney, then he must know more than he told me earlier."

Mitch's eyes shifted warily to the lawyer, but he refrained from speaking.

"My client has done nothing wrong," Mr. Jenner said firmly. "But in an effort to find the girl, we are cooperating."

Ellie detested the man's arrogance. "Then he needs to tell the truth. He claims he didn't know Kelsey well, but we have reason to believe he might have snuck into Kelsey's bedroom window at night."

Mrs. Drummond pressed her fingers to her lips as if she wanted to say something, but her husband placed his hand over hers, silently signaling her to remain quiet.

The attorney cleared his throat. "Mitch does not know where the girl is."

Ellie directed her question to Mitch. "Then what *can* you tell us?"

Mitch's eyes jerked to hers for a split second; something there indicated he did want to help, and the attorney gestured for him to speak.

"Okay, I did see her a couple of times. At first... it was kind of a dare. A bet. To see if I could get her to like me."

Ellie gritted her teeth. "Go on."

He shrugged. "But then... I got to know her and she was different. You know..."

"What do you mean?" Ellie asked.

"Well, she was... nice. Like to everybody."

"Did she have trouble with anyone at school?"

His face reddened. "Some of the mean girls... they picked on Kelsey's friends. But Kelsey stood up to them."

"Do you think one of those girls would hurt her?"

"I d... don't know," he said, his voice breaking. "It was just stupid stuff. They filled Ruby Pruitt's locker with tampons. And someone cut a hole in June Larson's gym shorts. But it wasn't like... violent."

Definitely bullying. "Tell me what happened last night. Did you go to Kelsey's house?"

He scrubbed his hands over his face then looked up at Ellie. "Last night she called, upset."

Now they were getting somewhere. "What was she upset about?" Ellie asked, thinking of the Virgin Pact photo and the meme challenge Landrum had found.

Mitch's gaze shot to the lawyer. "Do I have to say?"

Mr. Jenner leaned forward. "Is my client under arrest, Detective?"

"No," Ellie said. "But if he's hiding something or knows where Kelsey is and doesn't tell us and I find out, I will charge him with interfering with a police investigation." She fisted her hands to calm herself. "You don't want anything bad to happen to Kelsey, do you, Mitch?"

"No," he said earnestly. "And I didn't do anything to her. I'd never hurt Kelsey."

His statement held a ring of truth. Maybe he had liked Kelsey. Ellie showed Mitch the picture of the girls posted on social media and the Virgin Pact Challenge post.

"Is this what she was upset about?" Ellie asked.

Mitch's bronzed skin turned a pasty white. For a long minute, he lowered his head and stared at the floor as if he didn't want to look at the picture.

Mrs. Drummond clenched her husband's arm.

"Tell me about this, Mitch," Ellie said. "Did you post it?"

"God, no," he said on a shaky breath.

"If you didn't post the challenge, do you know who did?"

A pained sigh escaped him. "I... don't know. It just showed up last night."

"You had nothing to do with it?"

"No," Mitch said gruffly. "I... wouldn't do something like that."

Tension stretched in the room as Ellie gave him a moment. "And you talked to Kelsey about it?"

The lawyer squeezed Mitch's shoulder. "Go on, Mitch."

Mitch exhaled. "Kelsey texted and was upset, said she'd meet me outside. She insisted she didn't post those pics on social media. So I snuck out and walked over to her house and she climbed out the window."

"Mitch," the mother said, her voice pained.

"I'm sorry, Mom," Mitch said, shooting her an apologetic look. "But when I saw that post, I was worried about her. She sounded hysterical."

Ellie gave him a small smile of encouragement. "Then what happened?"

"We went into the woods so her mother couldn't hear what we said or see us together. Then Kelsey got all mad and accused me of posting it," he said. "Said she thought that was the reason I asked her to Homecoming."

Mrs. Drummond buried her head in her hands, but Mr. Drummond simply shrugged. "Boys will be boys," he said with a flash of something sinister in his eyes as if he'd probably done something similar as a teen.

Ellie stiffened. "Is that how it played out, Mitch? You wanted to break the virgin pact but Kelsey refused and the two of you argued and things spiraled out of control. Maybe you pushed her and she fell and hit her head." She paused a second, watching his face as it contorted with emotions. "If something like that happened, Mitch, you need to tell me where she is."

TWENTY-FOUR

"No, no, that's not the way it happened." Mitch blinked, knotting and unknotting his hands.

"Then fill me in," Ellie said sternly.

Mitch heaved a breath. "Some of the other guys texted last night. They thought that pact... that it was funny and... well, yeah, they kind of bragged that they'd be the one to break it." His breathing grew labored. "I told Kelsey that I wasn't part of it, that that's not why I asked her to the dance. But she was so upset... she screamed that she couldn't face going back to school again, that her parents would be ashamed and that she was afraid it would mess with her getting a scholarship." His voice cracked. "I told her it would all blow over but then... another picture was posted on social media."

"Let me see it," Ellie said.

He handed her his cell and her pulse hammered. The photo showed Kelsey, Ruby and June in their underwear. It looked as if it had been taken in the gym locker room at school but she couldn't tell for certain.

"Did they pose for this?" Ellie asked Mitch.

He shook his head. "No. That was another reason Kelsey was so upset."

Now she understood why Ruby had looked so wary.

Mitch gulped. "She ran into the woods. I followed her, but she told me to go away. I told her it was no big deal, but she... she said her life was over, that her dad would kill her."

"Was Kelsey frightened of her father?"

"I don't know. I never met her parents. But she said that they were adamant that she was too young to date. She was so hysterical it scared me. When she reached a drop-off, she threatened to jump if I came closer."

"So you left her?" Ellie asked.

"I didn't know what else to do." He heaved a breath. "I figured she'd calm down and go home."

"But she didn't." Ellie crossed to the window, uneasy over Mitch's account of the night before. Teenagers could be dramatic, but still, it was hard to believe Kelsey would commit suicide over a prank.

She stepped aside and quickly called Cord's number. A second later, he answered and she relayed Mitch's statement. "Expand the search in the woods behind Kelsey's house, Cord."

A sick fear rippled through Ellie. They might be looking for a body.

TWENTY-FIVE

WHISPERING PINES

At Ellie's request, Cord and the team divided into search grids to cover more territory.

He kept thinking about what Ellie had said about Kelsey and her friends being bullied. He knew how that felt. He'd been an outcast at school. Called horrific names because he'd lived above a mortuary. Some kids had even been scared of him.

They should have been. He was an angry, messed-up teenager.

But he'd gotten his revenge in the end. He didn't regret it either. His bastard foster father had deserved worse. But at least now he was six feet under and couldn't hurt anyone else.

He shoved his memories to the back of his mind.

The woods were deep and wide, trees standing so close together their limbs touched in places, blocking out light. Shadows flickered through the haze of gray. With the dark clouds hovering above, the forest seemed ominous. The wind whipped through the trees, cracking limbs and twigs and hurling them to the ground.

Cord wove around a thicket of briars and passed clumps of wild mushrooms. The wet earth sucked at his boots, making the ground soggy and slippery. He shined his flashlight across the brush near where he'd found Kelsey's phone, looking for a path of crushed weeds or footsteps to indicate the direction Kelsey had gone.

He knew the area, recognized the plants and wildlife, the fork in the trail that led to Blackwater Creek, an area known for the black tarry sludge that pulled your feet under like quicksand. A mile into his trek, he spotted a downed log near Pine Ridge. Brush had been crushed and as he peered closer, he spotted what looked like a handprint. He knelt to examine it and realized there were two partial handprints, as if someone had tripped over the log and fallen.

A few feet away, he noticed a trail of broken twigs and spotted blood on the side of a tall pine.

His instincts roared to life and he snapped a photo of it. Ellie would want a sample for forensics. He continued to follow the crushed weeds and found himself at the edge of the dropoff. Using his binoculars, he looked down below, spanning the terrain for Kelsey.

He didn't see her or a body anywhere. But to the right of where he stood by the boulder, he spotted a tennis shoe, a female shoe.

There was also more blood.

Dammit. He called Ellie's number. "Hey, I found a shoe that may belong to Kelsey, and blood on a rock. We need an ERT to process that blood and see if it belonged to Kelsey."

"I'll send one right away."

"Okay, I'll climb down to the bottom of the ridge and keep looking for her."

Cord's chest tightened as he gauged the distance from the top of the ridge to the bottom. At least two hundred feet. If Kelsey had jumped or fallen, she couldn't have survived.

TWENTY-SIX

KUDZU HOLLER

After Ellie left the Drummonds' house, she drove to June Larson's house. She'd done her homework and knew June's parents had died and she was living with her grandmother Louise.

Ruby hadn't mentioned the pictures or social media posts. But Mitch had been helpful. She wondered if June would be forthcoming.

Kudzu Holler was less than a mile from Whispering Pines and Backwater's Edge, meaning the girls all lived within walking distance of one another. Only Ruby and June lived on the poorer side of the tracks.

Whatever slivers of sun that had shone today had been obliterated now by dark gray clouds. The wind was blowing, leaves falling, disintegrating already, a sign of winter coming, continuing the cycle of life and death. Flowers in the hanging baskets were wilting on the small front porch, loose petals swirling across the wood floor. The blue shutters, porch swing and "Welcome" wreath on the bright yellow front door made the place look cheery and homey.

Ellie knocked and was greeted by a plump woman, probably early sixties with curly gray hair. An orange cat darted past her feet and raced toward a tree.

"Detective Ellie Reeves," Ellie said.

"Louise Larson," the little woman said.

"Is your granddaughter June here?"

"Yes, but she's pretty upset about her friend Kelsey who's missing," Louise said. "Have you found her?"

"I'm afraid not," Ellie said. "But I would like to talk to June."

"Of course, come in." Unlike Ruby's mother, Louise seemed openly friendly.

The older woman waved Ellie in, and Ellie spotted a thin girl with shoulder-length brown hair standing in the small living room. Sadness and fear darkened her brown eyes. She was dressed in jeans, a T-shirt and Converse sneakers.

Louise led Ellie into the room, which was neat, clean and homey, and smelled of blueberries and bacon. She invited Ellie to sit, and June took her place beside her grandmother on a blue sofa, huddling close to her.

"June, you understand why I'm here, don't you?"

The girl nodded, then chewed her thumbnail. "You didn't find Kelsey yet?"

Ellie gave her a sympathetic look. "I'm afraid not. I was hoping you could help."

Louise patted her granddaughter's leg. "Go on and tell her whatever you know, hon."

June clenched the homemade afghan on the couch in her arms like a security blanket. "I don't know where she is. Ruby and I texted her all morning, but Kelsey hasn't answered."

"When was the last time you did have contact with her?"

"Last night."

"I talked to Ruby and she mentioned that Kelsey had a boyfriend named Mitch Drummond."

June gave another little nod.

"I spoke to him also," Ellie said. "He told me about the pictures of you, Kelsey and Ruby someone posted on social media."

The grandmother frowned. "What pictures?"

June squeezed her eyes closed for a moment. When she opened them, tears filled her eyes.

"I'm sorry, June. None of this is your fault." Ellie turned to the grandmother. "Louise, someone took a photo of the girls in the locker room at school and posted it. You didn't know they were taken, did you, June?"

June shook her head vehemently. "No."

"There was also a meme," Ellie said. "Did you see it?"

June's face colored. "It was so mean."

"Yes, it was," Ellie agreed.

"I don't understand." Louise fidgeted. "What does this have to do with Kelsey?"

"I'm sorry to inform you of this, Louise, but your grand-daughter and her friends were being bullied." Shock registered on Louise's face when Ellie showed her the photograph. "According to Mitch, Kelsey was really upset about it and ran into the woods. She said her life was over and even threatened to jump off the ridge."

June gasped. "No... she wouldn't do that."

"She told Mitch that her father would kill her," Ellie continued. "Was she afraid of him? Did he ever hit her?"

Denial swept over June's face. "No, she was just being dramatic. I mean he was strict and didn't want her dating. But he never hit her."

"Do you have any idea who posted the photo of you and your friends in the locker room?"

June glanced at her grandmother, who looked shaken. Still, Louise squeezed her granddaughter's shoulder in a comforting gesture. "If you know, tell her, June."

"I'm not sure, but we thought it was Bianca Copenhagen.

She's one of the popular girls. She was really upset when Mitch asked Kelsey to Homecoming."

Ellie assured them she'd do everything she could to find Kelsey, then headed back outside. Phone in hand, she called Deputy Landrum. "I may know who posted the pic and meme of the girls. Another student named Bianca Copenhagen. Find out where she lives and bring her and her family in for questioning."

TWENTY-SEVEN

RED CLAY MOUNTAIN

Signs for Homecoming at the local high school mocked Digger as he maneuvered the switchbacks of Red Clay Mountain. The ten miles between the high school and his old homestead felt like a hundred, each mile steeped with tension. Dusk had come and gone and, with the storm clouds, the sky was as black as his soul.

For fifteen years he'd been haunted by his past. He had to see the house where it had all gone wrong. Maybe if he did, he'd remember details that had gotten lost in his befuddled brain a long time ago. Like what had possessed him to take his little sister's life.

The shocks were worn out on the old clunker, making every bump and pothole jar his back. He rolled down the window to breathe in the fresh air, something he'd never take for granted again.

A tractor trailer barreled around the curve, and for a brief second Digger thought about jerking the wheel toward it and plowing straight into it. But Caitlin O'Connor's voice fought through the darkness.

"I think you got a raw deal, Darnell," Caitlin said the first time she'd interviewed him for her podcast. "You were just a kid. All the evidence is circumstantial. I've watched the tapes of your confession, and something doesn't add up."

Truth was, he didn't remember confessing. All he recalled was the shock of looking down at his sister's pale dead face and hearing his stepfather's bark. *You killed her, Digger!*

Then his half brother's tormented face bleeding through the haze. *You killed Anna Marie.*

A horn honked from an ongoing car and his tires skidded toward the shoulder as he yanked his eyes back to the road. Raindrops began to ping off the windshield, slashing though his open window, but he still couldn't bear to close it all the way. He rounded a curve then spotted the rusted sign for Hog Hill, the dirt road leading toward his old homestead.

The tall pines and oaks boxed him in as he maneuvered the narrow stretch and he thought he spotted a wild boar rutting in the muddy brush. Fat raindrops collected on the windshield as the wind picked up, and he flipped on the defroster, then the rotting wooden house slipped into view like a monster rising through the fog.

Home sweet home, he thought with a sickening knot in his belly.

The place looked smaller than he remembered, the clapboard structure dilapidated, mud-splattered and overgrown with patchy weeds. Broken bare tree limbs and twigs had been scattered across the property. The sharp ridges jutted out over rocky terrain and the hard red clay.

As a kid, he'd thought the thin brittle branches on the trees looked like skeletal hands reaching out to snatch him.

This part of the mountain was known for rumors that its deep, Georgia red clay was the devil's land.

And he believed it.

He cut the engine, breath tight in his chest as he climbed out and walked up to the door. The shutters were sagging, paint peeling, the once white house a dirty yellowish color. He tried the door. Unlocked. Judging from the state of disrepair, it had been abandoned for years. Not that it looked much better when they'd lived here.

Evil whispered around him as he entered, shadows flickering as if Anna Marie's ghost had been awakened. For a second, he heard the tinkle of her laughter as she danced with the calico cat named Prissy that she'd dressed in baby doll clothes when she was little.

Heard the sound of his brother tossing the baseball back and forth in his glove as he practiced his pitching stance.

Felt the rage in his stepfather's pacing after his mother had deserted them.

Sweat beaded on his neck, his boots making the floors squeak as he walked past the dingy kitchen. His whole body tensed, bracing for an avalanche of memories as he made his way down the hall to his sister's bedroom.

The ancient iron bed still sat in the same spot, faded gingham curtains flapping from the breeze coming through the broken window. Rain slashed through the opening, soaking the floor in a puddle. A streak of lightning zigzagged through the room, illuminating the bed frame.

The mattress was ratty now as if animals had chewed it.

A clap of thunder bolted above the trees and startled him back to that night. He saw himself leaning over his sister, hands on the pillow.

He closed his eyes, struggling to recall walking into the room. If he'd been angry at her for some reason. If she'd heard him and awakened and looked at him and begged for her life.

But a black curtain fell over his mind, plunging him into an empty cauldron of nothingness.

TWENTY-EIGHT

GEORGIAN MANOR

From the back of the deputy's car, Bianca Copenhagen fidgeted. And she was not a fidgeter.

She shoved her hands beneath her legs to keep them still. Showing her jitters would make her look guilty of something.

The deputy hadn't mentioned the pictures when he'd shown up at their house. Just that the police were talking to all of Kelsey's classmates and teachers.

She would play it cool. Be charming. All the girls at school thought she was the *it* girl.

She'd been growing a following as a teen influencer with her trendy clothes and makeup tips. Already, one of her posts showcasing her closet and wardrobe was going viral. Soon, designers and brand name companies would start sending her free gifts, clothing, jewelry, makeup and other products to demonstrate to her followers. She might even end up on a talk show!

She was creative, too. The meme she'd posted was particularly clever. If the losers didn't know she had power over them, they would now.

Nerdy band freaks. She'd bet her Michael Kors bag that

underneath all that *we don't care what anyone thinks* attitude, those geeks envied her just like the other girls at school. She imagined them playing with makeup to cover the freckles and pale skin, trying to find the same shade of lip gloss Bianca used and struggling to tame their hair into a sleek glossy mane like her own. She almost felt sorry for them. *Almost.*

Kelsey was a different story. She could have fit in with Bianca's crowd, only Kelsey turned up her nose at Bianca from day one. She thought she was better than everyone with her righteous Virgin Pact. Who did that anymore? All the boys expected a hand or blow job and it was hard to get a date if you were a prude. Besides HJs and BJs weren't really sex.

Served that snotty goody-two-shoes right that the football team made bets to see who could get in her pants. The challenge was half the fun for them.

Maybe that was the reason Kelsey made the pact. She was more devious than anyone thought and *wanted* to challenge the guys to make herself more popular.

The boys couldn't resist. They all thought with their dicks.

Although, Bianca had the monopoly on them. Half of the football and baseball team were wrapped around her little finger. She was working on the soccer team next. Already, she'd been asked to Homecoming three times but she'd been holding out for Mitch—only he'd asked that bitch Kelsey.

Curse words rolled through her mind.

In the front seat, her mother pulled her compact and prettied up her lipstick. Her face and body were a shrine, makeup perfect, clothing all designer. She especially enjoyed showing off the double-C-cup body Bianca's father had paid for before the divorce. Her house—Bianca called it the glass house because she'd grown up being told not to touch anything or it would break—was as perfect and fancy as her mother. Nothing out of place. Glass and china everywhere. Polished marble floors. A two-story chandelier with a footlong waterfall of crystals.

How could Kelsey think she was better than that?

Ignoring the deputy who'd remained silent, her mother tucked her compact back into her Coach bag and gave a dramatic sigh. "I hope this doesn't take long, Bianca. I'm missing my spa appointment."

Bianca shrugged. "No idea, Mom." Although she had an inkling of a clue. She knew Kelsey was missing. Everyone did.

Not that she cared. Kelsey got what she deserved. And so did the others.

Frustration knotted Ellie's shoulders as she and Derrick entered the interview room, her worry for Kelsey growing with each minute that passed.

Bianca was a pretty blond with bronze skin and no tan lines that probably came from a tanning bed. Her bright pink lipstick matched the hot pink crop top she wore with jeans and black Converse sneakers. She sat, legs sprawled, arms hanging loose, a bored look on her face.

Her mother was the picture of a haughty trophy wife who frequented the country club, playing tennis, enjoying spa treatments and being catered to by the working class. She sat stiffly in the metal chair, hands folded in her lap as if she was afraid to touch anything for fear of being contaminated by germs. Obviously, the décor was subpar for an elitist woman like her.

Immediately, Ellie pegged Bianca as a mean girl just as the other girls had described her.

"Thank you for coming, Mrs. Copenhagen," she said. "Bianca."

"It's not like we had a choice." Disdain laced the mother's

tone. "That deputy didn't seem to care that I had plans this evening."

A seed of anger sprouted inside Ellie, and Derrick stiffened beside her.

"We're sorry your day has been interrupted," Derrick cut in with a hint of sarcasm. "But one of your daughter's classmates is missing and her parents are terrified something has happened to her."

The woman's face blanched. "Yes, I heard about that Amber Alert. But I hardly see what that has to do with my daughter."

"We're talking to students and teachers at the school to see if any of them can shed light on Kelsey's whereabouts and what happened to her."

Bianca squared her shoulders, a small smile tilting her mouth. A smile that hinted at evil thoughts beneath. "I have no idea where she is," Bianca said. "She and I didn't hang out together."

"Yes, I'm aware of that," Ellie said. "That's the reason we wanted to talk to you. You didn't like Kelsey and her friends, did you?"

Bianca shrugged again. "I have a lot of friends, I didn't need those losers leeching onto me."

"Actually Kelsey wasn't a loser. She was an honor student and had plans to attend Juilliard."

Mrs. Copenhagen tapped her manicured nails on her thigh. "Well, I hope you find her and I'm sorry we can't help you." She stood, the emerald on her right hand sparkling beneath the fluorescent light. "Now, we need to get going."

Derrick set a folder on the table. "Not before we ask your daughter about these."

Irritation flashed in the woman's eyes, but she sat, her fingers tapping impatiently.

Bianca simply raised a blond brow but showed no reaction

as Derrick showed them the social media posts. Mrs. Copenhagen angled her head to look at them, eyes crinkling as if she was trying to comprehend what was going on.

"If this girl wanted to get into Juilliard, she's a fool to post those," Mrs. Copenhagen said with a smirk.

"*She* didn't post them," Ellie said.

"The picture of the girls in the locker room was taken without permission," Derrick continued, his voice as cold as ice. "We believe your daughter took it and posted it to humiliate Kelsey and her friends."

Rage darkened the mother's eyes. "My daughter is too dignified to do something like that."

"We know for a fact that she bullied Kelsey and the other girls," Ellie said, watching Bianca for a reaction. "And that she was jealous because a boy at school asked Kelsey to Homecoming instead of her."

Bianca rolled her eyes.

Derrick pulled an envelope from his pocket. "Actually the FBI's cyber team is working on verifying who posted the locker room photo and created the meme. We'll need Bianca's phone and computer."

"Seriously?" Mrs. Copenhagen said. "You need warrants for those."

"Then we'll get them." Ellie gave Bianca a pointed look. "If you didn't post them, make it easy and hand over your laptop and phone and we can clear this up right away."

Confidence rang in Bianca's tone. "You won't find anything there. If I'd posted those, I wouldn't be dumb enough to leave them on a device."

Derrick quickly fired back, "You'd be surprised at what the FBI can recover."

Mrs. Copenhagen clenched her phone and started stabbing numbers. "Don't say anything else, darling. I'm calling your father."

Ellie flattened her hands on the table. "Bianca, listen to me and listen good. If you know where Kelsey is, now is the time to speak up."

Mrs. Copenhagen glared at Bianca, who rolled her eyes as if she was bored.

Ellie and Derrick left Bianca and her mother in the interview room to stew while she made the call to her husband.

Derrick went to Ellie's office to request warrants.

Ellie stopped by Deputy Landrum's office. "I'll have Bianca Copenhagen's phone and computer soon so we can search them. I think she posted the locker room, Virgin Pact pics and the meme that upset Kelsey Tiller."

He gave a nod, and she stepped into her office to call Cord. "Hey. Did you find her?"

"Afraid not," Cord said. "If she'd jumped or fallen here, El, there's no way she could have survived. And I've looked all around and there's no body."

Hope bubbled inside Ellie. "Then she could still be alive."

"Maybe. The ERT took DNA from the bloody handprint along with a photograph of it. The Tillers confirmed the shoe was Kelsey's." Cord's voice broke in the wind. "It's starting to storm here. The guys are beat, too. We're going to have to call off the search team for the night."

"Fine, we'll regroup in the morning." She hesitated, wanting to say more, to ask him about Lola and the baby but that was none of her business.

Ellie's boss rapped on the door. "Mr. Copenhagen is here."

Ellie gestured that she'd be there in a minute. "Talk tomorrow, Cord, get some rest." She hung up and she and Derrick returned to the interview room.

A short, stocky, dark-haired man with an attitude stood in the room, arms folded. Tension filled the air as the family exchanged looks.

"You will not speak to my daughter without my presence,"

Mr. Copenhagen stated, an underlying threat in his harsh tone. "If my daughter is under arrest, I'm calling my attorney. If not, I'm taking her home."

Derrick matched his tone to the lawyer's. "She's not under arrest, Mr. Copenhagen, but I will advise you to have her cooperate."

"Do you know where Kelsey Tiller is?" Ellie asked directly.

"How should I?" Bianca retorted.

"Because we believe you bullied her and made that post to embarrass her."

"Kids pass pictures along all the time," Mr. Copenhagen said.

"These were one of the girls in their underwear in the locker room at school, pictures the girls had no idea were taken, ones Bianca did not have permission to post." Ellie wet her dry lips with her tongue to wipe away the distaste she had for the spoiled girl in the room.

"We are working on warrants for her phone and computer," Derrick said.

Mrs. Copenhagen gasped, but the father simply straightened. "I'm sure whatever she did was harmless."

"Not if they pushed Kelsey into running away or drew a predator to her," Ellie said sharply.

Mr. Copenhagen gestured to the door and his wife and Bianca stood. "You have no proof of any such thing."

Bianca shot Ellie a victorious smile, although Mrs. Copenhagen looked shaken.

"Not yet, but if she did that, this won't be the end of it," Ellie said. "One of my deputies will be out to your house to collect Bianca's cell phone and computer shortly so I suggest you go home. And don't leave town."

Ellie didn't like or trust the Copenhagens. With their wealth, they could book a ticket out of the country and be gone by morning.

THIRTY

RED CLAY MOUNTAIN

He stood by his car for a moment. The storm was dying down, yet the wind screeched off the mountain like a wolf's death cry as he stared at the old house. The house where his life had changed forever.

The place had been deserted for years, and he was grateful no one was here now.

Maybe he should just burn the old place to the ground, let the flames eat up the walls and furniture and beds.

He closed his eyes and imagined it. Smoke billowing toward the clouds. Wood popping and crackling in the night. A fiery blaze exploding, drowning out the memories and the sound of Anna Marie's scream.

But Anna Marie's skeletal body floated through the smoky haze like a ghost ship rising from the underbelly of the sea. Her eye sockets were gaunt, eyes bulging at him with fear, anger and shock.

"Why did you kill me?" her soft voice cried. "Why?"

Emotions made his chest tighten. "I'm sorry, Anna Marie," he choked out. "So sorry."

He had a can of gasoline in his car. All it would take was to douse the dilapidated structure, strike a match and drop it onto the rotting wood.

But... not yet. He had other plans.

He opened the trunk of his car, grabbed his supplies and carried them into the house.

The moment he stepped inside, the scent of musk and death assaulted him, dragging his mind back to the hellhole of secrets he'd carry with him until the day he died. The floor squeaked, wind whined through the windowpanes and a tree branch slapped at the glass as a gust of wind railed outside.

The electricity had been off for years, the house pitch-black. Using his flashlight, he found his way to Anna Marie's bedroom. He carefully covered the bed in a white sheet, white for purity and innocence, then tucked the corners in military style and placed the pillow at the head of the bed. Satisfied with the way it looked, he walked back outside to the car.

He lifted the girl from the trunk and carried her inside, her limp arms dangling like a ragdoll's.

In Anna Marie's bedroom, he laid the girl on the bed and spread her shoulder-length blond hair across the pillow. Then he pulled the top sheet up to tuck her in. Her cheeks glowed alabaster white in the dim light, her pale pink lips soft and slack, her slim fingers cold and stiff as he lifted them and tucked the white teddy bear into her arms.

She looked so innocent, like a sleeping angel waiting to be lifted into heaven.

"Rest in peace," he murmured.

A dark laugh caught him in its clutches as he imagined the fear her family must be feeling at the moment. The hours that had dragged on today as the search teams looked for her and night came with no answers.

The sorrow they'd feel when they saw her posed in death.

He snapped a photo of her with the burner phone, then sent the picture to her parents.

THIRTY-ONE
CROOKED CREEK

Worry for Kelsey consumed Ellie as she walked out to her Jeep. Deputy Landrum had collected Bianca's phone and computer, and Derrick was taking them back to his cabin to examine.

The wind tugged at her ponytail as she stepped outside, a rumble of thunder echoing through the air. Leaves fluttered to the ground like red, yellow and orange snowflakes, dry brown ones crunching beneath her feet. The hair on the back of her neck prickled. Suddenly a figure ducked into an alley. She frowned and considered checking it out. Had someone been following her?

Instincts alert, she decided not to give chase. It was probably someone taking a shortcut through the alley to beat the rain. As she started walking again, she kept alert. Another gust of wind brought more leaves raining down, and she plucked one from her hair as she unlocked her Jeep and slid inside.

Her phone buzzed as she started to shift gears. The Tillers.

Ellie connected. "Detective Reeves."

A hysterical cry echoed over the line.

Ellie went bone still. "Jean?"

"Help... I... I... I think Kelsey's... dead."

Panic stabbed at every nerve ending in Ellie's body.

"I'll be right there."

THIRTY-TWO

WHISPERING PINES

Cord hated that they hadn't found Kelsey yet, but they'd had to call it a night. They'd been searching all day which led him to believe that Kelsey was not in the woods behind her house.

His gut had a dozen knots in it as he stopped at the Corner Café on his way home. Though it was getting late, it was a Saturday night and there were still a few patrons at the bar. He swung into a parking space and got out, tugging his jacket hood up to ward off the rain starting to drizzle.

Two young couples were sharing a piece of chocolate pie, the mayor and his wife were paying their check, and several teenagers were enjoying burgers and shakes. He heard them talking excitedly about the upcoming Homecoming game and dance.

He'd been tossed around from one place to the other and so those things hadn't been a part of his past. He spotted Lola as he entered and thought about the baby she was carrying. His baby.

He pictured his kid growing up with all those things he never had, having a normal life. A life she could give him.

But where did he fit in?

He grabbed a bar stool and she gave him a big smile and poured him a beer. "Did you find the missing girl?"

He shook his head. "Had to call off the search until morning."

"Hopefully the Tillers will hear something by then. She probably just got mad about something and ran off."

He took a sip of the lager. "Maybe."

She yawned and rubbed circles on her belly, making him suck in a breath. This really was happening. She had his kid growing inside her.

"I'll get you the special."

He nodded but he had a sudden flash of his past. Another girl, Melanie... young... after Ellie left for the police academy. A stupid drunken night with a stranger, but that night had dogged him ever since. When he'd closed his eyes, he'd seen Ellie in bed beside him instead of Melanie.

When she'd woken up in the bright light of day, Melanie had seen his scars and looked at him like he was a monster. Three weeks later, he'd learned she was pregnant.

She hadn't even told him. Emotions clogged his throat. She'd taken care of it.

Said she couldn't have a kid with a broken, scarred man like him.

Shame burned deep inside him at the memory. Shame because she was right.

"Here you go, honey," Lola said as she slipped a plate of meatloaf and mashed potatoes in front of him. "I'll clean up while you eat then we can go home."

His throat was too thick to speak. Was she delusional? Didn't she see a kid needed a better man than him as a daddy?

THIRTY-THREE

BACKWATER'S EDGE

Taking a second girl so soon after leaving Kelsey was risky.

But he wanted this all over with. His hands were still fresh with Kelsey's scent, his adrenaline running high.

He parked on the back side of Backwater's Edge mobile home park, closest to where Ruby Pruitt lived. The red-haired freckled-faced teen looked nothing like Kelsey, but her mother was a no-good drunk whore who never should have had kids. The tramp probably wouldn't even miss Ruby when she was gone.

He snuck through the woods to the edge of the trailer park, welcoming the night shadows as he approached the rotting shed behind the Pruitt mobile home. Rain fell, streaking the muddy windows with streams of brown water dripping down the dingy panes.

Voices from the trailer broke through the wind as Ruby's mother flung the front door open and turned, shouting at Ruby.

"You damn little slut," her mother shouted. "Showing off your body online!"

"But Mama," Ruby cried. "I—"

"Shut up. I wish I'd never had you."

Mrs. Pruitt ran down the cement steps wearing her uniform of a mini skirt and tank top, cursing and calling Ruby all kinds of vile names. Ruby burst into tears, which mingled with the rain on her reddening cheeks.

He almost felt sorry for the girl. She deserved better than that woman as her mother.

He'd been watching her off and on for weeks now and had seen Ruby help her mother stagger into the house and into the bed countless times. Had seen a couple of her lovers corner Ruby. One even grabbed her arm, but Ruby had kicked him then ran into her room and locked the door. Later that night, her mother had fussed at her. Told her she'd messed up her night and next time to be nice to her friends.

And now the pictures were revealed and the challenge to break the virgin pact had been issued, it wouldn't be long until she turned into her mother.

Mrs. Pruitt's old Chevy spat mud as she sped from the driveway and onto the road, and Ruby swiped at her wet face, then dragged her feet as she went back inside the dive where she lived.

He started to move forward, but a noise to the right made him duck behind the trees. The old woman who lived across from Ruby must have heard the commotion; she had meandered onto her porch and was watching Ruby's trailer.

He tugged his rain hood over his head and found cover. He had all night. He'd wait till the old biddy went back inside.

Then Ruby would be his.

THIRTY-FOUR

CABINS ON THE RIVER

Derrick gripped his phone tightly in his hand as he let himself into his cabin. "Listen, Lindsey, we caught a case," he said. "A teenager has disappeared here."

"Sorry to hear that, Derrick, but the kids were hoping you could come over tonight."

Derrick gritted his teeth and counted to ten. He loved his godchildren to the moon and back and was grateful Lindsey had finally come around and stopped blaming him for her husband —his friend—Rick's suicide. "I can't. I have to search the girl's computer. You know every minute a child is missing decreases the chances of finding them alive."

"I know. I just want to make it up to you for the other night."

He pinched the bridge of his nose. "Forget it. It was nothing."

The memory played through his mind in vivid clarity. He'd taken the kids for ice cream then stopped to drop them off. Lately, Lindsey had him on speed dial and this time she'd begged him to come in for a drink.

"I'm just so lonely," she said as she poured him a whiskey and herself a tall glass of Merlot.

"What about your girlfriends?" he asked.

"Their husbands all worked with Rick," she said. "I... It's just hard being around them."

He understood. Sort of. She hadn't wanted to be near him when she first lost Rick.

Debating how to respond, he sipped his whiskey and before he knew it, was tucking the kids in bed. When he came down the stairs, Lindsey clasped his hand and pulled him onto the sofa.

Then she tried to kiss him.

That had come as a shock, and he'd bolted up and walked to the door. He stood there, shaken. Then she burst into tears.

"You're so good with the kids," she said. "We'd be good together, too."

He shook his head. There was no way he could be with his best friend's wife. He wasn't a replacement for Rick. And he told her that.

Her tears came hard and fast and she shouted at him to leave.

So he had.

But now she wanted him to come back. Hell, nothing good could come of that.

His phone beeped. Ellie. "I have to go. It's work."

He didn't wait for a response. He connected to Ellie.

"Derrick, I'm headed to the Tillers. I don't know what happened, but Mrs. Tiller called, hysterical."

Derrick pulled his keys from his pocket. "I'll meet you there."

The missing teen took priority. He'd figure out what to do about Lindsey later.

THIRTY-FIVE

WHISPERING PINES

Ellie parked at the Tiller house, her stomach in knots. The cloud cover cast the property in an eerie gray, making the woods look even more ominous tonight.

Derrick pulled in behind her, and they shared a worried look then headed to the house.

She heard Jean crying as her husband opened the door. His face looked ashen, eyes glazed. A hint of bourbon wafted from him.

Kelsey's father motioned them to come in with a shaky hand. "My... wife... in here."

Ellie's chest tightened as she and Derrick followed him to the living room where Jean sat gripping her phone in her hand, her body trembling, huge gulping sobs erupting from her.

The couple had sat divided earlier this morning, but tonight Mr. Tiller rushed to his wife's side, sank down beside her and put his arm around her in comfort.

"What happened?" Ellie asked softly.

He took the phone from his wife's hands and shoved it toward her. Derrick leaned over her shoulder and they looked at it together.

A sick feeling stole through Ellie. Kelsey was lying on a bed with white sheets, hair fanned across the pillow. Another white sheet covered her lower body.

And a white teddy bear was tucked in beside her.

Eyes closed. Skin pasty. Pale lips pressed together.

Not moving.

"My... baby... She's d... dead," Jean choked out.

Ellie chewed the inside of her cheek. The girl looked as if she was sleeping. But the lack of color in her face and her still body did seem lifeless.

"When did you receive this?" Derrick asked.

"Just a few minutes ago," Mr. Tiller said. "We tried to call the number back but there was no answer."

Ellie wanted to give the couple hope, but she couldn't lie. "Do you have any idea who sent this?"

"No," Mr. Tiller said. "If I did, I wouldn't be sitting here. I'd have gone after the bastard."

"Does the teddy bear belong to Kelsey?" Ellie asked.

Jean shook her head no.

"She wasn't the teddy bear kind," Mr. Tiller added.

"Where is she? Who took her?" Jean cried. "What did he do to her?"

Ellie wished to hell she had some answers. "Have you had any repairmen or workers come to your house in the last few months?"

The couple shook their heads.

Ellie studied the photo more closely. She didn't see any visible wounds.

"Let me send this to the lab," Derrick said. "Maybe our cyber team can determine where the photo was taken."

"Send it to Deputy Landrum, too," Ellie said. "His computer skills might come in handy."

She snagged her phone and called the sheriff. If some

maniac had been stalking Kelsey, he might live in the vicinity of the Tillers.

"Sheriff Waters," she said, then explained about the photo. "We don't know where he left her body so have your deputies start searching abandoned properties. Focus first on properties within a twenty-five miles radius of the Tillers."

If Kelsey was nearby, they had to find her. They had to.

THIRTY-SIX

BACKWATER'S EDGE

Tears burned Ruby's eyes as she finished scrubbing the kitchen and piled fast food wrappers, empty cigarette packs, Mountain Dew cans and sticky old magazines from her mother's hoarding into a garbage bag to carry outside.

Her mama's words taunted her. *Trash. Slut. You've ruined your life, girl. I oughta kick you out now.*

"I didn't do anything," Ruby had argued.

"Don't lie to me, girl. Now I gotta get to The Hungry Wolf. You stay in that trailer and don't cause me any more trouble." Her breath sounded wheezy from the last drag of her Camel. "I'll deal with you when I get back."

Ruby shivered at the thought.

Shoving the blackened bananas into the trash bag, Ruby tied it closed and carried it outside to the bin in the mud hole the trailer park called a yard. Rain dripped from the trees and pinged off the metal can, and somewhere nearby she heard a cat fight. There were half a dozen feral strays around, pawing for scraps and marking their territory. They climbed under the trailer, making the sagging back stoop reek of cat pee.

The trash stunk just as bad and there was a mountain of it

overflowing. Flies swarmed around it; a couple of bags on the ground had been ripped apart by wild animals.

Thunder rumbled above and Ruby ran back to the trailer. Footsteps sounded behind her and she glanced over her shoulder. A dark figure moved between the trees.

Probably just old man Huddie two doors down. He was a meth head and she stayed away from him. She picked up her pace and ran, slipping in the mud and falling on her butt. A limb cracked off from a nearby tree and flew to the ground at her feet.

She pushed herself up, slipping and sliding until she made it up the concrete steps to the back door. She wiped her muddy feet on the old doormat, then grabbed a kitchen towel to wipe her hands as she stepped inside.

But suddenly she thought she heard a voice. But it was so low she couldn't tell if it was a man or woman. Or... maybe Kelsey?

Praying it was, she stepped back onto the porch and scanned the yard. The swing creaked at the old playground. The one where she and Kelsey and June liked to hang out.

Hope and curiosity drove her, and she ran down the steps and headed to the playground.

THIRTY-SEVEN
RED HAWK RIDGE

Deputy Heath Landrum had had a bad feeling ever since he'd seen the news of his brother Digger's release from prison. That do-gooder O'Connor woman with the Innocence Project had dredged up all the horror when she'd questioned him about his sister's murder.

Something he never talked about. Had tried to forget.

Could not outrun.

That one night had completely destroyed his life.

Actually, his family life had blown up even before that when his mother deserted them. Just left one day and never came back. Not a single damn word in years, not birthdays or holidays or even Heath's graduation.

After their mama left, Anna Marie had cried for a week then had become sullen and refused to talk. Digger was just plain pissed off. He and Heath's father had butted heads something bad. His father accused Digger of being just like Digger's real old man, a sadist who liked to hurt people.

Turned out he was right.

Heath had not seen it coming.

Guilt for not protecting Anna Marie haunted him.

She was around the same age as Kelsey Tiller. And now Kelsey was missing.

He poured himself an IPA. This damn day had felt like a hundred rolled into one. Sympathy for the Tillers filled him. They must be suffering not knowing where their daughter was, just like he'd suffered not knowing where his mama had gone or why she'd left him and his siblings behind.

He stepped outside on the back deck of his cabin, gazing out over Red Hawk Ridge. He'd moved here to escape the scandal of his past and was drawn to the red-tailed hawks known to hover and soar over the ridges on this side of the mountain.

His phone rang, cutting into the silence. He was tempted to ignore it. But what if it was work? Or what if the O'Connor woman had given Digger his number and Digger was calling?

Now he was free, would he come looking for Heath? Did he expect forgiveness?

Instead of the O'Connor woman, Detective Reeves's name appeared on his screen.

Hopefully they'd caught a break in the case, and this girl would be saved.

He took a sip of beer then connected. "Landrum."

"The Tillers received a picture of their daughter," Ellie said, her tone grim. "I'm forwarding it to you now, Landrum. I can't tell where it was taken. Special Agent Fox is sending it to his cyber team as well."

Heath inhaled a deep breath, bracing himself for whatever he was about to see.

His pulse hammered when the photo came through.

Kelsey was lying on a bed of white sheets, a white teddy bear tucked in her arms. Eyes closed. Mouth slack. She looked as if she was sleeping.

Or... dead.

Just as Anna Marie had been. Anna Marie with her hair fanned across the pillow. Anna Marie and the white teddy bear...

Dear God, Digger. What have you done?

THIRTY-EIGHT
BACKWATER'S EDGE

Ruby's heart thumped wildly. Was Kelsey alive and out here on the playground where they used to meet? The muffled voice—was that Kelsey calling to her to sneak out and meet her?

Wind whipped her hair around her face and she tucked the tangled strands behind her ear, turning in a wide arc. The streetlight for the entrance to the trailer park was broken, the sky dark and stormy, making it hard to see. Wet leaves swirled to the ground. The sound of twigs snapping set her teeth on edge. A dog's howl echoed from old man Huddie's yard. The swing moved back and forth but there was nobody in it.

A chill rippled through her and she turned to search the jungle gym. Her feet skidded over pine straw and wet leaves. Mud sucked at her shoes.

No one on the jungle gym.

"Kelsey, where are you?" she whispered.

A noise sounded from behind her. Then the sound of breathing. She started to turn around but someone grabbed her from behind, then shoved her so hard she fell into the mud.

She clawed at the ground to get up and spit out debris as she fought to get away. Hands snatched at her, yanking her backward. She struggled and screamed for help, but her attacker gripped her around the neck, pressed his hand over her mouth and dragged her into the woods.

The acrid odor of garbage and her own fear swirled around her, making her dizzy. He was holding her so tight, she felt her windpipe being shut off, felt her lungs straining for air and the darkness sucking at her.

Car lights flickered across the dirt drive. Hope speared her. Maybe they'd see her. Help her.

But her attacker dragged her between the trees and shoved a rag over her mouth. She smelled something strong, like acetone.

She yanked at the man's hands, but suddenly the world blurred and she sagged to the ground. She tasted mud just before the world faded into darkness.

THIRTY-NINE

CROOKED CREEK POLICE DEPARTMENT

Sunday

Dawn broke with no news of Kelsey.

Ellie strode into the conference room for the debriefing she'd called, anxious and exhausted from lack of sleep. All night she'd wondered where the killer had left Kelsey's body and if she'd ever find her. The Tillers needed that, needed closure.

Captain Hale, Derrick, Deputy Eastwood and Sheriff Bryce Waters filed into the conference room minutes later. Cord loped in with coffees for everyone.

"Lola sent this over, said she was up early baking." He dropped a bag of pastries on the counter along the far wall at the coffee station.

Ellie bit her tongue, fighting resentment. Lola was the perfect little woman. And she would be the perfect mother. Ellie should be happy for Cord. He deserved that kind of love.

Bryce's jaw hardened and he looked down at his hands, which she noticed had a slight tremble.

Was he drinking again?

"I'm all in," Shondra said as she grabbed one of the coffees then dug in the bag and chose a cinnamon roll.

"Nice of Lola," Ellie said, regaining her composure. "It was a long day yesterday. Probably going to be another."

The sheriff nodded. "You need to do a press conference, El," he said quietly. "People are already starting to spread rumors at the café."

Ellie grimaced. Meddlin' Maude was probably the leader of the pack. But he was right. She had to inform the public of the facts. "I'll give a statement when we finish here."

Captain Hale grabbed a cheese croissant and walked toward the door. "I'll arrange it now."

Cord snatched a coffee and muffin for himself and took a seat. Everyone else followed suit and joined him at the table. She glanced at the clock on the wall.

Eight o'clock sharp. Where was Deputy Landrum? Typically, he was the first to arrive.

Didn't matter. She had to get started.

On the whiteboard, she displayed a copy of the photograph of the girls in the locker room then the picture of the virgin pact, and the meme with the balloon words depicting the countdown for Christmas. "These were posted Friday night and Kelsey called Mitch Drummond upset, leading us first to think Kelsey might have run away."

In another column, she listed the people they'd questioned and their comments, then attached the picture of Kelsey the Tillers had received.

"This morning, we're working on the theory that Kelsey was abducted. And judging from the picture the Tillers received, that she was murdered."

A collective rumble of shocked reactions followed. Cord's look darkened and Shondra gasped softly.

"The FBI's cyber team is analyzing the photo the Tillers received and trying to pinpoint who it came from," Ellie said.

Footsteps sounded and then the deputy's voice as he entered. "Sorry I'm late."

Landrum's eyes looked bloodshot, his sandy-blond hair mussed as if he hadn't bothered to comb it, and beard stubble grazed his jaw.

His gaze landed on the photo on the board with a flicker of unease. She'd never seen the deputy emotional but she could have sworn he was upset.

"I checked into the Tillers' financials," Deputy Landrum said. "Nothing out of the ordinary, middle-class income. No bad investments or recent big withdrawals. No hidden money or offshore accounts."

"If they can enhance the photo enough to see a landmark or location from where the message was sent, I might be able to identify the area," Cord said.

"Will keep you posted on what the cyber team turns up," Derrick said matter-of-factly.

"Why send a picture instead of just letting us find the body?" Shondra asked.

Ellie wondered the same thing. "Good question. Perhaps he wants the Tillers to suffer for some reason. Or he could be planning to dispose of her in a way we could never find her."

"Or he's sadistic and playing a game with us. He wants us to know she's dead and that he's smart enough not to leave any clues, even her body behind," Derrick suggested.

"The way she was posed is significant," Ellie said. "Why white sheets? Why the white teddy bear?"

"Did the bear belong to her?" Shondra asked.

Ellie shook her head. "No. Which means the perp must have bought it."

"That means it's part of his MO and that the murder was premediated," Derrick pointed out. "A profiler might suggest that posing her as if she's sleeping means he wants her to rest in peace. Or that he cares about her."

Ellie followed his train of thought. "And the white sheets and white bear could represent innocence or purity."

"That would fit with the virgin pact," Derrick agreed.

Ellie nodded. "Which means that if our killer saw it, it may have had something to do with the reason he chose Kelsey."

"I traced the posts back to Bianca Copenhagen," Derrick said.

"You want me to call them and tell them to come back in?" Deputy Landrum asked.

Ellie quirked her head in thought. "No. There's no way Bianca could have kidnapped Kelsey, moved her body and orchestrated this. But Landrum, analyze the photo the Tillers received."

"Copy that," he murmured.

"How did it go with the counselor and teachers?" Ellie asked Shondra.

"Counselor said Kelsey had not requested a meeting or confided that she was upset about anything. Her teachers gave glowing reports about her, both academically and personally. Her computer science and technology teacher, Mr. Jones, confirmed that he saw Bianca Copenhagen bullying her. And that Bianca was a whizz with technology."

"Sheriff, anything on the search for abandoned properties?"

"Nothing yet," Bryce said. "But we're back at it this morning."

Cord stood. "I'll organize search parties for the more remote areas."

Ellie rapped her knuckles on the table. "Let's get to it."

Captain Hale stepped into the doorway. "Detective Reeves, Angelica Gomez is here."

"Tell her I'll be right there." Time to face the music. Unfortunately, she had nothing good to tell the public.

FORTY

Heath Landrum couldn't erase the image of the girl in the sleeping pose from his mind as he returned to his desk. Ellie was right about one thing—this murder was not carried out by a teenage girl.

It had taken planning and muscle.

The way Kelsey had been posed taunted him.

Digger was out of prison at the moment. Could he be demented or brazen enough to commit a similar crime so soon after his release?

Antsy, he phoned Caitlin O'Connor with the Innocence Project. His pulse hammered while he waited for her to answer.

"Caitlin O'Connor," she said on the third ring.

"It's Deputy Landrum, Digger's brother."

"Yes," she said a little tightly. Probably because he hadn't exactly been cordial to her when she'd requested an interview for her podcast. He'd told her he thought she was wasting her time trying to clear Digger, that he wanted nothing to do with it.

"I saw you got Digger released," he began.

"Yes, on parole with time served. But we're requesting a new trial to exonerate him."

"You really think he's innocent, don't you?"

A tense second passed. "I think there are holes in the story that are worthy of being investigated. That he was a kid and was railroaded."

"He confessed," Heath said.

"I've reviewed the transcripts and watched the interrogation," she said. "Something was off. And what was his motive for killing his sister? There's no mention from any of the people I've talked to that he harbored animosity toward Anna Marie."

"He was a loose cannon," Heath finally said. "He and my dad butted heads a lot."

"But to attack someone in their sleep is different from being provoked or killing someone in the heat of the moment. And if the stepfather was the problem, why not go after him?"

"He suffered from night terrors. Maybe he thought she was someone else, that he was fighting someone. Or maybe he knew the best way to get to my dad was to hurt his pet child."

"I suppose that's possible," she said. "But the police were quick to accept his confession without pursuing other leads. We have an investigator doing that and some questions are being raised."

"What type of questions?" Heath asked.

"I can't say at the moment," she said. "But when the podcast is released and if the case is retried, it'll all come out."

Frustration knotted Heath's neck muscles. "Do you know where he is?"

The woman hesitated. "Why are you asking?"

"Because he's my brother," Heath said, barely containing his irritation. That was the only reason he hadn't shared his suspicions with Ellie earlier.

"That may be so, but you've made it clear that you're still angry at him and don't believe he's innocent. At this point, the last thing he needs is to be provoked."

Heath's temper rose, but he forced himself to take slow deep breaths. Being a hothead himself wouldn't earn her cooperation. "I assume with your job that you watch the news and that you're aware a teenage girl named Kelsey Tiller went missing yesterday morning."

"Yes, I heard. Did they find her?"

"Not yet." He hesitated, knowing he shouldn't share details with anyone. But she was close to Digger and if he confided in anyone, it would be her. "Police are not releasing this information to the public yet so keep this under wraps. Last night Kelsey's parents received a photograph of their daughter posed as if she was sleeping. She's lying on a bed with white sheets and holding a white teddy bear."

Her long-winded sigh echoed back. "What are you saying, Deputy Landrum?"

"The girl... She's posed exactly like my sister was found."

Another heartbeat of silence. "Are you insinuating Digger is involved?"

"I don't know," Heath said. "But I don't like coincidences."

"When we hang up, I'll contact him," she said. "But Deputy, ask yourself this. Why are you so convinced that your half brother was guilty of your sister's murder?"

The image of Digger being hauled away by police fifteen years ago flashed in his head. "Just find him and see if he has an alibi for when the girl was taken. Then let me know what he says."

Not that he would believe him. Not until he talked to him himself.

FORTY-ONE

Although Ellie hated press conferences, they were a necessary evil. People needed to know facts, not spread gossip or speculation that stirred panic. Sometimes posting a tip line brought out the crazies, but other times they received valuable information.

At the moment, they needed all the help they could get.

She inhaled a calming breath as she joined Angelica Gomez and her cameraman, Tom, in the press room. In spite of the grave situation, Angelica looked flawless as always, her long, dark brown hair pulled back in a pearl clasp, accentuating her sharp cheekbones. The black pencil skirt and lacy white blouse were professional, just as her demeanor was.

"Are you ready?" Angelica asked.

"As ready as I'll ever be," Ellie said wryly.

Angelica knew how much Ellie hated to be in front of the camera and had been confrontational when they'd first met, but over the last few cases they'd settled into a working understanding of each other. During one case, they'd also discovered they were half sisters.

Ellie took her place by the reporter and signaled to Tom that they were ready to begin.

"Angelica Gomez, Channel Five News, here with Detective Ellie Reeves at the Crooked Creek Police Department," Angelica said. "Yesterday an Amber Alert was issued for fifteen-year-old Kelsey Tiller, who disappeared from her home in Whispering Pines." She tilted the microphone toward Ellie. "You have an update for us, Detective Reeves?"

"Yes," Ellie said. "Unfortunately, Kelsey has not yet been found. But we have reason to believe she was kidnapped. At this point, we are conducting a statewide search for her and are pleading with the public for information that might lead us to the person responsible for her disappearance." Ellie swallowed hard as the image in the photo played through her mind.

"Do you have any persons of interest?" Angelica asked.

Ellie wished to hell they did. "I'm not at liberty to discuss details at this point. But again, please help us find Kelsey and bring her home."

She silently indicated that she was done, and Angelica wrapped up the segment with phone numbers for the police and a tip line. Tom took his cue and left Ellie with Angelica while he carried his equipment out to the news van.

"Now, tell all," Angelica murmured.

Ellie sighed and shook her head. "There's not much to tell." Ellie showed Angelica the picture the Tillers received.

"Oh my God. I feel for that couple," Angelica said.

"I know," Ellie said. "The sheriff, his deputies and Ranger McClain are searching abandoned properties for her body now."

Angelica narrowed her eyes as she studied the photo again. "Something about the way she's posed seems familiar."

"How do you mean?" Ellie asked.

Angelica smoothed a strand of her chignon that had escaped the clasp. "I don't know. I just feel like I've seen it before."

Ellie's pulse jumped. "As in another murder?"

Angelica shrugged. "Maybe."

Ellie breathed out as a seed of an idea sparked. "Thanks, Angelica. If this bastard has done this before, the MO might show up in the system."

FORTY-TWO

LAST CHANCE MOTEL

The ding of his phone jarred Digger from a frenetic sleep. He growled, rolled over and checked the clock. Ten a.m.

Damn. Again, he'd had a nightmarish night and hadn't fallen asleep until dawn.

The ding sounded again, and he checked the number. Caitlin O'Connor.

Hell, he had to answer. She was his ticket to keeping his freedom. And now he'd had a taste of the fresh mountain air, he never wanted to leave it, especially to return to that hellhole prison. The animals there were more dangerous than the bears, wild hogs and snakes on the trail.

Rubbing his hand over his eyes, he sat up, grabbed the phone and connected. "Hello."

"Digger, it's Caitlin O'Connor. Where are you?"

He frowned at her tone. "At a motel. Was sleeping."

"How about night before last?" she asked.

The hair on the back of his neck prickled. He knew what this was about. "Same," he lied. Telling her he'd woken up in the woods wouldn't look good for him. "You want the number?"

"Yes, I do," she said.

He silently cursed. She wanted to check his alibi. "Last Chance Motel," he said. "Room Nine. What's up?"

"Are you aware a teenage girl disappeared from a neighborhood named Whispering Pines night before last?"

"Yeah, I heard it on the news." Frustration knotted his gut. When something bad happened or a crime occurred, the first person police looked at were ex-cons, especially ones whose crimes were similar. And he wasn't exactly an *ex*-con since his conviction hadn't been officially overturned. If he screwed up, he'd be right back in the pen.

"Were you anywhere near Whispering Pines Friday night?" Same question. Different wording. Didn't she believe him?

Stick to as much truth as possible so you don't have to remember your lies. "Like I said, I was here at the motel."

"Okay, I had to ask. Apparently, the parents of the girl received a photograph of her posed on a bed, the scene similar to the way Anna Marie was found."

"What?" Panic tightened his throat and he glanced at the scars on his hands, the ones he'd gotten in prison defending himself. "You think I got out of jail and was dumb enough to kill a girl and leave her like my sister? Lady, the last thing I want is to go back to that snake pit."

A heartbeat passed, and Digger realized he'd come off too strong. Caitlin was the only person who'd been on his side. He couldn't alienate her. "I'm sorry," he said. "I... didn't mean to snap at you."

"I know," she said. "And I realize this is difficult. If police start looking at you as a person of interest, it won't help our case. But it was your half brother who called me."

Heath? "He thinks I did it," Digger said flatly.

"He's a deputy in Crooked Creek," Ms. O'Connor continued. "And he's working the case. When he saw the photograph the parents received, a photo where the girl appears to be dead, he—"

"He instantly assumed it was me." A sense of despair washed over Digger. If his own brother thought he was guilty, the rest of the police would bury him.

"He wants to talk to you," Ms. O'Connor said. "I told him I didn't think that was a good idea."

Digger shoved the bed covers aside, stood and walked to the window and looked out at the sprawling mountains. The gloomy sky mirrored his mood.

Yesterday when he'd revisited his childhood house, he'd hoped he'd remember some detail to jumpstart his memory and help himself. Didn't happen though. That night was still a blur.

What would happen if he talked to Heath? Would he be able to fill in some of the blanks?

The sky was dark and stormy as Cord parked at the base of Bald Eagle Mountain. He'd been benched for nearly a month now and it was driving him bone-ass crazy. He was not used to being weak or being taken care of, and Lola tended to smother him.

She was going to be a great mother though. The kid was damn lucky to have one sane, stable parent.

He, on the other hand, had no idea how to be a father.

Or... a partner to Lola. Should he offer to marry her?

Did she want that?

Hell, he did care about her. But... when he closed his eyes at night, he saw Ellie's face in his mind instead.

Dammit, what was he going to do?

He knew what the hell it was like to grow up without a father. He couldn't do that to his own kid.

But wouldn't the child eventually realize he was a broken man? Flawed? Sense that he'd done bad things?

A blast of wind jarred him back to the reason he was here. To find the missing girl. He'd decided to search this area because it was near the Tillers. The area was sparse with tourists, offering remote places that would make a perfect place to dump a body.

He threw on his backpack, grabbed Benji from the cab of his truck and gave him a pat. "It's me and you, boy."

Benji ran his wet tongue over Cord's hand and Cord's heart warmed, the dark voices in his head quieting.

They were a team. Always had been. Always would be.

Benji was the one he counted on. He'd give his life for that sweet, loyal dog.

Just as he would for Ellie.

Sucking in a breath, he locked his truck and set off on the trail to climb Bald Eagle Mountain where eagles soared and life was free and he could hear the cry of the falcon overhead. As he maneuvered the steep ridges, raindrops dripped from shaking trees, wind rustled fall leaves and the scent of damp moss and lichen filled his nostrils. Thunder rumbled in the dark sky, raising the demons from deep within him, demons wrestling to get out so they could drag him to hell.

He already had one foot in the door.

Maybe finding Kelsey would bring him one step back from the darkness.

FORTY-FOUR

KUDZU HOLLER

June was trying to hold on to hope that Kelsey would be found okay. But so far nothing, and now Ruby wasn't even answering her.

Worse, June's grandma had told her horror stories of real-life abductions and murders that she'd been watching on Lifetime. Her grandmother's fretting made June feel like a dog about those stupid pictures. She'd had a nightmare herself, terrified that all those bad things Grandma had said might be happening to Kelsey.

Had some monster taken her? Was she tied to a bed or locked in a basement somewhere? Being tortured by some sex-crazed lunatic?

Would the police find her in a ditch or in the woods where the animals had chewed on her body...

Chill bumps skated up her arms, and she looked out the window at the kudzu-infested holler. Snakes and insects and God knows what else were hiding in the overgrown mass. The kudzu had taken over, winding together like a braided rope, twisting up the side of their house, crawling over the roof and slithering over the windows.

"We have to have faith," Grandma said as she scooped blueberry pancakes and bacon onto a plate for her. "The police will find Kelsey, I just know it. And then they'll lock up whoever took her."

"I hope so," June said as she poured syrup onto the pancake mound. "But I can't go back to school tomorrow."

Her grandma gave her a sympathetic but firm look. "You will go back to school and you'll hold your head up high, and this shall pass."

June stared at her in horror. There was no way she could face the laughter, teasing and name calling. They already called her the poor kid from the holler.

Grandma patted June's shoulder. "Now eat up. I'm going to church to pray about this. I think you should come, too."

June stabbed her fork at her pancake. "Please, Grandma, don't make me go to church. Everyone will be talking. Just let me stay here."

Her grandmother heaved a wary breath, the wrinkles around her pudgy face deepening. "All right. You can skip church, just this one time. But sooner or later you'll have to face this. And if that girl Bianca did this, you have to stand up to her and show her that she can't squash you like a bug with her bullying."

June knew she was right, but she wasn't ready to do that yet. The only friends who'd seen her in her underwear were Kelsey and Ruby. But now all the kids at school had.

Humiliation stung her cheeks. She choked down another few bites of her breakfast so as not to disappoint her grandmother. She was the most positive person June knew and refused to let anything get her down. She might be old, but she had a circle of church friends that would do anything for her. June wanted to have that kind of faith and friends; she *had* had it with Kelsey and Ruby.

"I'll clean up, Grandma," June offered. "Go to church and enjoy lunch with your women's group."

"Okay, thanks, hon." Her grandma gestured toward the Bear Paw quilt on her quilting frame. "Maybe we can work on the quilt when I get back."

June nodded. Her grandma's quilts were like pieces of art. She sold them at the local flea markets and took custom orders. June thought the hand stitching was tedious, but she enjoyed sorting the fabrics and helping her grandmother lay them out and piece them together. They fit like a colorful puzzle and told a story.

Some of the kids at school thought arts and crafts, especially sewing, was old-fashioned. But June thought it was cool. At thirteen, her grandma had taught her to sew, and June had made a patchwork purse. She'd been so proud, but Bianca and her friends had poked fun at it. One of Bianca's friends had grabbed it one day and unraveled the threads until it fell apart.

She felt like her life was unraveling around her now just like that thread.

Still, June admired her grandma. She might not have graduated high school but she had the kind of talent you didn't get from book learning.

"Sure, Grandma, I'll help you," she murmured and gave her grandma a hug. She'd have been lost to the foster system after her parents died if her mother's mother hadn't taken her in.

Her grandmother gave her arm a squeeze, then waddled down the hall. June picked up her plate, scraped the uneaten food in the trash and carried it to the sink. She quickly rinsed it, put it in the dishwasher and then cleaned the skillet.

Her stomach churning, she slumped on the couch and called Ruby. Her hands felt clammy with sweat as she waited for Ruby to answer, but the phone went to voicemail, so she left a message.

"Rubes, call me, please. I'm worried about you."

She bit her bottom lip with her teeth as fear took hold. It wasn't like Ruby not to respond.

Ruby's mama worked late at night. Brought strange men home. Sometimes she didn't come home at all.

Had Ruby been home alone all night? What if something had happened to her like it had Kelsey?

She glanced at the clock on the wall as her grandmother returned with her purse. She waved goodbye. "See you later. Now be sure to stay inside and keep the doors locked."

"Okay." June waved and waited until her grandmother's car rolled down the drive. Her grandma would be gone for a while. Preacher was long-winded and always went over. And the church ladies could make the buffet last for hours.

Making a snap decision, she snatched her rain jacket from the hook by the door, pulled it on, stuffed her phone in her pocket and dashed out the door. She'd check on Ruby herself and be back without her grandma ever knowing she'd left the house.

FORTY-FIVE
BOULDER CREEK

Adrenaline pumped through him as he maneuvered the switchbacks. He had to swerve to steer around a pothole then jerked the wheel to the right to avoid a deer that shot out of nowhere. The cloud cover created ghostly black shadows above the ridges, the bare trees swaying with the force of the wind.

He heard Ruby thrashing around in the trunk of his car and cursed. If someone heard the commotion, they might call it in.

He could not get caught.

Knowing he was closer to his own place than the house where he planned to leave her, he sped onto the road leading toward it. The boulders and ridges of the mountains surrounded his nest, sheltering him from outsiders. Creek water gurgled in the background as he pulled down his drive, parked then strode to the back of his vehicle. When he opened the trunk, Ruby was kicking and trying to untie her hands. Her scream was muffled by the rag he'd stuffed in her mouth, her terror palpable.

He grabbed the chloroform he'd bought, doused another rag with it then pressed it over her face. She pushed at him with her bound hands, kicking and flailing, but the drug finally dragged her into unconsciousness.

He opened his duffel bag with the sheets and teddy bear to set the scene, laughing as he imagined her mother's reaction. Torturing her with the picture would be worth sacrificing Ruby.

FORTY-SIX

BACKWATER'S EDGE

In spite of the chilly wind, June was sweating as she cut through the woods to Ruby's trailer. A sick feeling crawled up her spine like icy fingers raking over her.

A dog howled from somewhere close by and the smell of rotting garbage hit her. Her stomach roiled. At first, Ruby hadn't wanted any of them to see where she lived. The yards were littered with trash, the weeds overgrown. Her mama was the worst kind of housekeeper and the tiny trailer overflowed with junk that Mrs. Pruitt never threw out. Stacks of dusty magazines, knickknacks, old makeup, and boxes of junk she'd bought at the thrift store were everywhere.

At one time, Ruby said she'd counted fifty-two cans of tuna fish in the small pantry. And that was just the tuna fish. Other outdated canned goods filled the shelves along with homemade canned vegetables that, judging from whatever was growing inside them, had probably been there years.

Her mama was home, June realized as she spotted the rusted Chevy in the graveled drive. A black pick-up with muddy tires sat next to it.

She had company. June shivered. Ruby hated her mother's

friends, especially the men who slept over. More than one of them had given her the creeps by brushing up against her and cornering her. Another had grabbed her wrist and even left a bruise when she'd yanked her arm away from him. She'd taken to hiding in her room or running to June's or Kelsey's house some mornings to avoid them.

June halted at the door and called Ruby's phone again, but it went straight to voicemail. Worry made her clench her teeth, and she braced herself for Ruby's mother as she raised her fist and knocked. She hunched her shoulders against the wind as raindrops splashed the ground from the trees. A black cat darted past the house with a loud screech, another one chasing it.

June knocked again, scanning the yard and hoping Ruby would run around from the back so June wouldn't have to face her mother. She was sloppy and rude when she'd been drinking, which was most of the time.

A thin man wearing baggy jeans and a holey T-shirt opened the door, a sleeve of tattoos covering his hairy arms. He reeked of beer and cigarettes. His glassy eyes barely flitted over June and he grunted as if she was in his way, then he shouldered past her and stumbled to his truck.

Behind him, June spotted Ruby's mother, tugging a flowered bathrobe about her. Her hair was mussed as if she'd just crawled from bed. Disapproval darkened her scowl indicating June had interrupted her morning.

Was Ruby hiding in her room with her earbuds to keep away from them?

If she was, why not answer her phone?

"What are you doing here so early?" Mrs. Pruitt asked, her voice slurred.

Early? It was almost eleven o'clock. "I came to see Ruby."

"She's probably in her room." Mrs. Pruitt turned and wove

back through the mess. "You tell her she better get in there and clean that mud off the kitchen floor."

June watched her stagger down the narrow hall to her bedroom and she darted to Ruby's room. But when she looked inside, Ruby's bed was made as if she hadn't slept in it.

Nerves on edge, she hurried to the kitchen and spotted the mud on the floor. It looked like it had been tracked in from the back door. Maybe Ruby was outside, hiding until her mother's latest creepy guy left.

June sidestepped the mud on the floor as she made her way to the back door and stepped onto the stoop. The wind brought the stench of garbage and cat pee again. She covered her nose and followed the footprints in the mud in the direction of the old playground where they met to hang out.

Suddenly, she spied Ruby's silver headband a few feet away from the garbage cans. Then she saw drag marks on the wet ground and what looked like handprints in the mud.

Fear clogged her throat as she followed the drag marks around the dumpster to the edge of the woods. Holding her breath, she crept into the thicket of trees, peering left and right. "Ruby!" June called.

Another few feet and she called out again. "Ruby, are you out here?"

A dog barked nearby. The wind whistled off the mountain and hurled a tree limb down in front of her. June jumped back, scanning the playground, but it was empty.

She eased around a few more trees, searching and calling again until she reached the creek. There, she spotted Ruby's friendship bracelet. It was just like the one she and Kelsey wore. They never took them off. Never.

June pressed a hand to her chest. She had to get help.

She turned and ran back to the house, careful not to step into the muddy print. Just as she reached the back porch door, she heard a shriek from inside. Terrified, she sprinted up the porch steps.

Ruby's mother was standing in the kitchen, staring wide-eyed at her phone.

"Mrs. Pruitt," June whispered.

The woman blinked several times, her hand shaking as she dropped the phone. With a groan, she collapsed into the kitchen chair.

June picked up the phone to hand it back to her and gasped at the picture.

It looked like Ruby was... dead.

FORTY-SEVEN

Ellie had just settled into her office to search for cases with similarities to Kelsey's when Captain Hale knocked on the door.

"Detective Reeves, 9-1-1 call from some girl named June Larson. Said she's at her friend Ruby's mobile home and she's scared something happened to Ruby."

Ellie and Derrick both stood abruptly, and Ellie snatched her keys. "June and Ruby were Kelsey's best friends." She and Derrick rushed from the station and hurried to Ellie's Jeep.

"Two girls missing in two days," she said to Derrick as she drove past the Corner Café. "We may be dealing with a serial predator."

"I know," Derrick said. "But what is he doing to them? And why target these girls?"

"That virgin pact. It's going viral on TikTok," Ellie said. "Maybe he saw it and became obsessed with the girls because of it."

"That's possible, I suppose," Derrick said.

"That could mean June is also in danger." Ellie thumped her fingers on the steering wheel as she veered onto a narrow dirt road that disappeared in an overhang of trees that formed a tunnel.

The temperature in the mountains was already dropping, and the gray gloomy sky added a desolate feeling to the run-down mobile home park. The muddy pockets, weeds and dingy-looking trailers backed up to the woods, providing endless miles of trails to hide a body.

Her tires ground over the gravel, mud slinging as she rolled to a stop. A mangy dog lay sprawled on the porch of the double-wide next door, an old man rocking in a chair beside the dog. Junker cars were parked at neighboring mobile homes and just as the first time she'd come here to question Ruby, blue tarps covered several roofs that had been damaged in recent storms.

She spotted June on the porch stoop of Ruby's home, looking shell-shocked. Wind hurled trash across the ground near the steps as Ellie and Derrick strode to the front door.

"Hi, June," she said.

"Ruby's mama told me to stay out here and wait for you," June said.

Ellie climbed the steps and patted June's shoulders. "This is not your fault. You did the right thing by calling me."

"What happened, honey?" Derrick asked.

June wiped at her eyes. "I've been texting and calling Ruby all morning but she didn't answer. Then I got scared and ran over to see her."

"Go on," Ellie coaxed.

June's eyes filled with tears. "I looked out back and saw Ruby's headband near the garbage cans then some drag marks leading into the woods..." June traced her fingers over the friendship bracelet on her left arm. "Then I found Ruby's friendship bracelet by the creek. She never takes it off. None of us do."

Ellie and Derrick exchanged a look. "I'll check out back," Derrick said.

"I'll talk to the mother and look in Ruby's room." She gave June a sympathetic look. "When was the last time you talked to Ruby?"

"Late yesterday," June said. "I wanted her to come over, but she said her mom would ground her if she did."

Ellie bit her tongue as she recalled the shape of the interior of the home.

"Did you see anyone else or hear anything when you arrived?" Ellie asked. "Maybe a car?"

June fidgeted. "There was a man here with Ruby's mother."

"Was it Ruby's father?"

June shook her head. "No, she doesn't know who her father is."

"Do you know this man's name?" Ellie asked.

June chewed on her other thumbnail. "No. Ruby's mama stays out late, sometimes all night. And she... has strange men over. Different ones."

A clear picture of Ruby's home life formed in Ellie's head, and not a pretty one. "Let me talk to Mrs. Pruitt. Stay out here, honey, and don't go anywhere. We'll escort you home in a little bit, okay?"

June murmured okay then Ellie knocked gently on the door and opened it. Her pulse clamored as she surveyed the crowded, messy room. Every corner and space held stacks of junk, old magazines and collections of ceramic cats.

She walked past piles of laundry and found Ruby's mother smoking at the kitchen table with a tumbler of what looked like whiskey sitting in front of her.

FORTY-EIGHT

CROOKED CREEK POLICE DEPARTMENT

Deputy Heath Landrum did not want to believe his half brother had killed another girl.

Although Digger might have become even more violent in prison. Perhaps he'd nursed his memory of taking Anna Marie's life to the point that he wanted to relive the euphoria some killers experienced after a kill. Once their appetite was whetted, they wanted more.

Was that the case here? Was his need so strong, his ego so cocky, that he thought he could get away with it? Did he think the O'Connor woman would find a way to clear him no matter what he did?

Painful memories flooded his mind. When Anna Marie had died, he'd gone into shock. The days blurred together in a mindless sea of reporters, lawyers, police officers asking questions, probing into their family. Where was their mother? Did they know Digger had been violent? Had he hurt animals? What was his beef with his sister?

Why hadn't Anna Marie cried out for help?

Did Heath resent his half brother? Or did Digger resent

Heath and Anna Marie because they were his father's blood kin and Digger wasn't?

He closed his eyes and landed back in time to the night before his mother left them.

He was eleven. Heard his parents arguing that night. Heard something crash. His mother crying. Then his daddy's pick-up truck firing up, tires screeching as he roared away.

Anna Marie had heard it, too. She'd snuck into Heath and Digger's room and stood at the door in her nightgown, wide-eyed and scared.

"It's okay," he'd told her although he had no idea if it was. Was his father coming back? What were they yelling about?

"Is Mama all right?" Anna Marie whispered.

Heath climbed from bed. "I'll check on her." His stomach clenched as he tiptoed into the hall. Digger stood at the door to the living room, an odd smile on his face.

Crying echoed from his parents' room, and he turned away from Digger and walked down the hall. When he reached his parents' room, he pushed at the door.

"Mama?"

The door squeaked and he saw his mother picking up the lamp that had been overturned on the floor. Tears streaked her cheeks as she looked up and spotted him. Moonlight shimmered through the window, illuminating the teardrops sparkling on her eyelashes.

"Go to your room," she said, her voice shaky.

"But—"

"I said go. Everything will be fine."

Heath's fingers dug into the door jamb but he turned and fled. Digger stepped in front of him just before Heath reached his room. His teeth were bared like a wolf's as he grinned, his eyes vacant. Menacing.

Heath ducked inside his room and found Anna Marie huddled in the chair in the corner. "She's okay," he assured her.

"*I'm scared, can I sleep in here?*" *Anna Marie said, her voice pained.*

He didn't want her in the room with him and Digger, but she was shivering and looked terrified, so he pulled the comforter from his bed and threw it on the floor. He tossed a pillow onto it and Anna Marie crawled on it and curled up, twisting the blanket in her fingers.

Heath waited until she fell asleep before he lay back on his bed and closed his eyes. He didn't like the way his father had left. Or the way Digger had seemed to enjoy the fight his parents had had.

Mama's okay, he reminded himself. They've argued before. In the morning, everything will be fine.

But in the morning when he'd gone to the kitchen to find her, she wasn't there.

"*Your mama left us,*" *his father said.* "*And she's not coming back.*"

He'd stared at his daddy in shock, certain he was wrong.

But that was the last time he'd ever seen her.

FORTY-NINE

BACKWATER'S EDGE

With the heavy black clouds above casting the property in shadowy grays, Derrick shined his flashlight along the ground as he searched the drive and front of the trailer park for indications of foul play.

The driveway consisted of mud, gravel and dead leaves. Fresh tire prints marred the ground. Two sets. He made a mental note to follow up on who the second prints belonged to.

Around back, he spotted the girl's footprints then another set. The girl's were small but, judging from the size and ridges of the second one, they looked like a man's boots.

A scrap of trash and an empty cigarette pack lay on the ground so he snapped photos of those. ERT would collect them and process for forensics. The cigarette pack could belong to Ruby's mother or a visitor or the killer. Although, with trash littering the other properties, it could belong to someone else who lived in the mobile home park. As he reached the rear, he noticed the overflowing dumpster. Loose trash had blown across the yard and the glow from his flashlight lit up more footprints that came from the back stoop. The indentations in the soil looked like sneakers. Probably Ruby's.

He followed them to the trash bin and realized they were fresh as if she'd been tasked with emptying the garbage. Wind carried the acrid odors of waste and spoiled food and he found a larger partial print that looked like a man's. This one was slightly different from the one out front.

Maybe from sneakers, not work boots?

Crushed weeds and drag marks caught his eye. Carefully, he maneuvered around the tracks, not wanting to destroy any evidence. He tracked them to the edge of the woods by the creek. A bracelet like the teens wore had snagged on a rock. A few feet in, the drag marks ceased, but he saw what appeared to be tire marks from some kind of ATV.

If Ruby had been abducted, no telling where she was now.

FIFTY

Ellie approached Ruby's mother at the table, her hands circling the tumbler of whiskey.

"Billy Jean," Ellie said. "I can call you that, can't I?"

The woman's bloodshot eyes stared at Ellie, her pale skin blotchy from tears or lack of sleep. Or both. She nodded, then pushed her phone toward Ellie.

Ellie's pulse clamored at the sight of the picture. Just like Kelsey, Ruby lay on a bed of white sheets, hair fanned across the pillow, a white teddy bear in her arms. She looked almost angelic, as if she was sleeping.

Ellie had a bad feeling that was not the case.

"Who... would do this?" Billy Jean asked in a voice that warbled.

"I don't know but we will find out," Ellie said.

Anger sharpened the woman's tone. "You probably promised Kelsey's mama that but you haven't found her."

Ellie's lungs squeezed for air. "We're still looking for Kelsey." And now they'd have to add Ruby to the missing persons database. "I understand this is a difficult, terrifying time. But I need to ask you some questions." Ellie strived to be gentle. "When did you last see or talk to Ruby?"

The ice in the tumbler clinked as Billy Jean took a sip of the whiskey. Then she ran her fingers through her tangled hair.

"Yesterday before I went to work."

Her accusatory look made Ellie's stomach churn with guilt. She understood the woman's silent message. If she'd found Kelsey and her abductor, Ruby would have been safe.

"Did you talk to her on the phone while you were at work?"

She shook her head. "No, we were too busy."

"What is it you do?" Ellie asked.

"I'm a waitress at The Hungry Wolf." Her eyes cut to Ellie, daring her to comment on the fact that the place was a seedy bar known for strippers.

"What time did you get off work?"

Annoyance flashed in the woman's eyes. "What does that matter?"

"I'm trying to establish a timeline for when your daughter disappeared," Ellie explained.

Billy Jean's finger released the strand of hair she was twisting then began the nervous gesture all over again.

"I worked late, that's the way to make tips."

"And you got home about what time?" Ellie continued.

She glanced at the clock on the wall, then heaved a sigh. "About three."

Ellie nodded. "Did you check on Ruby when you got here?"

Her tone was defensive. "No, I figured she was in bed. She's used to me working late and takes care of herself."

Ruby was a defenseless fifteen-year-old girl who couldn't weigh more than a hundred pounds.

"How about this morning?"

"Look, I'm a single mother doing the best I can," Billy Jean snapped. "I got home late and slept in," she said. "Ruby gets up and fixes her own breakfast."

Ellie nodded. Sounded like both mother and daughter had it hard. "Where is Ruby's father?"

Billy Jean swirled the liquid in her glass with a disgusted grunt. "He ran out the minute I told him I was knocked up." She gave Ellie an angry look. "Now stop asking me all this shit and find Ruby."

"I'm sorry the questions upset you but it's part of the investigative process," Ellie said. "Did you notice anything odd when you got home last night?"

"What do you mean odd?"

"Did you see a car hanging around? Hear a noise outside or inside?"

Billy Jean rubbed her hands over her face. "No... I was tired and... had a guest and we just went to bed."

"What was your guest's name?"

"Jim Roberts, the manager of The Hungry Wolf. But he didn't do anything to Ruby."

Still, they'd check him out.

"Did he talk to her?"

"No, I told you she was in her room, and we went straight to bed."

"Is it possible that he got up while you were sleeping and could have done something to Ruby?"

She slammed her fist on the table rattling the glass. "He's not like that. He doesn't like young girls." She leaned forward. "Now listen to me, don't you dare go accusing him of this. I can't afford to lose my job." She knocked back the rest of her drink. "You know the creep who took Kelsey probably took Ruby, too. Now go find him."

"I intend to," Ellie said. "Was the door locked when you got home?"

Ruby's mother cut her eyes toward the front door. "Yes. I remember dropping my keys and having to pick them up."

"How about the back door?"

She slanted a look toward the rear door which Ellie noticed stood ajar. "I... didn't notice."

A knock sounded and Derrick lifted a hand from the doorway, motioning he wanted to talk to her. "Excuse me," Ellie said. "I'm going to issue an Amber Alert for Ruby. And I need to speak to Agent Fox."

The woman stared into the whiskey glass as Ellie maneuvered the crowded room to the door.

"Anything from the mother?" Derrick asked.

Ellie shook her head. "She worked late, had an overnight guest, didn't check on Ruby when she got home in the night, so we don't have an exact timeline for when Ruby was taken."

Ellie inhaled. "Text Deputy Eastwood and ask her to talk to the manager of The Hungry Wolf. He spent the night here last night. If he didn't take Ruby, he might have seen something this morning when he left."

Derrick nodded and sent the text.

"I found a friendship bracelet and headband that may have belonged to the girl and saw footprints," Derrick said. "I've called an ERT. There were also ATV tire marks near the creek, indicating her abductor may have used it to get away."

Dammit, where had he taken her?

FIFTY-ONE

While the ERT searched for evidence outside the property, Ellie texted Cord to search the woods behind the trailer park. Next, she phoned her boss and filled him in.

"It looks like the same person who took Kelsey Tiller abducted Ruby," Ellie said. "Issue an Amber Alert." Although, most likely this was a recovery mission, not a rescue. The best she could hope for was that someone saw the photograph of Ruby and had information on who would hurt these girls.

"On it," Captain Hale said. "I'll let the sheriff know we're looking for two girls, not just one."

She thanked him then took a look around in Ruby's room. A single bed was covered with a worn spread, a shelf of books, sheet music and a couple of well-loved stuffed animals that must been favorites from childhood.

A math book and English Lit book sat on her desk, a spiral notebook beside it. Ellie glanced inside and found scribbled musical notes as if Ruby was working on writing her own song.

She dug inside the desk in search of a diary but didn't find one, so she checked beneath the mattress. Nothing.

Her closet contained a few pairs of jeans, T-shirts, sweatshirts and an old pair of tennis shoes. Band and orchestra uniforms occupied another rack.

Inside a red and black backpack, she located Ruby's laptop. Hers was an older model, most likely issued by the school.

Ellie carried it to the living room to give to Derrick for analysis. Ruby's mother still sat at the table, the tumbler filled again, a cigarette glowing between her fingers.

"I told that girl to stay home," she mumbled. "Now look what trouble she's caused."

Ellie gritted her teeth. The woman blamed her daughter for being abducted?

Her mind struggled to shift the pieces of the puzzle into place. Two girls who were good friends had been kidnapped and appeared to be dead. The perp had to have known both of them.

Other than being friends, band, and the virgin pact, what else did they have in common? Kelsey was from a middle-class family, Ruby from a single-parent low-income one. They lived in different neighborhoods, but both attended Red Clay Mountain. The staff at the school was the only common factor. Shondra had already researched the teachers and staff and found no red flags.

"Billy Jean, did Ruby mention having problems with a teacher at school?"

The woman shook her head. "Hell, no. That girl was a bookworm."

"Did you have any workers come around here? A repairman or handyman?"

Billy Jean gestured around the room at the mess. "Does it look like I've had work done around here?"

No, but she desperately needed a cleaning service.

A knock sounded and Ellie hurried to the door. Cord stood on the stoop with Benji beside him, concern on his face. June was still on the steps, watching the chaos as the ERT searched the property. "June, I'll take you home as soon as we tie things up here. Or do you want to call your grandmother?" Ellie asked.

June swiped at her damp cheeks. "She's having lunch with her lady friends after church," she said. "And she's gonna be mad at me for leaving the house."

"Your grandmother seemed like a sweet lady, June," Ellie said softly. "If she gets angry, it's because she loves you and is scared for you."

June's shoulders lifted in a small shrug.

"I need to talk to Ranger McClain," Ellie said. "I won't be too long."

June nodded, crossed her arms on her knees and laid her head on them.

"Cord, ERT will process the scene, but maybe you and Benji can search the woods, in case he left her body there."

Glancing back at June, Ellie's mind went to dark places. If this maniac was targeting Kelsey and her friends, June might be next.

FIFTY-TWO

It was almost two p.m. by the time the ERT finished. Deputy Landrum arrived, his face pinched as Ellie showed him the photograph of Ruby.

He also looked tired and troubled. His brows lifted, his face strained. For a moment, he simply stared at the picture, then looked away quickly and back again.

"Are you all right?" Ellie asked.

He grunted. "Yeah. You have anything to go on?"

"Not much. But judging from the way she's posed, we're dealing with one perp," Ellie said. "Take Ruby's computer back to the station and scrub it and her social media accounts." Although so far, Kelsey's and Bianca's hadn't led them to the perpetrator.

The deputy took the computer from her and headed back to his squad car just as Cord returned looking grim-faced, Benji by his side. Derrick was on his heels but the two men stood at least a foot apart and hadn't seemed to acknowledge one another.

"ERT is finishing up," Derrick said.

"Anything in the woods, Cord?" Ellie asked.

"The tire marks lead about four miles north and stop at the road. From there, he could have gone any direction."

"Damn," Ellie muttered. They needed a break.

June stood and walked toward her on shaky legs. "Detective?"

Ellie forced a calming voice. "Yes, sweetheart?"

"I should go home. My grandmother will be back from lunch and she'll be worried if I'm not there."

"Okay, I'll run you over," Ellie said. "I need to speak with your grandmother anyway."

Now June had a target on her back, there was no way she'd leave her alone and vulnerable. She stepped over to relay her plan to Derrick and Cord. "I'm going to ask the sheriff to put a guard on June and her grandmother."

"I'll stay here until the ERT finishes," Derrick offered.

"Call me if you need anything else," Cord said, his voice thick as his gaze met hers.

Unspoken words lingered in his tone, but she simply nodded.

The wind whipped his shaggy brown hair around his rugged face as he walked to his truck. When he reached the vehicle, he paused and turned to look back at her. It took every ounce of Ellie's restraint not to yell at him to stop, to say they needed to talk.

But Derrick was watching her intently, Cord had a baby on the way and she had a case to solve. Families who needed her.

Cord didn't. He was having one of his own.

"June, stay here with Special Agent Fox while I talk to Ruby's mama for a minute, then we'll go." She ducked back inside the trailer, the musty smell assaulting her as she made her way toward the kitchen.

Ruby's mother wasn't at the table. She called out her name and walked down the hall, expecting to find the woman crying in her room. Instead, she was passed out on the bed, the tumbler of liquor spilled across the bedding and dripping onto the dingy carpet.

FIFTY-THREE

CROOKED CREEK POLICE DEPARTMENT

The images of the girls posed as if they were sleeping with that white teddy bear in their arms played through Heath's mind like a horror show. Anna Marie had had a white teddy bear she'd named Snowflake.

The years fell away as if he was thrust back in time.

Thunder clapped. Rain pounded the roof. The walls shook with the force of the wind.

He heard his daddy shouting. "What the hell have you done, Digger? Get off her!"

Heath jumped from his bed, certain he was having a nightmare. The room was dark and he stumbled as he ran into the hall. A low dark wail echoed from Anna Marie's room. He froze, body shaking. What was going on?

"You're a monster," his father screamed. "You killed her!"

Fear bolted through Heath as he peeked in his sister's room. Lightning zigzagged across the sky, visible through the window. His father stood by Anna Marie's bed. Digger was leaning over Anna Marie, a pillow clenched in his hands.

Anna Marie—even though she was his big sister, she'd always been thin and seemed frail. Now she wasn't moving.

"You killed her!" His father shoved Digger backward, knocking him to the floor.

Digger's head hit the corner. His eyes looked glassy. His breath came out in pants.

Her lips were parted in a silent scream. His father started CPR on Anna Marie.

Heath blinked away the memory yet it still haunted him. The sirens wailing. Police storming in.

Digger had gone to jail for murder.

But now he was free. And two other girls were dead, their bodies posed the same way they'd found Anna Marie.

He had to track down his half brother. Stop him from this madness.

Maybe tell Ellie.

His chest tightened. No, not yet. He wanted to confront Digger himself.

Hands sweating, he called Caitlin O'Connor again. "I have to talk to Digger," he said when she answered.

"I gave him your message," Ms. O'Connor replied.

"This is not a request, send me his phone number," Heath said, his tone angry. "A second girl was abducted. Her mother received a photograph and she's posed exactly as Kelsey Tiller was. Exactly the way we found my sister."

"Oh my God," Caitlin mumbled.

"You understand I have to bring him in for questioning," Heath said, his heart pounding.

"I do," she admitted. "But his attorney and I should be present."

"What for? You think I'm going to railroad him back to prison?"

"I don't know. Are you?"

He sucked air through his teeth. She had no idea what Digger had put their family through. His mom had left the week before. Then he'd lost Anna Marie.

His father had changed after that. He'd lost him, too.

Rage cut through Heath like the blade of a hunting knife. Maybe Digger had kissed Caitlin's ass when she'd come to see him. Maybe he'd pretended innocence. Maybe she'd fallen for Digger's lies.

But Heath remembered...

And he was a cop. He should tell Ellie. She'd have him fired if he withheld valuable information.

But some reason, some semblance of loyalty to his brother surfaced, and he had to investigate himself before turning him in. If Digger had done this, he had an idea where he might have left the bodies.

If he found them, there might be evidence to either clear Digger as a suspect or send him back to prison.

FIFTY-FOUR
KUDZU HOLLER

As June settled into the back of Ellie's jeep, Ellie called the sheriff, careful to remain outside her vehicle so June couldn't overhear their conversation. No teenager should have to fear for their life or face the death of not just one, but two friends. She was surprised June was holding up as well as she was.

"Bryce," Ellie began when he answered the call. "Any luck with abandoned houses or cabins?"

"Afraid not," he said. "We've searched all the ones in Crooked Creek and are working around Red Clay Mountain, but that's a huge area."

"I know," Ellie sighed. "But we have to keep looking. We may have another serial killer on our hands. One who's killed two girls now."

He muttered an obscenity. "These girls are not that much younger than my own daughter."

"I know, it has to be difficult for you. I'm driving June to her grandmother's house." She explained that June might be targeted next. "Can you spare a deputy to guard her twenty-four seven?"

"I'll send one of my officers over ASAP," Bryce agreed.

"Thanks. Expand your search, too. If we find the girls, we may be able to get forensics from the bodies."

He agreed, and she hung up then slid into the driver's seat. June's ashen face stared back at her, a taunting reminder Ellie needed to work faster. Clenching the steering wheel in a white-knuckled grip, Ellie silently vowed to keep her safe, even if it killed her.

"Why is someone doing this to us?" June asked as Ellie started the engine and pulled down the drive.

"I don't know, sweetie, but I promise to catch whoever it is."

June gave a slight bob of her head and wiped her damp cheeks with the back of her hand.

Ellie's anxiety mounted with every mile she drove. As a kid, she'd thought Kudzu Holler was a jungle, even scarier than the woods. She'd imagined the vines twisting around her ankles, like a life-eating plant, and dragging her beneath the mountain of suffocating leaves. Sometimes she'd imagined the devil lived below with his fiery fangs ready to snatch her and take her with him.

The people who lived here were often poor and uneducated and bred generations of the same, repeating the cycle.

Maybe June would break it.

One clapboard house after another flew past, the older small houses decaying and in need of repair. Yards were overgrown with weeds and shutters hung askew as if damaged in the last storm.

June's gaze darted toward the driveway. "Oh, no, my grandma's already back. She's gonna be mad."

Ellie parked and they got out, Ellie's arm curved around the girl's shoulder.

June's grandmother raced out, her eyes widening. "Oh, my word. Where have you been? I've been worried sick."

Ellie offered her a smile. "June is fine," she said, although that wasn't exactly true. "But there's been a new development in the case."

Louise folded her chubby arms around June and pulled her close, her gaze frightened. "What kind of development?"

"It's best we talk inside." Ellie gestured she would follow, and June and her grandmother led the way.

Although the house was older, unlike Ruby's trailer, it was clean and smelled of blueberries and bacon.

"June, are you really alright?" Louise asked.

June's face crumpled. "No... Ruby's gone."

Alarmed, her grandmother pulled her to the couch. June sank onto it and leaned into the older woman's bulk.

"Please tell me what's going on," Louise said, her voice breaking.

Ellie relayed what had happened.

Terror streaked the woman's hazel eyes. "I told you to stay put," Louise said. "It's too dangerous for you to go out alone right now."

"I agree," Ellie said. "Sheriff Waters is sending over one of his officers to stand guard until we catch this man." She addressed June. "You have to stay here, June. No more running through the woods or neighborhoods on your own."

"Don't you worry," Louise said. "I'll make sure she stays here with me."

Ellie stood to leave. Knowing the girls were safe meant she could focus on finding this bastard.

FIFTY-FIVE

CROOKED CREEK POLICE STATION

Angelica Gomez was waiting for Ellie when she arrived at the station. Derrick was still supervising the ERT at Ruby's while Landrum was supposed to be searching Ruby's computer.

"I heard another girl is missing," Angelica said.

Ellie pulled a frown. "Yeah, give me a minute. You and your cameraman can set up in the press room."

Angelica motioned for Tom to follow her. Ellie looked for Deputy Landrum but he wasn't at his desk.

She adjusted her ponytail as she strode to the press room. Angelica offered her a tentative smile although Ellie found no comfort in it.

"Let's get started." Angelica signaled her cameraman. "This is Angelica Gomez, Channel Five News, coming to you live from Crooked Creek Police Station. Once again, Detective Reeves is here to update us on the investigation into Kelsey Tiller's disappearance."

Ellie swallowed hard and stepped up to the mic. "As we reported previously, fifteen-year-old Kelsey Tiller is still missing. We now believe she was abducted. Sadly, this morning another teenager Ruby Pruitt was taken. Anyone with information about these abductions should contact the police."

"Do you have any leads or suspects?" Angelica asked.

Ellie paused at the sound of a commotion in the front of the station. "We are pursuing every possible angle."

Suddenly heated voices grew louder, and she looked up to see the Tillers storming toward her.

"What the hell are you doing to catch our daughter's killer?" Mr. Tiller barked.

Ellie clenched her hands. She hadn't divulged to the press that they suspected the girls were dead. But now he had.

Mr. Tiller stormed over and grabbed the microphone from Angelica. "How many more kids have to die on your watch, Detective, before you stop this maniac?"

FIFTY-SIX

SOUTHERN LIGHTS STUDIOS

Caitlin O'Connor knew what it was like to be accused of a crime you hadn't committed. She'd spent five years locked up herself for burglary when she was younger. Her early twenties wasted behind bars.

Although she had nothing to do with the break-in at her ex-boyfriend's rich father's estate, no one believed a scrawny poor girl from the wrong side of the tracks. She'd needed money, they'd said. She was from a broken home. She wanted to pay off her daddy's drug dealer.

All true. But that didn't make her a thief. Well, technically she was. She had stolen bread and peanut butter from the store once when she was starving. But she'd been desperate. Her daddy had been on a bender for days, there was nothing to eat in the house, and after six days with her stomach cramping, she'd given in. Even then she'd been ashamed and vowed never to do so again. She'd also vowed to get herself out of her crappy life and make something of herself.

Then rich, spoiled Keith Unger had pointed the finger at her for stealing an expensive painting from his father's estate. A sarcastic laugh caught in her throat. Like at twenty, she would have known anything about how to fence stolen art or its value.

Finally, after five years of hell and screaming her innocence, Ethan Baldwin with the Innocence Project had taken on her case. Within months, he'd proven she was right—that Keith's father had made some bad investments and was in dire financial straits so he'd arranged for the painting to be stolen to collect insurance money.

She'd walked free, completely exonerated. And mad as hell at the justice system and how it had failed her.

Now she devoted her time to making things right for others. That was why she'd taken on Darnell "Digger" Woodruff's case.

The first time she'd read the transcript of his interrogation and confession she'd sensed something was off. The fact that the arresting officer had accepted it so easily when Digger's statement sounded jumbled raised her curiosity. He hadn't considered the possibility that Digger was innocent or the fact that he had a history of insomnia and sleepwalking and had been prescribed Ambien to help him get through the night.

She'd done some research, and after interviewing Digger and learning his memory of that night was still fuzzy, she'd started talking to neighbors, Digger's teachers and other kids at school.

She glanced at her notes of her conversation with a woman named Hilary Johnson. She'd nannied for the family when the kids were small. Although the woman had allowed her to record her statement, she'd asked Caitlin to use a different name and to alter her voice for the podcast.

A noise sounded outside the studio.

Probably just the wind. Dismissing it, she turned back to the notes.

The floor creaked in the front office. She pivoted in her chair and called out. "Is someone there?"

Silence for a second. Then another sound… footsteps? She

stood and held her breath for a minute, listening, then tiptoed to the door. She scanned the reception area. Nothing. Then she ran to the door and looked outside.

She didn't see a car. Only the trees bending in the wind. Exhaling in relief, she secured the door. But suddenly the lights flickered off. She brushed her fingers along the wall in search of the switch. She found it and flipped it but the lights didn't come on.

The floor creaked again. Footsteps. Heavy breathing. And an odd smell.

Then everything went black.

FIFTY-SEVEN

CROOKED CREEK POLICE STATION

Ellie struggled to control her emotions. Mr. Tiller's accusation stung. He had a right to be angry though. His daughter was presumed dead and Ellie was no closer to finding her killer than she was the day before.

Angelica looked slightly shaken and Tom stopped filming.

"I'm sorry, Mr. Tiller," Ellie said. "We are doing everything in our power to find Kelsey and the person who took her."

Jean tugged her husband away from the camera. "Please, you aren't helping," she cried.

Captain Hale must have heard the outburst and appeared, his face a mask of stoic calm. "Sir, please come with me." He coaxed the irate man back toward the bullpen and his wife followed, tears streaking her cheeks.

Ellie squared her shoulders and addressed the camera. "Naturally, emotions are high for the families of the missing teens, so I implore anyone with information regarding their disappearance to please call the police." She'd be remiss if she didn't warn the public to protect their children. "Also, it's possible that this perpetrator may strike again, so parents and girls, be hypervigilant about your surroundings and who is around you. Please travel in pairs and let your parents know if you see someone suspicious or think someone is watching you."

Still shaken, she ended the interview then strode back to her office. She had work to do. Nothing was going to stop her from getting justice for Kelsey and Ruby.

FIFTY-EIGHT
CORNER CAFÉ

Digger tugged the Braves hat low over his eyes, careful to avoid eye contact and to blend in with the locals, who were glued to the TV and the news report. Two girls missing in two days.

A sick knot hardened in the pit of his stomach. Did Heath think he was responsible?

"Another serial killer on the loose," a woman in the booth behind him gasped.

A brunette woman yanked her daughter up against her as they passed him. "I'm not letting you out of my sight, honey."

Other frantic whispers floated through the room.

"Why do you think these killers keep coming to our mountain?"

"I hope that detective finds this one before another girl is murdered."

"Maybe we should get her fired. Let the sheriff take the lead."

"Or that young deputy Landrum," an older woman said. "Get some fresh eyes on things around here."

The diner owner, a pretty woman named Lola, passed an

order to a cute little waitress in her teens, her eyes haunted as the reporter stated the number for the police department.

Digger stared down into his meatloaf, his pulse thumping wildly. He felt like he had a laser aimed at him. It was just a matter of time before the police connected these cases to him.

If they hadn't already.

Knowing his stepfather hated him, he wouldn't be surprised if he called them and pointed them in Digger's direction. He was shocked Heath hadn't already had him arrested. Maybe that was the reason he'd called Caitlin.

His fingers tightened around his fork and for a brief second, he felt like stabbing someone with it. His breath panted out, sweat beaded on his skin and his hand shook.

He was so close to being free. But once the spotlight turned to him with these new suspicions, the people with the Innocence Project would probably drop him like a hot potato.

"Your half brother wants to talk to you," Ms. O'Connor had said when she'd phoned earlier. Which meant Heath had already honed in on him as a suspect.

His appetite gone, he pushed his plate away, then laid cash on top of the bill. Just as he stood, the sheriff walked in, his badge glinting beneath the overhead light, his gaze scanning the room.

Digger's stomach clenched, and he pulled the hat lower and waited until the sheriff reached the counter. His head down, he walked to the door and stepped outside.

He'd done some homework at the library in prison before his release. He knew where Heath lived. Red Hawk Ridge. A wry laugh caught in his throat. No surprise that he'd moved there. As young boys they'd hiked the area and watched the red-tailed hawks soaring above the mountains. Had admired their grace and freedom.

Heath wanted to talk.

Maybe it was time they did.

Ellie wanted to scream. She was pissed as hell. Not at the Tillers, who she watched her boss escort out.

At herself for not finding this sick monster before another girl was hurt.

Nerves on edge, she sank into her desk chair, contemplating the details they knew about the case.

Derrick rapped on her door, then stepped inside, his expression solemn. "I heard about the interview. Tiller shouldn't have gone off on you like that, Ellie."

Ellie made a wry sound. "I don't blame him. If it was my daughter missing and presumed dead, I'd be shouting to the rafters, too."

"I know, but we—you—are doing everything you can. We have to follow the leads and at the moment, we don't have any."

She drummed her knuckles on the desk, wracking her brain for avenues to pursue. "Did ERT find anything at Ruby's?"

"They collected samples of the blood on the rocks and made casts of the shoe prints outside. Ruby's mother confirmed that the friendship bracelet and headband were her daughter's."

Ellie flipped open her laptop. "If this is a serial predator, he may have killed before."

Focused now, they both set to work, the silence thick with the urgency to stop this madman. She ran a nationwide search for murders of teenage girls in the last year bearing the same MO but found nothing so she went back two years.

One teen had been smothered by her father and was found the next morning by her mother. But there was no mention of a white teddy bear. The girl's father confessed via a suicide note.

She searched back another five years and found one case of a five-year-old girl dead, found wrapped in a white sheet with a blue teddy bear. Police had eventually arrested a pedophile who lived four doors down from her.

The next hour, she continued searching, tension knotting her shoulders and neck as she extended the search to ten years, then fifteen.

Her pulse clamored when she got a hit for a murder, fifteen years ago, of a teen who attended Red Clay Mountain High. She studied the photo of the victim, her heart racing. The girl had an uncanny resemblance to Kelsey Tiller.

Ellie skimmed the police report. Sixteen-year-old Darnell Woodruff arrested for killing his half sister, Anna Marie.

Ellie's breath quickened as she read the news report for details. The fifteen-year-old sophomore was smothered by a pillow in her bedroom while she was sleeping. Her father stated that he found his stepson standing over the girl holding the pillow he used to kill her.

Ellie's mind raced. Anna Marie not only looked like Kelsey, but she attended the original Red Clay Mountain High.

In the crime scene photos, the girl looked posed as if she was sleeping, just as Kelsey and Ruby had been. The sheets and bedding were white as was the teddy bear tucked in her arms.

Ellie skimmed the obituary next.

A memorial service for fifteen-year-old Anna Marie Landrum will be held Sunday, at two p.m. at Red Clay Mountain Chapel. Anna Marie is survived by her father, Gilbert Landrum, and brother Heath Landrum.

Ellie froze, her head reeling. The murdered girl was Deputy Landrum's sister.

SIXTY

Ellie tapped her fingers on her temple. If Heath's sister was found in a similar manner to Kelsey and Ruby, why hadn't he spoken up?

Questions pummeling her, she searched deeper and found another story offering more details.

> *Sixteen-year-old Darnell Woodruff confessed to the murder of his half sister and was sentenced to twenty years in the federal state prison. His stepfather testified that he heard a noise around midnight and raced into the bedroom where he found Darnell standing over Anna Marie's bed. The girl was unconscious, clutching a white teddy bear in her arms. Mr. Landrum performed CPR but was unable to save his daughter while his eleven-year-old son Heath called 9-1-1.*

No wonder Landrum had looked pale when he'd seen the photograph of Kelsey and Ruby. But he should have told her instead of letting her waste time.

She studied the photograph of Darnell Woodruff then realized she knew the name. He'd been at the center of a recent news report, his release instigated by true crime podcaster Caitlin O'Connor, who worked with the Innocence Project.

Dammit. She had to talk to the deputy.

"Derrick?"

"Yeah?"

"There was a similar case fifteen years ago. Sixteen-year-old Darnell Woodruff has been serving time for the murder and was just released. The victim was his fifteen-year-old half sister, who was found in bed clutching a white teddy bear."

Derrick jerked his head up. "Now we have a suspect."

Ellie wiped perspiration from her forehead. "Yes," she said. "And that man is Deputy Landrum's half brother."

Derrick swung his gaze to her. "What the hell?"

"I know. I can't believe he didn't mention that detail." And she would find out the reason. "Derrick, the murdered girl attended the original Red Clay Mountain High." Was that significant?

Derrick pulled a hand down his chin. "Now that is interesting." He turned back to his computer. "Let me see if there are any employees at the school who might have been working at the original high school fifteen years ago."

"Good idea," Ellie said. "I'm going to find Landrum."

Jaw clenched, she pushed away from her desk. On a mission to know why he'd failed to mention his sister's murder, she hurried to find Landrum, but the deputy wasn't at his desk.

She checked the break and conference rooms then hurried to the captain's office. "Excuse me, sir. Have you seen Deputy Landrum?"

"He left, said he had something to do. I assumed he was following a lead for you."

Ellie bit her tongue and decided to talk to Landrum before she confided in the captain. She at least owed him that.

"Right. If you hear from him before I do, please tell him I need to see him."

The captain nodded and Ellie made her exit. She pulled her phone and called the deputy's number, but he didn't answer so she left a message.

Annoyed and hoping he was looking for Darnell for questioning, not hiding him out somewhere, she returned to her office. While Derrick dug for information on the teachers, Ellie found Caitlin O'Connor's phone number through the Innocence Project.

It went straight to voicemail so she left a message. Frustration bubbled inside her. Damn. Didn't anyone answer their phones anymore?

"Ms. O'Connor, this is Detective Ellie Reeves from the Crooked Creek Police Department. I understand you've been investigating convicted felon Darnell Woodruff for your true crime podcast. If you've seen the news, you're probably aware that two teenagers from Red Clay Mountain are missing and presumed dead. What I did not reveal to the press was that the girls were posed in a similar manner to the way Mr. Woodruff's half sister was found, both holding a white teddy bear in their arms." She tucked a strand of her hair back into the ponytail holder. "Mr. Woodruff is wanted for questioning in this case. Please call me back with his contact information."

She hung up with a sigh. "Anything on the teachers?"

Derrick shook his head. "None have records, and no one at the school was employed there at the time of Darnell's arrest. But I'm looking into Woodruff. No juvenile record. He lived with his stepfather, Gil, his half brother, Heath, and half sister, Anna Marie. Mother abandoned the family before Anna Marie's death."

"That could have been his trigger," Ellie said as she accessed the trial transcripts.

Derrick's chair squeaked as he shifted. "Sixteen at the time of his arrest. Confessed. Open-and-shut case."

Ellie rubbed her forehead. "Then why does the O'Connor woman think he's innocent?"

Silence stretched for a few minutes, while Derrick continued his research.

"The podcasts haven't been released yet, but at his parole hearing, Ms. O'Connor cited a lack of evidence and contradictory details in Darnell's confession. The investigating officer was named Stan Traylor and still works at Red Clay Mountain Police Department. He was promoted to Lieutenant after he closed Woodruff's case."

"I want to talk to him." Ellie called him, explained to the dispatch officer why she was phoning and was patched through immediately.

"Lieutenant Traylor," he said in a deep baritone. "I've been expecting this call," he said. "Ever since that O'Connor woman opened up a can of worms with her podcast, everyone's interested in Digger Woodruff."

"Digger?" Ellie asked.

"Yes, that's what his family called him. Stepfather said he earned the name cause he was always trying to dig his way out of trouble." He made a sarcastic sound. "Went too far when he killed his half sister."

"How were you sure he was guilty?" Ellie asked.

"Damn kid confessed. When we got to the scene, Digger kept saying, 'I killed her. I killed her.'"

"Was there a witness?"

"According to Gil Landrum, he heard a noise and went to see what it was. Found Digger hovering over the girl holding the pillow that was used to smother her."

"Did Digger say why he killed her? Did they not get along?"

"Never said why. Just said he did it. There were fibers from the pillow under his nails and a strand of her hair on his T-shirt."

"Did he have emotional problems? Prior arrests?"

"No arrests, but teachers at his school said he had a temper. Got into a couple of fights and was suspended twice in the six months prior to the murder."

"I'd like to look at the video of your interview with him and the murder book you compiled detailing the investigation," Ellie said.

"Why? You aren't calling because you think he's innocent," he groused. "You like him for the disappearance of two teens in your area. Guess that O'Connor woman had it wrong. He got out and went right back to killing."

SIXTY-ONE

Where the hell was Landrum? It wasn't like him not to answer her calls. Which told Ellie that he was avoiding her. That he didn't want to discuss the truth about the possible connection to his half brother.

Maybe he was even hiding Darnell from the law.

When she did talk to him, she planned to give him a piece of her mind.

The video of Darnell's interview she'd requested from Traylor came through and she and Derrick watched it together.

Darnell Woodruff, AKA Digger, was a gangly sixteen-year-old with a slight case of acne, a bony frame and pale skin. She could easily guess that he'd been awkward socially, a loner and had been bullied himself at school which could have triggered the fights he'd been in.

Had he taken out his rage on his little sister? If so, why her?

Ellie watched intently, searching for impropriety on the police's part. Traylor paced in front of Darnell, his six feet towering over the kid as he glowered down at him.

Darnell sat hunched over the table in the interrogation room with his head down, hands splayed in front of him, staring at them with glazed eyes. His knuckles looked bruised, skin dry, his body jittery.

"Darnell, I need you to tell me exactly what happened at your house," Detective Traylor said, his tone harsh.

Emotions choked Darnell's voice. "I... did it," he mumbled. "I... smothered Anna Marie."

The detective claimed the seat across from Darnell, the chair legs clacking against the floor as he arranged his wide frame into it. "Why?" he asked.

Darnell's thin shoulders lifted into a shrug as if his mind was someplace else. Was he reliving the crime?

"Darnell," Traylor repeated. "Did you and your sister fight? Did she do something to anger you?"

His brows were pinched as he worked his mouth from side to side. Then he shook his head.

"You don't remember if she made you mad or you don't want to say?" Traylor asked, his voice booming.

Darnell shrugged. "Everything last night is fuzzy."

Traylor made a clicking sound with his teeth. "What *do* you recall? Do you remember going into Anna Marie's room?"

Darnell ran his trembling hands over his face. "No..."

"Was she awake when you went inside her bedroom?"

He narrowed his eyes in confusion. "I... told you I don't remember going in there."

"But you were in her room," the detective said. "You were standing by her bed."

Darnell nodded.

"Did she fight you or try to scream when you attacked her?" Traylor pressed.

"I..." Digger closed his eyes and pinched the bridge of his nose. Either trying to remember or trying to forget, Ellie wasn't sure which. "I don't know. Maybe."

"Maybe she fought you," Traylor said. "Is that how you got those scratches on your knuckles?"

Ellie made a mental note to check the ME's report and confirm that his DNA was underneath Anna Marie's fingernails.

Darnell studied his hands, tracing one finger over his bloody knuckles. "I... don't know."

"So you don't remember how you were scratched or going inside the bedroom or if Anna Marie screamed. But you know you killed her?"

Slowly, the kid gave a nod, then dropped his head into his hands and began to sob.

Silence stretched between Ellie and Derrick as they considered what they'd seen.

"What do you make of the confession?" Derrick asked.

"He looks like a scared kid in shock. I can see why Ms. O'Connor wanted to dig deeper into the case."

Derrick pulled up the police report. "No other suspects were ever mentioned. Just as Traylor said, Darnell's stepfather stated that he heard a noise, went to check on things and found Darnell standing over Anna Marie. He yanked the boy away and Darnell fell backward. Father tried to perform CPR but it was too late."

"Traylor had his confession, so he didn't feel the need to consider other suspects." A bad feeling niggled at Ellie. She ran a search for news articles about the trial and arrest and skimmed the contents. All reported similar statements made by Traylor. Photographs showed Darnell being hauled away from his house in handcuffs with his father and a younger boy watching as he was shoved in the back of the police car.

Heath was so young in the picture. His eyes haunted.

Did he believe Digger was guilty?

SIXTY-TWO
RED HAWK RIDGE

As night set in, Heath grew more and more antsy. He'd called the O'Connor woman again and left another message. He'd also asked her to send contact information for Digger's parole officer. But no word yet.

He'd followed Detective Reeves's orders and tried to trace the source of the photographs of the dead girls, but they'd come from burners and were untraceable. Finally, he'd narrowed down the tower they'd pinged off.

Shit. It was near his childhood home. The house hadn't been visible in the picture. The shots were simply close-ups of the girls. But if Digger was reliving his first murder by killing Kelsey and Ruby, he might have left them in the house where he killed Anna Marie.

Cold fear caught him in its clutches.

He should call Ellie. Tell her everything. But he swung his vehicle onto the road leading to the old house instead. He'd wait. Check out the place first. He could be wrong.

Sweat beaded on his neck. He hoped to hell he *was* wrong.

Except for a sliver of moonlight peeking through the storm

clouds, the sky was as gray as his mood. Wind whined through the tall pines and oaks as he sped around the switchbacks.

The house was dilapidated now, boards rotting, paint peeled off, a couple of windows cracked. The roof was in disrepair, and sticks, tree branches and debris had accumulated.

There were no cars in sight. No sign anyone was here.

Still déjà vu struck him. In his mind he saw Digger being hauled to the police car that horrible night fifteen years ago. Heard the slamming of the door and screeching of the siren as the police car carried him away.

After Digger was locked up, he and his father had moved around every few months to escape the media circus. Once other kids' parents learned about his brother, they warned their kids away from Heath.

He's too dangerous.

His brother is a murderer.

That family is trouble.

Stay away from him.

What if he's a killer, too?

The gossip and stares had seared him though, the stigma a festering sore that wouldn't heal. His phone buzzed. Ellie.

Dammit. He ground his teeth so hard his jaw ached and ignored the call as he slogged through the overgrown brush. Scratches marred the front door as if animals had clawed at it, and the rancid odor of cat pee filled the air. Feral cats probably lived under the porch.

He pulled on gloves, then found the door cracked and pushed it open. The stink assaulted him—mold, decay, animal feces... the smell of death.

Stomach churning, he fought his memories and prayed the smell was an animal.

What little furniture was left was broken and rats had gnawed at the orange vinyl sofa. He walked past it and the empty kitchen, then down the musty hall to Anna Marie's bedroom.

Covering his mouth at the stench, he eased open the door, his heart hammering.

Fuck. Kelsey Tiller was lying on the bed where Anna Marie had died, posed as if she was sleeping, that damn white teddy bear tucked in her arms.

SIXTY-THREE

SOMEWHERE ON THE AT

He could hear Ruby's body bouncing around in the trunk as he swerved around the switchbacks. The old homestead loomed ahead, surrounded by the woods and mountains that had hidden the secrets within the house.

And the secrets in the forest that should never be told.

The closer he got images of Anna Marie with her golden hair and sunny smile taunted him. She'd meant so much to him.

He hadn't wanted to kill her.

Had planned a different life for himself. She'd been planning, too.

Then it had all fallen apart.

The scent of pine, sunshine and rain washed over him, the rustling of the leaves in the wind a soft melody compared to the storm on the horizon and the raging of his tortured soul.

He hated himself for what he'd done.

But he'd had no choice. In a way he'd saved her from herself. Just as he'd saved Kelsey Tiller. And now Ruby.

His tires chugged over the graveled road and as he climbed the hill and rounded a curve, he spotted the house of his nightmares. He tightened his hold on the steering wheel, his breath rasping out at the sight of a police car in the drive.

Curse words rolled off his tongue and he sped up and raced onto the turnoff for the creek. His foot stomped on the gas pedal so hard he nearly cut a circle but managed to right his car before he careened into a ditch.

Panicked at the thought of getting caught, he raced on. They must have found Kelsey.

He'd planned to leave Ruby with her so they wouldn't be alone. That plan was trash now.

Laughter mushroomed inside him as he thought of the perfect place. Another place where Anna Marie's memory would live on.

He hadn't been back there in ages, but he drove on autopilot, exhilarated with memories of his teenage years. Isolated and perched on top of the mountain, the area looked as desolate as a ghost town.

He parked and sat for a moment, soaking in the sight of it. A tree branch fell from a skinny pine and hit his windshield, jarring him back to his task, and he climbed from the vehicle.

When he opened the trunk, his pulse hammered at the sight of Ruby lying curled on the floor, motionless, her skin such a milky white you could see the spidery blood vessels beneath her paper-thin skin. Her bones looked too big for her slender body as if she was half-starved, her hair tangled around the sharp features of her youthful face.

The girl had been a scrapper, just like Kelsey. He liked the fight in her, that she had grit. Of course, she had to in order to survive with that trampy hoarder of a mother. Through the window, he'd seen shit piled so high you could barely walk through the rooms.

Swallowing back the rage that lived deep inside him, he slung his backpack of supplies over his shoulder, then scooped up Ruby. She weighed next to nothing, legs and arms limp and dangling as he carried her inside the building.

Wind whined through the eaves as he walked down the hallway, the empty rooms and spaces echoing with the feeling of abandonment. He laid her down then raked her tangled hair from her face.

"I'm sorry, Ruby," he whispered.

Sorry she had been given a raw deal in life. Sorry she had to be sacrificed.

SIXTY-FOUR

HOG HILL ROAD

What the hell have you done, Digger? Why would you kill again?

Careful not to touch her or anything in the room, Heath dropped his head into his hands. His body trembled with the memory of seeing his sister just like this. His father counting as he performed CPR. Digger standing in a stupor with the pillow in his hand.

Only it was too late for her. It was too late for Kelsey, too.

Bile rose to his throat, and he turned and fled the room. The pulled pork sandwich he'd eaten earlier was about to come up.

He hit the outside and flew down the steps, then over to the giant oak where he puked into the bushes. A groan erupted from deep within him and sweat streamed down his face. Coughing, he pulled a handkerchief from his pocket and dragged it across his mouth. Then he sank to the ground and stared back at the house, pain wrenching his gut.

Seconds turned into minutes as a silent debate thrashed in his mind. He didn't want to believe his half brother had done this. Had taken another innocent life.

But the scene, the way the body was posed, the place where Kelsey had been left... it all pointed to Digger.

Shit. He'd become a cop because of Anna Marie's death. He'd taken an oath to serve and protect.

The Tillers deserved to bury their daughter and to know that the person responsible was in jail.

He hadn't told Ellie anything about his past.

He reached for his phone with a clammy hand.

But he had to tell her now.

SIXTY-FIVE

CROOKED CREEK POLICE STATION

Ellie muttered a choice word at the sight of Deputy Landrum's name on the caller screen. She jerked the phone up, vying for patience when her tank was running on empty.

"Deputy Landrum, where have you been?" she barked.

A sharp breath echoed back. "Working the case."

"Really? Because I've been trying to reach you and—"

"Just listen, Detective," Landrum said.

Ellie stiffened at his curt tone "Then this had better be good." *Because I know about Darnell.*

"I found Kelsey Tiller's body," he said gruffly.

Ellie rapped her knuckles on her desk to get Derrick's attention then put the phone on speaker. "What? Where?"

"It's a long story."

Anger threatened to make Ellie lose her temper. She didn't want to play games. And she would put him through the ringer when she saw him. "What about Ruby?"

"She's not here." His voice cracked. "I'll text you the address. Send the ME and an ERT..." He paused, another breath wheezing back as if the call was costing him.

"Landrum—"

"Not now," he said. "I'll explain when you get here."

The phone went silent, and Ellie stood, snagging her keys. A second later, the text came through and she and Derrick hurried to the door.

Battling grief and guilt, Ellie peeled from the parking lot and headed toward Red Clay Mountain and the address the deputy had sent. Derrick phoned for an ERT and the ME, Dr. Laney Whitefeather, to meet them at the scene, then she called Cord and put him on speaker.

"We found Kelsey Tiller's body."

"Aww hell, I'm sorry, El."

"Me, too. We're meeting Deputy Landrum at the scene. Can you meet us to search the property in case the killer left Ruby in the woods nearby?"

"Of course. Text me the address."

"Derrick is sending it now."

She ended the call, her stomach churning at the thought of having to notify the Tillers of their daughter's death.

Tension stretched painfully long as the Jeep ate the miles around the mountain. By the time they reached the house, Ellie had wrangled her emotions under control. She couldn't bring Kelsey back, but she would find her killer.

She and Derrick scanned the property as they got out. Other than Landrum's squad car, no other cars were in sight. The house was set far off the road, the forest backing it. The house looked small and crumbling, as if it had been vacant for over a decade.

Landrum sat hunched inside his car as they approached it, his face ashen, the door ajar. He looked up and her breath caught at the pure anguish in his eyes. The news photo of him after Digger's arrest taunted her. He'd only been a kid when that happened.

"The minute you saw the photo of Kelsey posed with the teddy bear, you suspected your half brother, didn't you?"

He gave a nod and cleared his throat. "You know about him?"

"Yes," Ellie said. "When Ruby was taken, I suspected we might be dealing with a repeat offender. I did some research and it led me to your sister's murder."

Landrum groaned. "It was a long time ago, but I still remember that night."

Compassion for him flooded Ellie. "I'm sorry, that must have been awful."

Derrick swallowed hard. "I know what it's like to lose a sister. You never get over it."

Landrum's eyes swam with emotions. "I know Digger looks right for this, but I don't see how he'd be so stupid to kill right after he was released from prison." His voice sounded like he'd swallowed gravel.

"We need to ask him. Do you know how to reach him?"

"I've been calling Caitlin O'Connor, the woman who helped arrange his release, but she hasn't answered."

"Try her again while we take a look at Kelsey."

He wiped his hand over his mouth then clutched his phone while Ellie and Derrick started toward the house. With each step, her anxiety mounted. The porch creaked as they crossed it and entered. The stench made her cover her mouth, growing stronger as they walked down the hall.

They found Kelsey in the first bedroom. "Poor baby," Ellie murmured as she pulled on gloves.

Footsteps and voices sounded from the front of the house then in the hall, and Dr. Whitefeather appeared, her kit in hand.

"The ERT and Ranger McClain are outside," she said.

Derrick gave a nod. "I'll go talk to them."

Ellie clenched her jaw. "Tell them I want this place searched inch by inch. Maybe the bastard left some forensics in here and we can nail him."

SIXTY-SIX

Dr. Whitefeather stepped over to examine Kelsey and two crime techs began searching the house for evidence while Cord and Benji combed the property. Ellie snapped pics of the scene on her phone for studying later, then phoned Captain Hale and explained the situation. "Issue an APB for Darnell Woodruff. And get his picture on the news. But hold off mentioning the homicide until I have time to notify the Tillers."

"Agreed."

As she ended the call, she joined Laney by the body. "Do you have cause of death?"

Laney lifted Kelsey's eyelid. "See the petechial hemorrhaging?"

Ellie nodded. "He strangled her?"

"There are fibers matching the pillow indicating he smothered her with it."

The same MO Darnell had used when he'd killed Anna Marie Landrum.

Laney examined Kelsey's fingernails. "I'll scrape for DNA."

"Any other injuries?" Ellie asked.

"Some bruising on her legs and torso where he probably put his weight on her to hold her down while he smothered her."

"Any signs of sexual assault?"

Laney shook her head. "Thank God he spared her that."

Yes, thank God.

"Time of death?"

"I can't say for sure until I get her on the table."

Ellie checked her watch. "Which means Kelsey was dead as she'd appeared to be in the picture her mother received."

Although questions mounted in her head. If the unsub left Kelsey here because the place was significant and he was copying Anna Marie's murder, why not leave Ruby at the same place he left Kelsey?

SIXTY-SEVEN

Heath braced himself for an interrogation as Ellie approached him.

"Did you reach the O'Connor woman?" she asked.

He shook his head. "She's not answering but I left another message."

Ellie folded her arms. "Have you talked to Darnell since he was released?"

"No."

"Do you know why the O'Connor woman thought he was innocent?"

"She said the evidence was circumstantial and that there were inconsistencies in his confession. I was planning to look at the tapes of it myself."

"I realize you were only a kid," Ellie said. "But did you believe Darnell killed your sister?"

Pain radiated in Heath's long-winded sigh. "At the time, I did. I was in shock myself and I saw him in Anna Marie's room. Dad was already in there and pushed Digger away from the bed, then Dad shouted, 'You killed her,' and Digger just stared at him."

"You didn't actually witness him smother her?"

He shook his head. "No, I heard a commotion in the bedroom and then ran to the room. Then Dad yelled at me to call 9-1-1."

Ellie wanted to study the taped confession again. "What happened next?"

"The police and paramedics showed up and... they said Anna Marie was dead. And then they arrested Digger."

"Did you or your father visit Digger in prison?"

Heath shook his head. "Hell no. Dad went off the deep end after the trial. Said Digger was dead to us, that we had to cut him out of our lives."

"Where's your father now?"

Heath gritted his teeth. "Red Clay Mountain. He works with a construction crew there. A few months after Anna Marie died, he dropped me at his mother's, and I haven't seen or talked to him since."

"Do you think Darnell would go to see him?"

"I have no idea. Dad was pretty hard on Darnell, even before that night. He always favored Anna Marie."

"And then your father helped send him to prison. Darnell might hold a grudge."

Heath hadn't considered that. "I guess he might." He had issues with his old man himself, but Digger had reason to hate him. "I'll keep trying to contact him."

Ellie shook her head. "You're too close to this, Landrum. You can work behind the scenes to locate him, but you have to let me and Agent Fox handle the rest."

"But—"

"I mean it, Deputy. We have to play this by the book. Your relationship with Darnell and your father could compromise the investigation."

Heath silently cursed. He understood what she was saying.

But he didn't like it. He wanted to do something, help find Ruby. Question Digger himself.

Ask him why the hell he started killing all over again when he'd just gained his freedom.

The ME and medics appeared at the door with Kelsey. He'd seen body bags before, seen other victims. Watched a scene just like this when his sister had been carried from that very same house.

If Digger was responsible, he couldn't just sit on his ass. No matter what Detective Reeves said, he would help them find his half brother. And if he was guilty, he'd haul him to jail himself, lock him up and throw away the damn key.

SIXTY-EIGHT

WHISPERING PINES

Ellie left Derrick to deal with the ERT and Cord searching the woods, knowing the notification to the Tillers couldn't wait. They'd been on pins and needles with fear.

They deserved to know the truth, although knowing it would only trigger a new kind of pain.

Derrick offered to go with her, but she assured him they'd be better off with him looking for evidence to catch the bastard who'd murdered Kelsey than babysitting her.

She didn't bother to call ahead but drove to the neighborhood, her gut twisting.

She pulled into the driveway, her heart in her throat as she walked up to the door. As soon as she finished here, she'd give another press conference.

Not the news she'd wanted to deliver to the family or the public. When Ruby's mother saw it, she'd assume Ruby was dead, too. She made a mental note to ask Shondra to check on Billy Jean later.

The whispering pines dropped pine needles onto the damp ground as she parked and walked up to the house. She rang the doorbell, then took a deep breath as Mr. Tiller opened the door.

He took one look at her and it was as if he knew. His face hardened and he spun around and led her to the living room, where she saw his wife curled on the sofa, her face gaunt.

The moment she saw Ellie, Mrs. Tiller lurched to a sitting position, and her husband sank down to her side.

"You found her?" Mr. Tiller asked, his voice a choked whisper.

Ellie nodded. "I'm so sorry."

Mrs. Tiller doubled over, her husband catching her in his arms, and they both began to sob, great heart-wrenching loud cries that made Ellie want to drop to her knees.

God help her, she had to find this sick monster before another girl died.

SIXTY-NINE

LAST CHANCE MOTEL

The flashing orange neon sign for the Last Chance Motel mocked Digger as he watched the news again. Apparently, there had been a break in the missing girl case. He hoped to hell it would clear him of suspicion.

The reporter introduced herself and handed the mic to Detective Ellie Reeves with the Crooked Creek Police Department. Digger had done his homework. The woman was Heath's boss.

"Unfortunately, this afternoon, we found Kelsey Tiller's body in an abandoned house on Red Clay Mountain where it appears she was murdered. At this point, the search for fifteen-year-old Ruby Pruitt remains active." She paused, then continued, "We're also looking for a man named Darnell Woodruff for questioning. If you have any information regarding this murder, Ruby Pruitt's disappearance or Darnell Woodruff's whereabouts, please contact the Crooked Creek Police Department."

Digger scrubbed his hands over his face with a groan as his photo flashed on the screen. Shit, shit, shit.

The girl was dead.

Furious, he kicked the side of the bed then paced across the dingy motel room to the window. Nerves clawing at him, he pushed the curtain aside and peeked into the parking lot.

What the hell was going on? His memory of the night he'd killed Anna Marie was foggy, but he hadn't killed Kelsey Tiller. That much he knew.

Desperate, he snatched his burner phone and called Caitlin O'Connor. The phone rang and rang.

By the time the voicemail picked up, he wanted to scream. "Ms. O'Connor, we need to talk. I know the police are looking for me. But I didn't kill that girl. I swear."

Maybe she'd figure out a way to get to the truth. Talk to the police. Find out why they were looking at him as a suspect.

Fear crawled through him. Maybe someone was setting him up. That had to be the answer. But who would go to that much trouble?

He wracked his brain for names of enemies he'd made in the pen.

Had one of them decided to get revenge on him by framing him for murder?

SEVENTY
KUDZU HOLLER

June pressed one fist to her mouth to keep from screaming as her grandmother turned off the news. "No, no, no..." June cried. "Kelsey can't be dead. She can't be..."

Her grandmother's gnarled hand shook as she hugged June to her side. June fell against her on a sob and her grandmother rocked her back and forth, stroking her hair.

"Oh, hon," her grandmother whispered. "I'm so sorry, so sorry..."

"I can't believe it." June's lungs felt like they were on fire as she tried to breathe. "Why would someone kill her?"

"I don't know," her grandma murmured. "There are just bad people in the world."

June's chest ached. "And if she's dead, what about Ruby? She might be, too." She had looked dead in the picture Ruby's mother received.

Her grandmother didn't seem to know what to say to that. She just tightened her hold and together they cried for Kelsey.

"We pray for her family now," Grandma said. "And we pray hard for Ruby now."

June knew her grandma had faith. But she'd been praying for Kelsey and that hadn't worked.

Her grandmother plucked some tissues from the box on the end table and stood, brushing her hands over her apron as she crossed the room to the window. The curtain fluttered as she pushed it back and peered outside. A shiver ripped through June at the sight of the police car. The detective had put a guard outside for a reason.

Because she thought the killer might come after *her* next.

Heath parked at his cabin, grabbed his laptop and hunched his shoulders against the cold as he hurried to his front door. A noise made him jerk his head to the right and he saw a stick banging against the house.

The mountains stood ominous and unforgiving in the background, the sound of the hawks' wings flapping echoing from above. He ducked inside his house, the floor creaking as he closed the door.

Tonight, he'd review the case against Digger and see if he could locate his father in case Digger had contacted him.

He made his way to the breakfast bar, set his computer on top of it and flipped on the light. The hair on the back of his neck stood on end. The faint scent of sweat and cigarette smoke made his nose itch.

Someone was inside his house.

He reached for his weapon. Heard a footstep near the back door.

He turned and swallowed hard. Digger was inside by the sliding glass doors, his broad shoulders thrown back, his eyes cold and hard.

Heath barely recognized him. The last time he'd seen Digger, he'd been a scrawny, awkward teenager with big wary eyes and glasses.

Now he was over six feet, at least two hundred pounds, with muscles that indicated he spent time in the prison yard working out. Scars crisscrossed his arms and a long jagged one slashed his left cheek running from his temple all the way to his ear. His head was shaved but a goatee grazed his chin, a few early gray hairs poking through the brown.

"Hello, little brother," Digger said.

"You broke in," Heath said. "Isn't that a violation of your parole?"

Digger's scowl matched his tone. "You gonna arrest me?"

Heath searched for some semblance of the boy Digger had once been. Instead, all he saw was a cold, angry man with a grudge against the world. "Should I arrest you?"

Digger shrugged. "I figure you want me locked back up and out of your way."

Heath ran his gaze over the length of Digger's body. "You armed?"

Digger cursed then raised his arms to his side like Heath imagined him having to do constantly when they searched him in the pen. "See for yourself."

Heath considered it but finally gave a shake of his head. "I want to talk."

"Now, you do," Digger snapped. "You sure as hell didn't want to talk to me the last fifteen years."

"You killed my sister and blew up all our lives," Heath said, unable to keep the bitterness from his tone.

His brother pulled a hand down his chin. "I know. I... I'm sorry."

"Really? If you're so sorry and reformed like that O'Connor woman said, why would you get out and kill another girl?"

Digger hissed. "Already tried and convicted me, haven't you?"

Heath shot him a challenging look. "Prove me wrong. Did you kill Kelsey Tiller and kidnap Ruby Pruitt?"

A vein pulsed in Digger's neck, making his snake tattoo appear as if it was slithering up his throat. "You won't believe me no matter what I say."

"Try me," Heath snapped.

Digger walked to the front window and looked out, although he kept one eye on Heath as if he thought he might pull a gun and shoot him. "I didn't kill that girl or take the other one."

Heath jerked his half brother by the shirt. "Listen to me, where is Ruby Pruitt?"

"I don't know," Digger said. "I told you I didn't take her."

"Don't lie to me. If she's still alive and you cooperate, it could work in your favor. Just turn yourself in."

Digger made a sarcastic sound. "Yeah, right. So I can spend the rest of my life in a cell for a crime I didn't commit."

"If you're innocent, we'll find proof," Heath said.

"I am innocent," Digger said through clenched teeth. "But considering my record, you really think the cops will look anywhere beyond me? That female cop already put the word out to look for me."

Unfortunately, Digger was right. "If anyone will look for the truth, it's Detective Reeves."

"Then why did she put that APB out on me?" Digger asked.

"Because the murdered girl was posed like she was sleeping, with a teddy bear in her arms. Just like Anna Marie."

Digger fisted his hands. "I know but I didn't kill her," he insisted.

"He laid her on a bed of white sheets with a white teddy bear," Heath said.

Digger's Adam's apple bobbed up and down as he swallowed.

"How do you explain that?" Heath asked.

"Someone has to be framing me."

"How's that? When Anna Marie died, the cops didn't release photos of the crime scene to the public." Heath continued. "The only ones who knew how she was found were our family, the attorneys, jury and judge."

Digger shook his head in denial. "I don't know, man. I'm not the cop. You are."

Heath paused for a second, considering the possibility. "Okay, so who would want to frame you?"

Digger ran his fingers over his shaved head, drawing Heath's attention to the scars on his hands and arm. "Hell, I made some enemies in prison. Maybe one of them is retaliating against me."

"Give me some names," he said. "And I'll check them out."

"You believe me?" Digger asked, his voice cracking.

Heath's gaze met Digger's, a silent debate warring in his head. He didn't even know Digger now. Didn't know what he was capable of. Could he trust him?

"I said I'd look into it." He handed Digger a notepad and Digger scribbled a couple of names on it.

Heath accepted it, his gaze taking in the tattoo on Digger's neck. A gang tattoo. Heath knew what happened in prison. Violence led to more violence. Turned men into monsters. If you didn't fight back you'd die.

He glanced at the names, then back at Digger. His phone buzzed, and he walked over to the bar to pick it up. Hopefully it was the O'Connor woman.

No, it was Ellie.

The sound of the sliding glass doors opening made him jerk his head around. He had to keep Digger here.

But the wind barreled through the open door and Digger was gone.

SEVENTY-TWO
GEORGIAN MANOR

Bianca waited until her parents went to their room to check social media. They'd been upset about the accusations against her, she figured mostly because her mother would be embarrassed in front of her country club friends and her father with his colleagues.

Their prestige and social status were all they cared about.

That and the glass house.

Better not break a collectable figurine or one of her mother's precious Faberge eggs. Bianca had never understood her obsession with the overprized pieces of glass but her mother showed them off as if they were her babies.

Sometimes Bianca wanted to take a hammer and smash the stupid things to smithereens and strew the pieces across the floor so her mother would step on them when she slipped into the kitchen for her nightly bottle of Pinot Grigio.

When her mom was really being bitchy, Bianca imagined the prickly shards stabbing her delicate pedicured toes and her blood dotting the floor like the petals of a dead red rose scattered across the white marble.

A smile creased her lips. She tiptoed to the top of the

winding staircase in the monster house. The light in her father's study was on, the door closed. She imagined him talking quietly to one of his colleagues, planning his strategy to minimize the damage caused by her actions. Or planning a clandestine meeting with one of his young assistants. So clichéd. But if the Italian loafer fit...

She heard her mother humming and spotted her staggering toward their downstairs bedroom, carrying a bottle of wine and an empty glass in one hand.

Irritated they were still up, she waited until the bedroom door closed, then she tiptoed down the steps and into the kitchen. Her bare feet were cold on the slick marble flooring as she snuck a bag of Oreos from the pantry, one she'd hidden from her mother because sugar was the devil in her mother's eating-disordered world of tiny salads, tuna fish and spinning classes.

Sometimes, she couldn't believe her mother actually allowed herself to sweat. But she supposed she had to sacrifice somehow to maintain her size-two figure. Besides, she always rewarded herself with a massage afterward to relieve the stress.

What kind of stress did she have in her life? She'd never worked or had any purpose, other than to be arm candy for Bianca's father at his social events. Even so, she'd been cutting out of those lately with random excuses.

Tucking the Oreos under her arm, she grabbed a real Coke, not the diet ones her mother drank, and darted up the steps before anyone realized she'd been in the kitchen.

Shutting herself in her jail cell for the night, she crawled onto her bed, ripped open the package of cookies and stuffed two in her mouth. She popped the top on the Coke can and chugged it to wash down the crumbs.

Better clean it up in the morning before the housekeeper arrived or she'd rat her out. Sometimes she thought her mother paid the staff to spy on her.

She wolfed down four more cookies, knowing she'd have to purge tonight. Couldn't gain a pound or her mother would completely freak or put her in some fat camp like she'd threatened to do last summer when Bianca had suddenly developed hips.

She grabbed another cookie, bit half of it in one bite, then opened her laptop and searched social media. News about the disappearance of Kelsey and Ruby was blowing up the internet.

Oh, God... they were saying Kelsey was dead...

SEVENTY-THREE
SOUTHERN LIGHTS STUDIOS

Digger's head swam with confusion as he parked at the studio where Caitlin O'Connor taped her sessions. He had to talk to her. Assure her he hadn't killed that girl.

Heath had looked skeptical at the idea he was being framed. Caitlin was the only person who might believe him.

The last few months, his memories had become like a hurricane, thrashing and flooding his brain with images as fractured as shattered glass. Sometimes he saw himself, hands picking up the pillow to smother Anna Marie.

Other times he was certain someone else had been there.

His stepfather's shout. Accusations. His fists slamming into him. Himself hitting the floor, his vision blurring.

Then his stepfather leaning over Anna Marie, hands pressing against her chest in CPR. "You killed her!"

His little brother's cry of horror when he saw what was happening.

"Call 9-1-1!" his father shouted to Heath. For a minute, Heath just stood there. Paralyzed.

"Do it!" his father yelled.

Heath bolted from the room.

The room blurred again. His father's voice. "Come on, Anna Marie. Come on, breathe."

Seconds ticked by. Then minutes. A siren wailed.

Two medics rushed in and pushed his father aside and took over. One of them shook his head and muttered, "No pulse."

Footsteps pounded the floor. Police ran in.

"He killed her," his father screamed to the police.

An officer yanked Digger by the arm and dragged him outside.

Digger blinked, straining to recall more details. To remember why he would have hurt his sister. She was a pest, yes. Had followed him around like a puppy dog.

She was also pretty and sweet. The senior guys at school had started chasing her, asking her out.

He'd seen one asswipe pull her behind the bleachers and start groping her. She'd pushed him away and started crying.

Digger had beat the crap out of the guy.

He slid from the car now and walked up to the small building. A Honda Accord was parked in the lot. A light was burning inside. Caitlin must still be here.

Raindrops pinged off the ground as he approached the small wooden house. The signage swayed in the wind.

He needed to know everything she'd learned about his case. Why she believed in him when no one else had. Maybe she'd help prove his innocence now, with this latest murder.

Sweating, he reached the door, then tried the knob. Unlocked.

Not very smart, Caitlin. Anybody could walk right in.

Not wanting to frighten her in case she was armed, he knocked. No answer. He glanced around the property to see if anyone else was around. No one. Barring the howl of the wind, the place was quiet.

He knocked again and tapped his foot on the ground. No answer again. No sounds from inside. Then he realized if she was taping, she probably was wearing headphones or her studio was soundproofed for recording.

Slowly, he eased the door open. "Ms. O'Connor," he called out as he entered the small reception area. A desk faced the door, but it was empty. He called her name again, walked down the hall and found the sound room.

He knocked on it. "Ms. O'Connor?"

Outside, the rain beat at the roof. The floor creaked. He jiggled the doorknob and the door swung open.

He went still, the blood roaring in his ears. She was lying on the floor, face down, arms and legs at an odd angle.

A knot of panic seized him and he raced toward her.

SEVENTY-FOUR

Ellie's head ached as she parked in between some trees at the end of Red Hawk Road near Deputy Landrum's.

She'd tried calling but he hadn't answered so she'd decided to pay him a visit. She hated distrusting him. He'd worked for her for three years now, had been a solid deputy, was tech-savvy and followed orders.

But he'd withheld important information from her on this one. Had known the MO matched Digger's and covered for him.

Frustration gnawed at her gut as she watched through the fog for his vehicle. If he knew where Digger was, would he warn him to run?

The rain slowed to a drizzle, the sky black with night. A streak of lightning zipped over the tops of the trees and somewhere she heard a boom as if it had struck. A transformer could have blown. Or lightning hit a tree and knocked it down.

She tapped her fingers on the steering wheel impatiently. Exhaustion tugged at her, and she rolled her shoulders to alleviate the tension. Her body needed a bed and some sleep.

But how could she sleep knowing Kelsey's killer was still on the loose and that Ruby was probably dead?

The sound of an engine cut through the low rumble of thunder. Then Deputy Landrum's Ford Bronco appeared, spewing water from the tires as he raced onto the main road and headed down the mountain.

Ellie cursed, then eased her Jeep into drive, keeping her distance as she followed him.

"Dammit, Heath, you'd better not be going to meet Digger."

SEVENTY-FIVE

SOUTHERN LIGHTS STUDIOS

Digger froze, paralyzed at the sight of Caitlin O'Connor lying so still. She was the one person who'd tried to help him over the years. She couldn't be dead.

He inched toward her and checked for a pulse. Faint, but she was alive.

His gaze skimmed over her body, searching for injuries. No gunshot or stab wounds. Bruising discolored her neck, and the imprint of someone's fingers marked her skin.

No blood except for a streak of it that had run from her lips to her chin. Probably bit her tongue when she was attacked.

Was it his fault she was hurt?

He reached for his phone to call 9-1-1, but a noise outside made his pulse jump. Was her attacker still here?

He raced back to the front room and looked outside. Shadows darted around the property, slithering like the demons that chased him in his sleep.

Suddenly he saw a faint light like a cigarette being lit. A second later, the scent of gasoline seared his nostrils. Panic struck him as flames burst to life.

What the hell?

He dashed to the second window and looked through it, a cold sweat enveloping him. The flames jumped higher on this side, licking at the building and starting to climb to the bottom of the windowsill.

Pure rage heated his blood. Someone had attacked Caitlin and now they were planning to burn the building to cover it up.

Knowing the older wooden house would be totally engulfed in minutes, he ran back to Caitlin.

Shit. If he was caught here, he'd look guilty as hell, just as he had fifteen years ago.

Smoke began to seep inside the house and into the room though the openings below the doorways, and a coughing attack seized him. He covered his mouth with his hand, then started to grab her arms and drag her outside.

A siren's trill sound cut into the night, mingling with the sound of wood crackling and popping. Part of the roof crashed in with a loud bang.

Coughing again, he lifted her body and searched for a rear exit. Flames were starting to crawl along the floor, but he dodged them, jumping over patches as he went. Heat scalded the back of his neck as boards splintered and crashed down.

Sweating, he made it to the rear exit just as tires screeched and car doors slammed outside. Hell, the doorway was in flames. He pressed Caitlin's head to his chest and cradled her close as he darted through the burning door. Flames caught his shirt sleeve, but he ignored the sting of the burn as he rushed to a patch of trees at the edge of the woods. He laid her down by an oak, then beat at his burning sleeve.

Shouts erupted from the front of the house. Someone was here. They'd help her.

Emotions choked him and he darted into the woods.

SEVENTY-SIX

Ellie had maintained a safe distance behind Heath as she followed him, but when she turned onto the side street, she saw smoke plumes curling into the dark sky, flames shooting upward. Heath's Ford Bronco was parked sideways, the driver's door open.

The small house in front of her was engulfed in flames and Heath was running inside. She threw her Jeep into park, pulled out her phone and called 9-1-1 as she jumped out and ran toward the deputy. Heat scalded her as she neared the building, the fire climbing the exterior of the house and eating the wood.

"Landrum!" Ellie shouted as she drew closer. "Where are you?"

She reached the door, but the roof collapsed, wood splintering and shooting sparks across the ground at her feet. She jumped back to avoid getting hit while searching for Heath, but he didn't come back out. Her pulse hammered as she ran around the outside of the house, looking for another way inside.

Seconds later, Heath emerged, beating at the flames nipping at his shirt. He was coughing madly and soot dotted his face. She shouted his name, then helped him away from the raging inferno.

"What were you doing here?" she asked, her voice loud over the crackling fiery blaze.

He looked up, dazed and confused. "You followed me?"

The accusation in his tone infuriated her. "I came by your house to ask you about Digger and your father."

He coughed again, staggering slightly, and they hurried back around front. He collapsed into the driver's seat of his Bronco in a coughing fit.

"An ambulance is on its way," she told him. "Was anyone inside?"

He shook his head and ran a shaky hand over his face. "I didn't see anyone."

"Why did you come here?" Ellie asked.

"That podcaster Caitlin... Her studio... Wanted to talk to her... Thought Digger might have come to see her."

Ellie had put a call in to her earlier but she hadn't answered. "Was she here?"

"Don't know," he muttered.

A chill ripped through Ellie. "Wait here. An ambulance and fire truck are on the way. I'll take a look around."

Ellie grabbed her flashlight from the Jeep and set off to search the premises. Wind howled and brought the acrid odor of charred wood and ash. Heat blazed into the night. Sparks flew from the crumbling debris.

She circled the house, then found the back door. No way inside. It was completely engulfed. But she saw footprints near the back. One was probably Heath's. No, when he'd come out of the studio, he hadn't gone toward the woods.

But there was definitely another set. Brush crushed. Smashed weeds.

She followed the tracks to the edge of the woods, shining

the light around. A second later, she spotted the O'Connor woman lying on a bed of grass. She was so still Ellie thought she was dead.

SEVENTY-SEVEN

Ellie knelt beside the woman and checked for a pulse. Seconds ticked by. A minute then two. "Come on, Caitlin," she murmured. "Wake up."

She held her own breath, waiting. Listening. Finally, she felt a flutter of hope. She had a pulse. It was low and thready. But at least Caitlin was alive.

Ellie checked for wounds, a gunshot or knife, but no sign she'd been shot or stabbed. Gently she eased her tangled hair from her face, her breath stalling in her chest at the sight of bruises around the woman's neck.

Someone had tried to kill her.

She raced back to Heath where he sat still stunned and coughing in the front seat of his Bronco. "I found Caitlin O'Connor outside by the woods. She's alive, but barely breathing. Someone tried to strangle her."

"God." Heath scrubbed his hand over his face.

"Did you see Digger here?" Ellie asked.

"No... but why would he hurt that woman? She was helping him." He started to climb from the vehicle, but Ellie pressed her hand to his chest. "Wait here for the ambulance, call an ERT

and then search Ms. O'Connor's car. I'm going to look around."
She phoned Derrick as she walked around the back of the
burning studio. "It's Ellie." She explained about following
Landrum and that the O'Connor woman was injured.
"Someone set fire to her studio. I found her outside."

How was that? Ellie thought. Had she staggered out, then
collapsed?

"Ambulance and fire engine are on their way. Landrum's
calling an ERT."

"You think it was Woodruff?" Derrick asked.

"I don't know. Why would he hurt the one person helping
him?"

"Maybe she uncovered evidence that would put him back
in prison," Derrick suggested.

"That's possible, I suppose." Ellie glanced back at the fire.
"We need to know what she found, but whoever tried to kill her
set her studio on fire. Most likely to destroy evidence. Hopefully
she kept back-up copies of her research at her home?"

"I'll find an address and secure warrants," Derrick said.
"Then look at other cases she might have been working on.
Someone else may have had a grudge."

"True." Her gaze cut to the miles and miles of forest as they
ended the call. The perp was probably long gone by now. But
still, she phoned Cord. His voice sounded gruff when he
answered and she wondered if he'd been sleeping. "It's El. Did I
wake you?"

"No, what is it?"

She quickly relayed what had happened. "Do you mind
coming out and searching the woods?"

"On my way."

She could always count on Cord. He knew these mountains
better than anyone.

A siren trilled as she hung up, and the firetruck roared up,
lights twirling. The ambulance was right behind them. Voices

shouted as firefighters jumped out and started to work, rolling out hoses and attacking the blaze. Ellie rushed to the medics.

"This way." She gestured for them to follow and sprinted around back to Caitlin. "She's barely breathing." Ellie gently patted the woman's hand. "Help is here. Hang in there, Ms. O'Connor."

The medics snapped into motion, taking her vitals and giving her oxygen.

Ellie shined her light into the edge of the woods. An owl's hoot bled through the sound of the raging blaze. A lone wolf cried out. More thunder rumbled.

She stooped down to examine the area where Caitlin lay and saw footprints leading into the woods.

Questions mounted in her head as she tried to make sense of the scene. Why kill the woman and drag her out here instead of leaving her body in the fire? Had Caitlin somehow escaped her attacker and run out on her own?

She surveyed her body and clothing. Caitlin wore black slacks and a white blouse that was now stained with mud, but only one shoe.

She retraced the footsteps she'd seen in the dirt. Judging from the size, they were a man's. If Caitlin hadn't run out on her own, someone had carried her from the fire.

Although it was late, Derrick found the Hayes State Prison's warden's home number. "I know this is late, sir, but this is Special Agent Derrick Fox. I'm calling to inquire about one of your former inmates, Darnell Woodruff. Do you remember him?"

"Of course. What do you need to know?" the warden asked.

"We're investigating the murder of a teenage girl and another missing teen near Red Clay Mountain. Darnell is a person of interest in our case." He paused. "Did he have visitors while he was incarcerated?"

"His family never came, not even once. Until Ms. O'Connor with the Innocence Project took an interest in him, he was just another lifer on his own."

The fact that he had no visitors was interesting. "Did he connect with anyone in prison or make friends?"

"No, but he did get in several scraps. Had to spend time in the hole a few times."

"Did you consider him dangerous?"

"Everyone in this place is dangerous. They're locked up, angry and bitter. Even the ones who try to stay on the straight and narrow find it difficult. Gangs run the place and prisoners are attacked on a daily basis."

That answer didn't surprise him although it wasn't helpful either. "Was Woodruff an instigator?"

"A couple of times. But oddly, he wasn't defending himself. He took up for the scrawny green ones who came in, naïve, perfect targets."

"Could I speak with the prison counselor?" Derrick asked.

"She's gone home for the day," the warden said.

"Would it be possible for me to reach her at home? This is urgent."

"I suppose so." The warden gave him her number and Derrick thanked him then called her.

"Reba Boles," she said when she answered.

Derrick apologized for the late hour and explained the reason for his call. He'd talked to her several times regarding other cases and appreciated the fact that she was a consummate professional. "It's Special Agent Derrick Fox."

"Frankly, I'm surprised Darnell is a person of interest already in another crime. Especially one involving teenage girls."

Derrick exhaled, aware confidentiality limited the information she could share. But general impressions, especially hers, could add insight. "Why do you say that?"

A heartbeat of silence passed. "Because he exhibited remorse over what he'd done. In fact, he seemed tortured over it, and confused about the details."

Derrick ran his fingers through his hair as he considered her statement.

"I think that's one reason Caitlin O'Connor chose to take on his case."

"Sociopaths can be charming and fake remorse," Derrick pointed out.

"True, but I wouldn't describe him as a sociopath," she said with confidence. "Believe me, I've been doing this job a long time and I can usually spot them during our first session."

"He confessed to killing his sister," Derrick said. "And he was only sixteen at the time."

"About that..." she began.

He let the silence linger, a technique he used in interrogations.

"I'm not certain he was guilty."

She was the second woman who believed him. "Why do you think that?"

Her sharp breath echoed over the line.

"During our sessions, he seemed confused. He couldn't recall exactly what happened," she continued. "The details were inconsistent."

"According to the original report, his father found him smothering Anna Marie and shoved him off of her."

"I know," Ms. Boles continued. "But I did some memory recall work with him and once, he said *he* performed CPR to save his sister, not his father."

Derrick stewed over that. Shock could cause confusing memories. So could the Ambien in Darnell's system.

Was it possible someone else had killed Anna Marie and Digger did try to save her?

SEVENTY-NINE

RED CLAY MOUNTAIN

For the next hour, chaos ensued as the fire died down and investigators flooded the crime scene. Ellie instructed the medics to have a forensic nurse check for DNA on Caitlin's body. ERT searched for forensics while Cord and Benji combed the woods. The firefighters finally extinguished the last of the blaze but had to wait until the embers died down and cooled before they could go inside to search for evidence.

Ellie had a feeling they wouldn't salvage anything. Melted metal and plastic lay in the remains.

Heath approached, a desperate expression in his eyes, his hands in his pockets.

"Did you find anything in her car? Back-ups of her work?" Ellie asked.

He shook his head. "No laptop. Nothing."

"Hopefully she has back-up discs or tapes at her house. Or in the cloud."

Heath squared his shoulders. "I can go to her house."

Ellie studied him for a long moment. "No, it's a conflict of interest, Landrum."

"I want the truth," Heath barked.

Ellie gave him a warning look. "We've already been through this."

A vein pulsed in his neck. "Then what do you want me to do?"

Ellie pursed her lips. "Do you know where Digger is?"

"I told you I didn't." Anger sharpened his tone. "You're assuming Digger's guilty just like the cops did years ago."

"I don't assume anything," she said. "But you know we have to question him."

He remained silent. As a deputy, he understood. But she sensed he did have some semblance of loyalty to his brother.

The fire chief, Remy Broussard, a handsome, muscular guy in his late thirties with a thick head of jet-black hair, removed his mask to speak, his Cajun accent thick. "Definitely smelled an accelerant. Gasoline. Arson investigator will be here to determine point of origin in the morning when this cools down."

"Our victim hosts a true crime podcast—*Guilty or Not Guilty*," Ellie explained.

"Must have made enemies," Broussard said.

Ellie nodded. Just how many, though, and which one attacked her was the question. Obviously, Landrum didn't want to admit it could be his half brother, their only suspect at the moment. But he'd better not do something stupid like try to take the case on himself.

Ellie sent Derrick a text.

Contact the Innocence Project. See if they have copies of Ms. O'Connor's investigation into Darnell.

Maybe the podcaster had found something to lead them to the killer.

EIGHTY

SOMEWHERE ON THE RIVER

Digger had parked a half-mile away from Caitlin's studio, not wanting his car to be seen. Aware the police would be combing the woods, he'd dived into the river that backed onto the property. His arms ached as he swam across the choppy waves. The heavy rains had raised the water level to near flood conditions and the current was so strong, he felt it sweeping him downstream and dragging him under.

Knowing he couldn't fight its force, he gave into it and paddled his arms with the current, letting it put much-needed distance between him and Caitlin O'Connor.

Caitlin... A string of curse obscenities rolled through his mind. She was hurt. Because she'd helped him.

The police would assume he'd done it.

But they were wrong. Killing Caitlin would be like cutting off the hands that fed him. She'd given him hope when he hadn't had hope in years.

Pain seared his lungs as rain pummeled him and the current dragged him under the surface. He swallowed water, the darkness filled with fish and debris, loose tree limbs torn down in the wind. For a moment, he closed his eyes and considered succumbing to the pull below.

Ending it all.

He couldn't go back to prison, not for something he didn't do.

He sank deeper and deeper, his body growing tired, his arms weak, legs numb. His lungs felt like they were on fire.

But Caitlin's voice echoed in his head.

I think you were railroaded. We're going to fight this and prove to the world you deserve to be free.

Only he didn't feel free. His guilt held him prisoner.

And now he was a suspect in another murder and a kidnapping. He was virtually on the run, the cops nipping at his heels like a pack of rabid dogs.

And Heath... Did his brother believe him?

Digger blinked, choking on the muddy river water as he swam to the surface. Rain slashed his face and he gulped for air.

Caitlin's voice again. *We're going to fight them. You deserve to be free.*

Did he? Could he fight this without her help?

Her face broke through the darkness. Yes, dammit. He couldn't let her efforts be in vain.

She deserved justice. That meant finding the person who'd attacked her tonight and clearing his name.

EIGHTY-ONE
HOLLY LANE

Ellie was wiped out, but she couldn't go home yet. Her mind wouldn't shut down. One girl dead. Another missing and presumed dead. An attempted murder of a true crime podcaster.

All related to Darnell Woodruff and the murder of his sister.

Deputy Landrum's brother... their primary suspect.

Her phone buzzed. Cord. "Hey. Did you find anything in the woods?"

"Afraid not, El. Sorry."

"Me, too. Hopefully Ms. O'Connor can fill in the blanks when she comes to. Meanwhile, I'm on my way to Caitlin's house in case the man who tried to kill her is after her files."

"Is Fox with you?"

"No," Ellie said.

"I'll meet you there."

"Not necessary, Cord."

"You're damn well not going on your own, El. Too dangerous."

It was dangerous for him, too. And now he was going to be a father.

"What's the address?"

She sighed. "1024 Holly Lane."

Needing to focus on the road, she ended the call. The details of the case swam around in her mind, thoughts tangling together like the twisted vines in Kudzu Holler. Rain pounded the car and ground, fog blurring her vision. The wipers swished vigorously, the defroster blaring. Traffic lights of an oncoming car cut through the fog, nearly blinding her.

Night had set in long ago, bringing the shadows of doubt and fear. She had to untangle the pieces until they made sense.

Fueled by determination, she steered her Jeep toward Caitlin's house. She didn't have the warrants yet, but time was of the essence. The killer might already be there.

She cut the steering wheel, turning right into the drive of a small cottage. Painted yellow with a bright blue door, the cottage looked cheery as if a ray of sunshine was shining through the black gloomy skies.

Quickly, she surveyed the property for an intruder, but shivering trees and the heavy downpour made visibility difficult. Tree branches snapped off and the wind flung them to the ground. One hit the hood of the Jeep and she startled.

She pulled her flashlight and shined it around before she got out, but she could barely see two feet in front of her. She checked her weapon, pulled on her rain jacket, tugged up her hood and slogged through the rain to the front door. A "Welcome" wreath hung on the blue surface, the wind banging it and trying to tear it from the house.

Ellie ducked beneath the stoop, inserted the key she'd found in Caitlin's car and opened the door. She knocked water off her boots then stepped inside, the hum of the furnace echoing in the silence. The house layout was similar to hers with an open-concept living room and kitchen. A light glowed over the kitchen sink illuminating the room, which was painted a soft teal.

The big picture window over the pine table and color scheme looked airy and feminine, like Caitlin took pride in her surroundings. Lightning zipped outside, zigzagging in a fiery pattern and thunder boomed off the walls.

Ellie stood ramrod still for a moment, listening for sounds someone might be inside. She hadn't seen a car parked outside. And inside, things appeared still and quiet. She shined her light across the interior and noted blue coffee mugs on a tray along with a cutting board. Other than that, the counters were uncluttered.

No desk or computer in sight.

Another pop of thunder made her jump and her gaze shot to the picture window. Trees swayed and leaves swirled in the downpour. She froze, thinking she saw movement, maybe someone running through the yard, but then realized it was simply an animal.

Taking a steadying breath, she walked to the right, passed a bedroom and bath combination. On the opposite side was a second bedroom Caitlin was using as an office. A wooden file cabinet was flanked by bookshelves on one wall, which housed copies of podcasts, legal reference books and research material. A gray farmhouse desk held recording equipment, and a laptop.

As Ellie studied the rows of podcasts labeled by title and date, she noted many were copies of other podcasters' recordings, which Caitlin had probably studied for format and style. There were also tapes of transcripts of criminal trials.

Interesting. What had inspired the woman to explore the crime genre?

She thumbed through them and in the last section found two labeled Darnell Woodruff. Her pulse jumped. This was what she needed.

She and Derrick could analyze the material in the morning

along with the computer. She checked the file cabinet next and found numerous hardcopy files of the past cases she'd worked. Then one with Darnell's name on it.

She gathered it along with the podcast to carry to her car, but just as she reached the door, she heard a noise. A crash.

She swung around.

Another noise, glass shattering, and she froze, listening again. It had come from the picture window. She set the tapes onto Caitlin's desk, pulled her weapon and tiptoed into the hall. Footsteps sounded.

Heavy breathing echoed in the dark space. She gripped her gun at the ready, her body bouncing backward as a hulking dark figure charged her. She shoved at the man, desperate to see his face but he was masked and wore all black.

She struggled to push him away, but he grabbed her by the hair, stomped on her stomach then dragged her toward the closet. "Police, let me go," she screamed as she kicked and clawed at his arms.

He slapped her across the face so hard she saw stars and her head snapped back, then he hit her again. Pain ricocheted through her temple and he hit her over and over, punching her in the stomach until she gasped for air, choking on the pain.

Yanking the closet door open, he shoved her inside. She clawed at his leg, but the door slammed, plunging her into the darkness. A dizzy spell assaulted her and for a moment she thought she was going to pass out.

Footsteps pounded on the floor outside the door, then she suddenly smelled gasoline. Fear seized her and she pushed herself up and began to beat at the door, twisting and turning the knob. A crackling sound broke the silence then the odor grew stronger.

Oh, God, he was setting the office on fire! Panic shot through her and she held on to the wall and kicked the door to force it open. She tried again and again, to no avail. Smoke slowly crept inside. Her eyes stung and her lungs ached for air. Claustrophobic, she felt the walls closing in around her. Her heart raced, beating so fast she heard the blood roaring in her ears.

Tense seconds passed. Her vision blurred. The room spun as if she was caught in a tornado.

She coughed, fighting to breathe but lost the battle. Her body was weighted down, her head fuzzy, and her face hit the floor.

EIGHTY-TWO

"I'm still working," Cord said as he headed around the mountain toward the O'Connor woman's address.

"I'll wait up," Lola offered.

"No, you need to rest," Cord said. The last thing he wanted was for her to lose the baby because of exhaustion. He'd never forgive himself.

"The storm has really kicked up so it'll take me a while. I'll be there as soon as possible."

"Okay but be careful. This baby needs his daddy. I love you."

A clenching of his lungs made it hard for Cord to breathe. He knew Lola wanted him to use the L word, too, but he couldn't bring himself to lie, so he said good night.

A tree had fallen over the highway, forcing him to veer onto a side road. His tires slung mud, and he spotted Ellie's Jeep on the hill in front of a little yellow bungalow.

The wind beat at the truck as he pulled his jacket on and darted up to the house. His gaze scanned the property. Except for Ellie's Jeep, there were no other cars. No one around that he

could see either. Trees bent in the gust of wind as he got up and
darted to the front door.

A thin stream of smoke seeped from the bottom of the doorway, then he spotted a dark figure running toward the woods.

He started to go after him. But the house was on fire. What
if Ellie was inside?

Terrified of losing her, he pushed open the unlocked door
and scanned the living room. Smoke was starting to fill the
space, but he charged through the room, yelling Ellie's name.

The first room he came to was cloudy with smoke but he
didn't see Ellie. He pulled his bandana from his pocket and
covered his mouth as he glanced in the next room. The smoke
was thicker here. Flames licked the window and wood trim.

"Ellie!" Dodging the flames, he surveyed the space and
spotted a closet. He ran toward the closet and yanked at the
door but it wouldn't budge.

"If you're in there, El, step back!" Heat seared his neck as he
lifted his leg and kicked the door. The wood cracked slightly.
He kicked it again and again until it splintered.

His heart thundered. Ellie was on the floor, curled up,
unconscious.

He scooped her into his arms and ran through the smoke to
the living room. The smoke was so thick he could barely see,
and he stumbled, but he blindly found his way and raced
outside.

Behind him, the fire continued to blaze as he ran toward his
truck. He opened the door, slid in with Ellie in his lap and
checked for a pulse.

Dammit, he couldn't feel one. "Come on, El, you're a fight-
er." He snagged his phone, put it on speaker and called 9-1-1 as
he began CPR.

"9-1-1, how can I help you?" the operator said when she
answered.

"This is Ranger McClain, from SAR. Requesting immediate assistance at 1024 Holly Lane. Officer down. Unconscious, possible smoke inhalation. Performing CPR now." Her cheek was red and bruised. She might have other injuries, too. "Need an ambulance and firefighters ASAP."

"On the way," the 9-1-1 operator replied.

He gently brushed Ellie's hair from her face. "You are not leaving me," he whispered. "You're not, El."

Seconds stretched into a minute, then two, then three. Terror tore at his insides as he watched her for signs of life. Another minute passed, then finally her eyes fluttered and she gasped for a breath.

Cord wasn't much of a godly person, but he thanked him anyway, then cradled her against him and held on tight.

EIGHTY-THREE

Derrick's pulse raced as he parked beside Cord's truck and jumped out. McClain had called him just as he'd started home from the station.

"Ellie's okay," the ranger had assured him. "I got her out just in time and gave her CPR. Ambulance is on the way."

CPR. That meant Ellie hadn't been breathing. That she'd almost died.

A sick fear ripped through him as he climbed out. Then mixed emotions as he spotted McClain in his truck holding Ellie against him.

His boots squished in the mud as he strode toward Cord's truck. A fire engine was already on scene, firefighters attacking the blaze although he doubted there was anything they could salvage. A siren wailed, lights flashing as it rolled up and screeched to a stop.

Derrick had to see Ellie for himself. Had to look into her eyes and know she was really all right.

The ranger looked up, his face and hair sweaty from the fire. Ellie's face was bruised, skin pale, her breathing unsteady.

"You okay, Ellie?" Derrick asked.

She gave a weak nod. "I had the files, the podcasts. But... he must have taken them."

Derrick raised a brow. "He?"

"The man who attacked me," she said on another cough.

"Did you get a look at him?" Derrick asked.

She shook her head as the medic helped her onto the stretcher. "He came up behind me."

Derrick gestured for Cord to step aside with him while the medic settled an oxygen mask on her face. "McClain, did you see anyone when you arrived?"

Cord gestured toward the rear of the house. "Thought I saw someone back there running into the woods. But the house was on fire so I went in for Ellie."

"You did the right thing." Derrick sized up the scene just as ERT rolled up. Williams, the head of the team, gave a nod of recognition as he approached. "Looks like the scene we just came from."

"Because this house belongs to Caitlin O'Connor, the woman whose studio was just set on fire. She's on her way to the hospital now," Derrick said. "This time the unsub attacked Detective Reeves and almost killed her."

He curled his hands into fists. When he found the bastard, he'd make him suffer.

EIGHTY-FOUR

CROOKED CREEK

It was the middle of the night by the time Derrick reached his cabin. He'd wanted to go with Ellie to the hospital and so had Cord.

Of course, Ellie detested being hovered over, and refused. Infuriatingly stubborn woman.

"Get your butts to work," Ellie had snapped. "We have to find this maniac before he hurts someone else."

She was right.

A crime scene was no place to discuss personal feelings. He was trying to be patient. Still, he couldn't wait around forever. If it was really over between them personally, he had a right to know.

Now she was immersed in this case though, he didn't expect an answer anytime soon. Ellie was like a dog with a bone when someone was in danger, especially when that crime involved kids. Her tenacity was one trait that drew him to her.

She might not realize it but she'd actually be a good mother, a protective bear that would do anything to keep her cub safe.

He poured himself a bourbon on the rocks, stepped outside on his deck and looked out at the sea of trees and the night sky.

The image of that burned house taunted him. If McClain hadn't been there, Ellie could have died.

He tossed back a sip of his whiskey, the howling wind ripping through him with a chill as he pictured Kelsey's body. And Ruby being held hostage. Or... possibly, probably dead.

Knowing he couldn't sleep, he decided to work. Derrick found three other podcast series Caitlin had done, one a year for the last three years. The first one, a female accused of killing her husband. Caitlin had not only proven the woman's innocence but pointed the police in the direction of the husband's lover who'd killed him when he refused to leave his wife.

The second, a nineteen-year-old boy accused of murdering his girlfriend. Again, Ms. O'Connor's investigation led to his exoneration when she uncovered the truth—the girl had committed suicide.

In the third case, the perp was guilty but agreed to the interview because he'd been high on cocaine at the time he stabbed his friend. He wanted his story told in hopes of saving other teens from a life of drugs.

Curious about what motivated her, he researched her past. Understanding dawned when he learned she'd spent time in prison herself and was halfway through serving a ten-year sentence for burglary when Attorney Joleen Hunt from the Innocence Project investigated her case. Six months later, she'd been released, her name cleared. No wonder she now worked for the woman.

Then she'd chosen Darnell Woodruff's case. The podcast series had not yet aired, but if there were back-ups at her house, Ellie was right. Either her attacker had confiscated them or they'd burned in the blaze. He found the number for the office of the Innocence Project and phoned it. At this time of night he got Joleen Hunt's voicemail, so he asked her to return his call.

Exhausted, he rubbed his temple where a headache was pulsing. Something about this case didn't make sense.

Killing Darnell's sister was a personal crime; maybe Darnell and Anna Marie hadn't gotten along or they'd had a disagreement and tempers had flared and he'd killed her in a fit of anger. But to murder teenagers he didn't know personally was a different type of crime and was premeditated.

Ellie said Deputy Landrum was Digger's brother. What about their parents? Would Digger contact one of them?

EIGHTY-FIVE

SOMEWHERE ON THE AT

He'd almost gotten caught tonight.

That blasted O'Connor woman had been a problem.

The nosy bitch knew things, things that might lead to him. But... not everything. He still had time to finish this.

His heart raced as he drove by June Larson's house.

The sight of a police car guarding her place sent his blood boiling and he drove on. Taking June was way too risky at the moment.

His anger mounted as he drove back to his place. Shaking rain from his boots and jacket as he entered the house, he hung his jacket on the door peg, then poured himself a Scotch.

Homecoming was only four days away.

The students and families were all pumped up about the dance and the football game. Just as he'd been fifteen years ago. That was supposed to have been a special night.

But it had blown up in his face.

He picked up the Red Clay Mountain High yearbook and thumbed through it for another girl. So many young faces to choose from. So many innocents.

Only they weren't all innocent.

The girls on the Homecoming court. The cheerleaders. The tennis team. The drama club.

No... he had another in mind. Although she wasn't innocent. And she was nothing like Anna Marie.

God, how he'd loved that girl. Hadn't been able to resist her. Had to touch her and make her his.

But then...

He banished the ugly thoughts steamrolling him. The reminder of his sins. Her scream when he'd tried to touch her again.

He'd had to silence her.

And now he'd do whatever necessary to keep his secrets.

EIGHTY-SIX

CROOKED CREEK

Monday

Ellie woke with a headache to find Cord slumped in the chair by her hospital bed. She'd insisted he and Derrick work the case at O'Connor's house while she was transported to the hospital. That must have taken half the night.

So when had Cord shown up here?

A knock sounded and she blinked to focus, pushing herself to a sitting position although every bone in her body throbbed from the beating she'd taken the night before.

Derrick poked his head inside the door. A scowl darkened his face as he spotted Cord asleep beside her. Then he turned back to her with raised brows.

"How are you feeling?" he asked.

She rubbed her eyes. "Just peachy."

A teasing glint flared in his eyes. "Liar."

She shrugged.

Cord stirred and scrubbed a hand over the beard stubble grazing his jaw. "El?"

"I'm okay," she said, irritated. She probably looked like hell. "Derrick, did you find Caitlin's back-up files?"

"They were destroyed but her coworker Joleen Hunt is sending over her copies this morning."

Cord's phone buzzed, and he walked to the door with his head down, speaking quietly. "I'm sorry," Cord said. "Someone attacked Ellie. I'm at the hospital now."

Lola's voice grew louder. "Of course you ran to Ellie."

Ellie winced at Lola's irritated tone, and Cord quickly ducked out of the room.

She and Derrick exchanged a look, then she pushed the covers aside. "Find a nurse and get me out of here," Ellie said. "We need to look at those files."

She glanced at the clock on the wall. Ruby had been missing well over twenty-four hours now. "Check with the sheriff and tell him to expand the search area," she told Derrick. "Then get someone to sign me out of here."

Ruby needed her.

EIGHTY-SEVEN
RED HAWK RIDGE

Heath stared at the names of the prisoners Darnell had given him. He'd already researched one and learned he was dead.

The second; Sloan Mullins. A nonthreatening name. But he looked up the man's record and learned his nickname was Stone Sloan because he'd literally beaten his ex to a bloody pulp with a river stone. Smashed in the head and left her for dead on the bank of the Chattahoochee.

Did he really hate Digger enough to set him up by murdering young girls?

Or was Digger offering an alternative theory to draw attention away from himself?

He twisted his mouth in thought and called the prison. It took a few minutes, but he was patched through to the warden.

"I need information on one of your prisoners, Sloan Mullins?"

The warden cleared his throat. "Leader of the Bloods. Mean as a snake and shows no remorse."

"Is he still incarcerated?"

"Yeah," he answered. "Had a parole hearing two weeks ago but no way he's being released."

"He's still at Hayes?"

The sound of keys clicking echoed back, then the warden returned. "In solitary at the moment for stabbing another inmate."

Heath shook his head as he hung up. It was possible another gang member had put out word to seek revenge against Digger. But that was too far-fetched for him to buy.

Digger had thrown out his name just to sidetrack him. Still, he'd insisted he didn't kill Kelsey Tiller or take Ruby Pruitt.

All prisoners claim they're innocent.

Irritated, he accessed the recording of Digger's confession. If he hadn't killed Kelsey or abducted Ruby, someone else had. They'd also attacked Caitlin O'Connor's files.

Dammit, if the cases were connected, he'd find out how. Maybe that would lead to Ruby.

EIGHTY-EIGHT
CROOKED CREEK

Two hours later, after a quick shower at her house, Derrick drove Ellie into town. "You should have called me for back-up," Derrick said sharply.

Ellie sighed, his loud voice intensifying her headache. "You were busy and Cord met me there. I wanted to get those copies before her attacker did." Only she'd failed.

"All the more reason you call your partner," he said gruffly.

Ellie winced and rubbed her temple. "That would have been wasting time."

He cursed. "Look, Ellie, I know things are awkward between us right now because of personal shit, but if you're going to shut me out of the case because of it, maybe you need a new partner."

His angry words chiseled at her calm.

"I'm sorry," she said. "That's not what I'm doing."

He swung his car into a parking spot at the Corner Café, then turned to her, his eyes glittering with mixed emotions. "Isn't it?"

"No," Ellie said, her voice raspy. "I just thought you were busy and I could handle it."

"You always think that," he growled. "So what's it going to be?" he asked bluntly.

Their gazes locked, their shared history taunting her.

"I want us to work the case together," she said quietly. "We make a great team, Derrick, and I don't want to lose that." That much she was sure of. On a personal level, her emotions were a rollercoaster, winding and twisting and threatening to pitch her over the edge.

His gaze hung on to her for a moment longer then he seemed to accept what she'd said and didn't push it.

"Then let's get busy. But," he said with a stern look, "from now on, no going it alone. I will be staying with you twenty-four-seven until this maniac is caught."

Ellie pursed her lips although that movement made her jaw throb even more. "That is not necessary, Derrick. I can take care of myself."

He gently touched her bruised cheek. "Yeah, I know. But you're still getting a bodyguard."

A frisson of sexual tension passed between them. In the past, he might have kissed her, but the moment passed and he pulled away.

The pressure in her chest eased slightly and she climbed out just as her phone rang. "I saw the news about Kelsey," Ruby's mother's voice slurred, an indication she'd been drinking. "Is my daughter dead, too?"

Guilt suffused Ellie. "We're still looking for her. I assure you we're working around the clock to find her and the person who took her." She tried to inject confidence in her voice but failed miserably.

Images of that mobile home taunted Ellie. What kind of life did Ruby have? She knew some children of alcoholics grew up raising themselves and being the caretaker of their parents.

"I'll keep you posted," Ellie said. "Right now I'm working a lead."

The woman muttered an obscenity and hung up on Ellie. She texted Shondra.

Ellie: *Check in on Ruby's mother. She just called.*

Shondra: *Yeah, she's a mess. Talked to the school counselor. This morning the principal is holding an assembly to talk about Kelsey's death.*

Ellie: *Get over there, too. And warn the students about the consequences and dangers of circulating or posting half-nude or nude pictures.*

Shondra: *Will do. I'll talk to the teachers again.*

Ellie: *Copy that.*

Next, she called Landrum's number. Angry that he didn't pick up, she left a terse message for him to get to the station.

EIGHTY-NINE
CORNER CAFÉ

A hushed silence fell across the café as Ellie and Derrick entered the popular diner. The heavenly scent of bacon and ham frying, eggs sizzling and rich dark coffee made Ellie's mouth water, but the wary looks aimed her way killed the pleasure. Damning questions and comments were reflected in the eyes of the locals. She could hear the silent accusations.

Detective Ellie Reeves fails to protect the town again. How many more of our children have to die?

She saw Lola standing behind the counter at the same time Lola spotted her. Goosebumps skated up her arms at Lola's ice-cold look.

Cord's usual bar stool sat empty and Bryce, who'd been dating Lola for a while, looked angry as he took his bag of food and paid the bill.

Ellie nodded hello to him. "You okay?"

He muttered something under his breath that sounded suspiciously like *damn women*. "Heading out to check some properties north of here."

"Thanks. Keep me posted."

Shooting a scowl over his shoulder toward Lola, he strode

out the door. Ellie felt for him. Obviously, he was not pleased with the fact that Lola was pregnant with Cord's baby. He must have been more serious about Lola than she'd thought.

Whispers and stares circulated through the café as the table of gossipmongers watched the local news on the TV above the breakfast bar. Her interview with Angelica reporting Kelsey's death and her request for information on Darnell replayed, the photo of Darnell flashing.

"Looks like you got out of the hospital okay," Lola said, her tone sarcastic.

Ellie ignored her sarcasm. "Yes, I'm better."

Lola handed Ellie her to-go order. "Hope you find those girls soon. The town's in a panic again. There's gossip that the high school is postponing Homecoming."

"Trust me, Lola, barring the girls' parents, no one wants those teens found more than I do."

"Trust you?" Lola made a derisive sound, then rolled her eyes and moved on to another customer.

Ellie ignored the jab, and she and Derrick passed the table of gossipmongers as they headed back to the door. Meddlin' Maude, the queen of the rumor mill, gave her a hateful look, her voice intentionally loud enough for Ellie to hear her conversation with Carol Sue, the local hairdresser at the Beauty Barn.

"Those girls were tramps," Maude hissed. "Posting pictures of themselves half-naked on the internet. They were asking for it."

"You know the one named Ruby, well her mama's nothing but a common drunk and whore," Carol Sue said. "Like mother, like daughter."

Maude fanned her face with her napkin. "I heard they made a bet to see who could sleep with the most boys before Christmas."

Ellie halted, rage searing a path from her throat to her stomach. "You nasty, clucking hens," Ellie spat. "You have no idea what you're talking about. Those girls are exemplary, hard-working honor students and are talented and dedicated. Kelsey was working toward a music scholarship." She leaned toward Maude, almost touching noses as she stared into her beady little eyes. Eyes that always seemed to see the bad in people.

"I know you hate me for your granddaughter's death, Maude, and that's fine, but Kelsey's family deserves respect and our prayers right now, and so does Ruby and her mother." She cut a look toward Carol Sue. "They did not post those pictures. They were victimized." She straightened, her contempt almost rivaling what she felt for the killers she hunted. "Now shut your traps and stop spreading lies."

Both women gasped in shock.

"Well, I never," Maude mumbled.

"Oh, my word," Carol Sue gasped.

Derrick nudged Ellie's elbow. "Come on, Ellie. They're not worth it."

Ellie lifted her chin with a nod. "No, they're not."

Heated gazes scalded her back as she turned and strode to the door. Although, as she passed old Miss Eula Ann, the little old woman rumored to talk to the dead, she saw a smile twitch at her lips.

When they stepped outside, Derrick raised his hands and clapped. "I'm glad someone finally told off that old biddy."

The women's words taunted Ellie as she looked up at the gray sky. There was truth in what they'd said. She had let Kelsey and Ruby down.

And with another day dawning, would their killer take another?

NINETY

SUNNY GARDENS CEMETERY

His head throbbed like a mother.

Last night he'd driven by Bianca's house and realized she was a rich girl and her family had a security gate and security system so there was no way he could take her from her house.

After that he'd spent two hours trying to devise a plan to get her alone without drawing suspicion.

So far he'd remained under the radar and that had to be maintained.

Before he went to work, he drove to the cemetery to see Anna Marie. He wanted to visit her daily but couldn't chance anyone seeing him at the grave. Usually he came at night, but this morning he had the desperate urge to talk to her.

As he wound along the narrow drive, a ribbon of sunlight streaked the headstones as if to say God was watching over them. He passed a tent where gravediggers were working to prepare for a funeral and in the distance saw an older woman hobbling along carrying flowers for whoever she'd come to see.

He glanced at the fresh flowers on the passenger seat, flowers he'd plucked from his own yard. Anna Marie had loved sunflowers so he'd planted them in her honor.

Another section of graves and then he'd be there with her.

But as he crested the hill, a parked police car slipped into view. His hands tightened on the steering wheel and his lungs screamed for air. A man in uniform climbed out.

Deputy Heath Landrum. Not someone he wanted to see or be seen by now.

Sweat exploded on his skin and he turned his car at the fork and moved on. But fury burned in his gut.

His need to finish this thrived deep in his belly.

Tonight, he'd take Bianca. Then he could end it.

As soon as Ellie entered, she looked for Deputy Landrum but he was not at his desk. Sensing he was avoiding her, she called his number.

He didn't answer, so she left another terse message. "Landrum, get into the office ASAP. We need to talk."

"I called this morning to check on Caitlin O'Connor," Derrick said. "She's still unconscious."

Ellie sighed. They needed her to wake up and identify her attacker.

"Last night, I did some digging into her prior podcast series and discovered the reason she works with the Innocence Project," Derrick said as they spread their breakfast on the table in the corner of her office. "She served time in the pen herself. An attorney with the Innocence Project helped clear her."

"Ahh, so helping others became her passion project," Ellie said as she bit into her sausage and cheese biscuit.

Derrick sipped his coffee. "Yeah. I also spoke to Joleen Hunt, the female attorney who works with Caitlin. She sang Caitlin's praises, claimed she had no enemies. She'd worked three cases before Digger's and was successful each time."

"Then none of the inmates she represented had reason to kill her," Ellie said, still mulling over Digger's motive. *Innocent until proven guilty*, she reminded herself.

"I also asked Ms. Hunt to send over any notes or information she had on Digger then I did some research on him. Mary Landrum, Digger's mother, left him and the family the week before her daughter's murder."

"I read that in the police report," Ellie said. Which meant Heath had only been eleven when his mother deserted the family.

"According to the prison warden, the only visitor Woodruff had in the fifteen years of his incarceration was Ms. O'Connor."

Ellie tilted her head in thought. "You mean Heath never visited him?"

Derrick shook his head. "Not even once."

"Hmm. I guess there's no love lost between them." So why would he cover for Digger now? "I would have thought as he got older, he'd want to talk to him, find out why he killed his sister."

"Maybe he was too traumatized by the murder," Derrick suggested.

"What about Heath's father?" Ellie asked, her mind beginning to race.

"According to the police report, his name is Gilbert, AKA Gil, Landrum," Derrick said. "As Landrum said, Gil works for Red Clay Mountain Construction."

"We need to talk to him," Ellie said.

Her phone buzzed. Dr. Whitefeather. She quickly connected and put it on speaker so Derrick could hear. "You have news for me, Laney?"

"Yes, confirming that Kelsey was smothered. The fibers on the pillow match one from the interior of her mouth."

The poor baby had probably bitten it when the killer had crammed it over her face.

"There's something else that's interesting," Laney said.

"Don't beat around the bush," Ellie said. "Just tell me."

"Darnell Woodruff's DNA was not found anywhere on the body or the pillow or her clothing."

"He might have worn gloves," Ellie said, keeping an open mind.

"Probably, but it's still odd that there weren't any foreign clothing fibers, not a hair, or any forensics that lead to him. There was, however, another partial print on the bedframe. I ran it through IAFIS but didn't find a match."

Ellie swallowed hard. If another person's fingerprint was on that bed frame then someone else had been with Kelsey at some time and could have murdered her.

Which meant Darnell might be innocent and they were looking for the wrong man.

She phoned Cord and filled him in.

"It's starting to look like someone else was there that night. Go back to the Landrum house where we found Kelsey and turn it inside out. If there's evidence that can lead us to this person, I want it found."

She clenched and unclenched her hands as she hung up. *If you're still alive, hang in there, Ruby. I won't give up until I find you.*

NINETY-TWO

SOMEWHERE ON THE AT

Tears rolled down Ruby's cheeks as she stared into the darkness. Her head ached and she felt as if she'd swallowed cotton balls. The sound of water trickling made her shiver. A musty scent filled the space. The floor below her was slick and hard. And wet. Rats skittered across the concrete.

She struggled to move but her body felt heavy and achy. Where was she? How long had she been here?

Who was he? She hadn't been able to see his face with that black mask on.

But when she'd woken up here, she'd felt him nearby. Heard his breathing. Smelled some funky odor on him.

A shudder tore through her. He'd shoved that pillow toward her. Hovered over her, breathing hard. She'd thought he was going to kill her. She'd begged and pleaded for herself and for her mother.

Who would take care of her if she was gone?

For some reason, he'd pulled back and stormed away, angry. Was he coming back?

She jerked her head to the right searching for a door. More

water was running somewhere. She held her breath and listened for footsteps.

Had the police found Kelsey? Did they even know *she'd* been taken?

NINETY-THREE

RED CLAY MOUNTAIN HIGH

June clutched her aching stomach as her grandmother pulled up in front of the high school. The deputy guarding her had stayed in the driveway all night and now was right behind them in his police car. Could he be any more conspicuous?

"Grandma, do I really have to go to school?" June's voice caught.

Her grandma gave her a sympathetic look. "I know it's hard, June, but you have to stand up to the bullies. Giving in lets them win."

Tears blurred her eyes. "But Kelsey and Ruby..."

Her grandma's arms wrapped her in a big hug, and June burrowed into her. She wanted to stay there forever and hide from the world. She'd hated school when she'd first moved here, but Kelsey and Ruby had brought her into their circle, and she counted on them.

But Kelsey was... gone and Ruby might be, too.

And she was all alone and the kids at school had seen that picture of her in the locker room and she didn't know if she could face them. Everyone would be pointing at her and laughing about the Virgin Pact and that stupid meme challenge.

Her grandmother pulled back, tilted June's chin up with her finger and smiled. "I know you're sad and upset, sweetheart, but you're tougher than you think. Do you want me to walk you to the door?"

June backhanded her tears and shook her head. That would only make things worse. Then she'd look like a big fat baby.

Her grandmother kissed her hair. "I'll be right here to pick you up when school is over, and so will that deputy. After the bell rings, wait inside until you see my car."

June nodded and slid from the car, her legs wobbling. She slowly walked up the steps, her breakfast threatening to come up. When she finally reached the landing, she turned and saw her grandmother watching.

And the cop. A reminder that Detective Reeves thought the man who killed Kelsey and took Ruby might come after her.

She scanned the parking lot. The teacher's lot was full. Other kids piled out of their cars, students slinging their backpacks over their shoulder as they met in groups. A black car turned in to the student lot and seemed to slow. A chill went through June. The tinted windows hid the face of the driver.

What if he'd followed her here? Was he watching her now, just biding his time until he took her?

NINETY-FOUR

RED CLAY MOUNTAIN HIGH

Bianca had been dreaming about Homecoming Week ever since the first day of school. She'd made a vision board of the decorations and added a picture of her in her dress and shoes, then cut out a picture of Mitch and placed it beside her own.

As head of the Homecoming Dance committee, she and her tribe of *it* girls had chosen the best theme ever. Barbie Dreamland!

Last week the students couldn't talk about anything else. Girls were gushing all over the place at the decorations they'd bought. With the hot pink and black retro theme, the pictures would be fabulous. No doubt she'd be crowned Homecoming Queen. Even the teachers supervising the committee, Ms. Otton, the art teacher, and old Mrs. Wallaby, who was so ancient she probably grew up in the era of *The Jetsons*, blathered on that they wished their dance had been as lit as the one she was planning.

Not that either one of them actually used the word lit. Mrs. Wallaby said "far out" like she was one of the original hippies. Which... Bianca had to admit was kind of cool in itself. Talk about a retro vibe!

Whispers rumbled through the room and some classmates stopped and stared at her as she walked to her homeroom, but not with the admiring smiles they'd had last week when Homecoming talk was all the rage.

"Can you believe Kelsey Tiller was murdered?" one girl said.

"My mom thinks Ruby's dead, too," another girl whispered.

"My dad says some maniac probably targeted them because of those posts," another girl said as she gave Bianca an evil eye.

The reactions kept coming.

"My mom's so freaked she almost didn't let me come to school today."

"My father said I can't go to Homecoming or anywhere but school until this psycho is caught."

"Mine wants them to cancel the football game and dance."

"How can we celebrate when two of our students may have just been murdered?"

"Kelsey helped me with my English Lit paper."

"I feel sorry for Ruby. She lives in a trailer and her mama's a drunk and someone says she's a hoarder, that she probably has rats crawling in her bed."

Their voices quieted as June Larson walked into the room. June lifted her head and glared at Bianca.

Bianca dug her fingernails into her palms in frustration. This was not turning out the way she'd expected.

Even two of her cheerleading friends huddled close together, whispering and staring at her as if she'd grown three heads overnight.

All talk of Homecoming had been shoved onto the backburner because kidnapping and murder were hotter topics.

June slid into her desk and a girl named Tamika leaned over and whispered, "It's Bianca's fault."

Bianca huffed and claimed a seat on the opposite side of the room in the back. Pissed, she tossed her backpack onto the floor by her desk. June and Ruby and Kelsey were ruining everything!

The sound of static of the intercom burst into the room, followed by the assistant-principal's voice. "Good morning, ladies and gentlemen."

Bianca rolled her eyes. *Geesh. Get on with the announcements already. And don't you dare say Homecoming is canceled.*

"This morning, we're holding an assembly to discuss the death of one of our students and the disappearance of another. Deputy Shondra Eastwood of the Crooked Creek Police Department will address our student body. Teachers, as soon as you check the students in, send them to the gym."

A strained silence fell over the room and Bianca slid lower in her seat as she felt dozens of eyes burning holes through her.

What happened to Kelsey and Ruby was not her fault. It was not!

Captain Hale poked his head into Ellie's office. "This came for you from Attorney Joleen Hunt." He set a file box on the table in front of Ellie.

"It's her notes from Caitlin O'Connor," Ellie said as she opened it. "And there are copies of the podcasts. It'll take time to wade through them." She explained about Deputy Landrum's connection to their suspect and Laney's report. "Captain, let's put a guard on Caitlin O'Connor's hospital room. If someone wanted to kill her over the information she uncovered, they might try again."

Deputy Landrum strode in, looking rough around the edges as if he hadn't slept.

Captain Hale indicated the deputy. "You want Landrum to go?"

"No, ask the sheriff to send one of his deputies. I need to talk to Landrum."

The captain nodded. "I talked to forensics this morning and they couldn't salvage anything in her studio or home. So far no prints, but accelerant confirms arson in both instances." He narrowed his eyes at Ellie. "That bruise on your face looks bad. You need the day off, Detective?"

"Hell, no," Ellie said. "Someone didn't want us to see what she'd discovered about Darnell Woodruff's case. That means there's a clue in there that might lead us to Ruby."

She filled Landrum in on Laney's report. "There was a partial fingerprint on the bedframe where Kelsey was found, but it didn't match Digger's."

Landrum ran his fingers over his beard stubble and shifted uncomfortably. "Digger showed up at my house last night before I went to the O'Connor woman's studio."

"What?" Ellie said, her voice on edge. "Why didn't you bring him in?"

"Because when you called, he ran off. That's why I went to the O'Connor woman's studio. He told me he didn't kill Kelsey or take Ruby, that he was being framed. When he left, I thought he might have gone there."

Ellie shrugged. "Framed? Did he say by whom?"

"He gave me a couple of inmates' names. But I looked into them and they aren't behind this."

"Still, we need to bring him in for questioning."

Landrum gave a nod. "Maybe I'll find his number in Ms. O'Connor's phone records."

"I have copies of her files to review. Agent Fox is going to look at the tapes of Darnell's confession if you want to join."

"I saw the interview but haven't read the police notes yet," Landrum said, then he claimed a seat beside Derrick on the loveseat where he was perched in front of his laptop.

Ellie settled at her desk with the files from the box Joleen Hunt had sent over. The podcast series hadn't yet aired but she'd already taped several interviews. Ellie put in her earbuds and connected to the first episode in the series.

November 10, 2022

Caitlin: This is Caitlin O'Connor, Southern Lights Studios, true crime podcast: Guilty or Not Guilty. In conjunction with the team at the Innocence Project, this series explores the case of Darnell Woodruff, who was convicted of murdering his younger half sister Anna Marie Landrum on October 31, 2008.

Interview one with Dr. Anthony Curtis.

Dr. Curtis, you evaluated Darnell Woodruff after his arrest. What can you tell us about his condition?

Dr. Curtis: Darnel Woodruff, age sixteen, approximately five-eleven, one hundred and sixty-five pounds.

Upon examination, Darnell appeared to be in shock and was dazed and confused, mumbling incoherently, having sweats and shivering.

His medical records indicated that he suffered from a sleeping disorder that included insomnia and sleepwalking. He was prescribed Ambien, and at the time of his arrest, tested positive for the drug in his system, which could account for his incoherence and confusion. He also had unexplained bruises on his body.

When asked about them, he didn't seem to recall how he got them.

His memories were all over the place, inconsistent at the time. He stated that he didn't remember going into Anna Marie's room, but he heard his father shouting, "You killed her!"

That's when he looked down and saw the pillow in his hand. His father shoved him to the floor and started CPR.

Caitlin: Did he remember smothering his sister?

Dr. Curtis: Just that he was holding the pillow.

Caitlin: And you deemed him mentally competent to stand trial?

Dr. Curtis: Yes, he was confused, but not mentally ill.

Caitlin: Dr. Curtis, do you think Darnell was capable of

killing someone?

Dr. Curtis: I believe that given the right circumstances, anyone is capable of murder.

Ellie moved on to the second audio file.

November 11, 2022

Caitlin: This is Caitlin O'Connor, Southern Lights Studios, true crime podcast: Guilty or Not Guilty. Today we are continuing our series on the Darnell Woodruff case with an interview from Mr. Woodruff.

Mr. Woodruff, thank you for speaking to me. Please tell us in your own words what happened the night of October 31.

Darnell: I... uh, the details are foggy.

Caitlin: Please tell us what you recall.

Darnell: It was storming. I... heard a noise and got up, thought my mother might have come home.

Caitlin: Your mother? Where was she?

Darnell: She left us the week before... I don't know why but she just left.

Caitlin: And you wanted her to come back?

Darnell: Yeah. So did my brother and Anna Marie. She'd been crying for days. So... I hoped Mama was back and... I wanted to see if Anna Marie was okay.

Caitlin: You cared about your sister?

Darnell: Yeah... she was thin for her age and... fragile...

Caitlin: What happened next?

Darnell: It was thundering and lightning and... I heard the noise again and it was coming from her room. So I went to see what it was and...

Caitlin: I understand this is difficult, Darnell, but what happened then?

Darnell: I saw a shadow and thought someone was hurting her and I... I froze... and then the next thing I remember my stepfather was shouting, "You killed her!" And I looked down and saw the pillow and I thought I must have done it. Then my stepdad shoved me to the floor and I... think I blacked out... and then the sirens were wailing and the police burst in and dragged me outside... and I looked down at my hands and... I couldn't believe I killed her.

The interview ended with Darnell sobbing.

Caitlin: There you have Darnell Woodruff's account of the night in question. Police insist he confessed to the murder of his sister. But did he really? Or does his statement raise reasonable doubt?

Ellie pushed back from the desk, troubled by the statement.

"Derrick, I just listened to an interview Ms. O'Connor recorded with Darnell."

Derrick looked up from the police report. "And?"

"He told her he heard a noise and got up to check. He thought it might be the mother returning. That he saw a shadow and thought someone was in her room and he blacked out for a minute. His father's shouts brought him back and he saw the pillow in his hands."

"The prison counselor said he made contradictory statements in his sessions with her."

Ellie angled her head toward Heath. "What happened with your mother, Landrum?"

Anguish darkened the deputy's eyes. "I don't know. She just ran off one day. Dad said she left a note."

"Had your mother ever left before?"

Heath shrugged. "A couple of times after they had a fight."

"What did they fight about?" Ellie asked.

Heath rubbed his temple. "Normal stuff. Mom accused Dad of being too tough on Darnell."

"Was he?"

"Yeah," Heath admitted. "Anna Marie was definitely his favorite."

"But if your mother defended Darnell, why would she leave the family?" Ellie asked.

Heath twisted his mouth in thought. "Like I said, I don't know. Before, she'd be gone for a night or two, but she always came back."

"Did your father look for her?"

"He called her, but she didn't answer. Then Anna Marie died, and he fell into a deep depression and refused to talk about her again. Said she was dead to us."

Ellie frowned at the wording. He'd used the same phrase about Darnell when he went to prison.

Derrick raised a brow. "I may have found something in the police report and trial transcripts."

Hope sparked in Ellie's mind. "What?"

"Police canvassed three neighbors who claim not to have heard anything the night of Anna Marie's death. But one said she noticed a black car drive by the house several times that week and thought a squatter had been staying in the abandoned place next door."

"What?" Landrum asked. "I don't remember that."

"You were what? Eleven at the time?" Ellie asked.

"Yeah, but if there was someone stalking Anna Marie, the police should have looked for them."

"Did they?" Ellie asked.

Derrick shook his head. "There's no mention of it. But he could have been a person of interest."

The hair on the back of Ellie's neck prickled. "Officer Traylor dropped the ball."

"He thought he had a confession," Derrick said with derision.

"And he never looked any further." Ellie understood now

the O'Connor woman's interest in the case.

"Is his name listed?" Ellie asked.

"No. But if he was a squatter or drifter, once the news hit the media, he could have skipped town."

"And gotten away with it while Darnell rotted in prison."

Ellie's phone buzzed. Deputy Eastwood. "Hey, Shondra," she said as she answered.

"On my way to the school now. But I canvassed the neighbors at the mobile home park where Ruby lived again."

"And?" Ellie asked.

"One woman mentioned a crazy old guy named Huddie who gave her the creeps but when I visited him, he was so strung out he could barely talk. The neighbor said he stays that way. So I don't see him as a real suspect. No way he'd be able to pull off a murder and another kidnapping."

"Probably not," Ellie agreed. "Anything else?"

"The lady in the trailer across from Ruby said she saw a black car driving by the mobile home park the week before Ruby disappeared. And then again, the evening Ruby went missing."

Ellie's pulse jumped. "Make and model of the vehicle?"

"A sedan. That's all she knew."

Ellie gritted her teeth. "Did she get the license plate?"

"No," Shondra said. "She has cataracts, and her vision is limited." A tense second passed. "I went back and asked the other neighbors if they'd seen the car but no one had."

Ellie's fingers felt clammy as her hold on the phone tightened. "Damn. That would have been helpful."

"You think Ruby had a stalker?" Shondra asked.

"Maybe. In the original investigation into Anna Marie's death, someone saw a black car driving by the Landrums' the week she died. Could have been the same car."

Which meant the current case was tied to Anna Marie's murder.

NINETY-SIX

November 12, 2022

Caitlin: This is Caitlin O'Connor, Southern Lights Studios, true crime podcast: Guilty or Not Guilty. Today we're continuing our series on the Darnell Woodruff case with an interview with a young woman who once nannied for Darnell and his siblings. Although this witness reluctantly spoke to me and only by phone, she has asked for her real name to be withheld, so for the purpose of this podcast, we will call her DeDe.

DeDe, when exactly did you work for Darnell Woodruff's family?

DeDe: Let's see. Darnell was turning one and Anna Marie was born. Mrs. Landrum had some postpartum depression so I helped with the kids.

Caitlin: Please describe the family.

DeDe: Mrs. Landrum had Darnell from a previous relationship which she refused to talk about. Mr. Landrum accepted that, but when his daughter was born, he seemed to resent Darnell. Later, when Heath was born, Darnell started acting out to get attention and he and the father butted heads. Then Darnell started getting into fights and trouble.

Caitlin: Would you say Darnell's stepfather was abusive?

DeDe: That depends on your definition of abuse. He was certainly stern and didn't spare the rod with Darnell.

Caitlin: Did he discipline Anna Marie or Heath in the same manner?

DeDe: No, just Darnell. Anna Marie was his princess. He doted on her.

Caitlin: And the mother? Did she favor the daughter as well? Or did she defend Darnell?

DeDe: She loved all of her children and defended him when Gil came down on him.

Caitlin: Tell us about Darnell. How did he feel about his sister?

DeDe: He was protective of her.

Caitlin: He didn't resent the fact that she was the favorite?

DeDe: Maybe. He smarted off about it a few times but got backhanded so learned to keep his mouth shut and take it.

Caitlin: Did Digger ever hit Anna Marie? Or hurt her?

DeDe: Not when I was there. But I didn't see the family after I left. I can tell you though there was a lot of tension in that household. Something was definitely wrong, something they didn't want anyone to know about it.

Ellie drummed her fingers on her desk. What exactly was going on in that family?

NINETY-SEVEN

SOMEWHERE ON THE AT

Tears of frustration blurred Ruby's eyes. Her fingers were raw where she'd tried to untie the ropes. Blood trickled down her arm from where they'd cut into her wrists. She had to pee so bad she thought she was going to explode. And it was so cold in here, her hands were going numb.

The sound of water gushing above made her shiver, and she heard the ping of it on the floor as it dripped into the room. She squinted in the dark, desperate to figure out where she was. but shadows lurked everywhere. Biting back a sob, she dragged herself along the concrete wall, pressing her hands along the surface in search of a window or door.

Seconds ticked into minutes. Then longer. She had no idea how long she'd been here. But she was terrified he'd be back any minute. A noise above made her freeze and she leaned against the wall and held her breath.

Listened for footsteps.

Heard her heartbeat pounding in her ears.

Then... was it thunder outside? Or the man who'd abducted her?

Had he come back to kill her?

Students gave Bianca a wide berth as they exited the assembly. Stupid cop made it sound like she was a criminal and now everyone was treating her that way.

Bianca's heart hammered as she hurried to catch up with Mitch. When she reached him, she tapped his arm.

He turned, a scowl darkening his deep brown eyes.

"Mitch, please talk to me. Let's go to Homecoming together."

"Moron," he muttered. "I wouldn't go with you if you were the last girl in school."

Bianca stepped backward as if he'd slapped her.

Blinking away tears, she darted through the crowded hall to her first period class, Computer Science and Technology. Just as she sank into her seat and everyone settled down, Mr. Jones, or Bones Jones as the kids called him behind his back because his legs looked like toothpicks and he walked bow-legged, stepped to the front of the room. The brown rug on his egg head had slipped out of place, which usually brought giggles and whispers. Today, there were none.

Good grief. Big babies were too scared to even laugh.

The assistant principal rapped on the door then stepped inside. "Bianca Copenhagen, Principal Bentley and I need to speak to you now. And bring your backpack, you won't be returning to class today."

Bianca's cheeks burned with embarrassment as she wove through the rows of desks and stepped into the hall. She felt as if she was a prisoner walking the gangplank like the pirates once forced captors to do.

"Sit down, Ms. Copenhagen," Principal Bentley said as they entered his office.

Bianca slipped into the chair across from the principal and twisted her hands in her lap.

"The FBI confirmed that you posted those pictures of Kelsey Tiller, Ruby Pruitt and June Larson. For that reason, the school ethics committee has decided to suspend you for the remainder of the school year."

Bianca gasped. "But... you can't do that. Homecoming is this week, and I headed the committee—"

He raised a hand. "Stop. The decision has been made. I've already called your parents."

As Derrick skimmed the autopsy report, his pulse quickened. "Ellie, this is interesting. Anna Marie was seeing a nephrologist."

Heath leaned forward. "What?"

"It's a specialist who treats kidney disease. According to the autopsy, Anna Marie was in the early stages of kidney failure but would eventually require dialysis until a donor could be found."

Ellie traded a look with him. "You didn't know, Landrum?"

"No," he said, his voice weak. "Are you sure she was sick?"

"Yes." Derrick checked Anna Marie's medical records. "She was diagnosed a few months before she died."

"What else does it say?" Landrum asked.

"Cause of death was asphyxiation due to being smothered by a pillow. Cracked rib consistent with CPR attempt." Derrick straightened. "Hmph. Wait a minute. This is not right."

"What is it?" Ellie glanced at the file.

"The entire family's DNA and blood types are in here." Derrick leaned back in the chair. "Anna Marie was not Gil Landrum's biological child."

Landrum's head jerked up. "What?"

Derrick pushed the report in front of the deputy and he paled as he looked down at it. "This makes no sense."

"DNA doesn't lie," Ellie said gently.

Landrum strode across the room, his agitation palpable. "I don't understand. Dad and Mom never told us that either."

"Maybe your father didn't know," Derrick said.

Ellie snapped her fingers. "Or maybe he did and just hadn't shared that information with you and Darnell. If he'd been in the dark, he could have just discovered the truth when he learned Anna Marie needed a kidney transplant."

"The big argument they had the night before Mom left," Heath murmured, as he sank back into the chair. "Good god. That's what that was probably about."

And the reason she left, Ellie thought. But why would a mother leave a sick child?

ONE HUNDRED

The fact that Anna Marie was not Gil Landrum's daughter sent Ellie's thoughts racing. The neighbor had seen a black car around the house the weeks prior to Anna Marie's murder, the nanny said there was something off about the family. The black car and paternity issue could have created reasonable doubt for Darnell by offering another suspect.

The fact that Landrum's mother abandoned the family raised more questions. Had she really left them, especially with her daughter's illness? Or... could something more nefarious have happened? Something that had to do with the daughter's birth father?

"Do you have the note your mother left?" Ellie asked.

Landrum's pallor had gone completely gray. He was obviously contemplating the implications of the new information. "No. I never saw it. But my dad... might have kept it."

"There's also someone else we need to look at," Ellie said.

"Anna Marie's biological father," Derrick said.

"What if the mother looked for him to see if he was a donor match?" Ellie asked. "If he didn't know he had a daughter, and she told him..."

Derrick heaved a breath. "He may not have been happy about it."

ONE HUNDRED ONE
GEORGIAN MANOR

Bianca's eyeballs ached as she stared out the window. There was that black car again. She'd seen it drive by her house a half dozen times lately. Once, it had even driven up to the gate but then quickly pulled away. A man had been inside although she couldn't see his face.

Although now, with Kelsey dead and Ruby missing, what if it was the bad man who'd taken them?

The car drove on and she breathed out. *You're being paranoid.*

She heard her father's Mercedes start up, went to the window and watched him drive away from the house. Her parents' room was downstairs and she figured her mother was on the phone with friends or having a second cocktail.

Two in and she'd be snoozing until dinnertime.

Bianca paced the room, waiting it out, watching the clock. The last school bell should be ringing.

She tugged on her rain jacket, pocketed her phone then tiptoed down the staircase. The kitchen was empty. Her mother was stretched out on the chaise by the fireplace, her hand over her eyes, snoring softly.

Bianca crept to the back door, closed it as quietly as possible then ran to the garage. She glanced down the street for the black car but she didn't see it, so she climbed on her bike and pedaled down the drive then onto the street and headed toward the school. With the wet fields, the football team wouldn't be practicing outside, so she and Mitch would be alone.

The rain started up again, the wind stirring the trees. Her fingers tingled from the cold. She tugged her hood over her head, hating to show up looking like a drowned rat. But she couldn't sit in that glass house, locked away, any longer.

Cars whizzed by, spraying her with rainwater, and her bike skidded in a puddle. She caught herself before she toppled over and pedaled faster, ignoring the strain in her calves as she pedaled up hill.

Huffing for a breath, she rode the two miles, determined to convince Mitch she wasn't a bad person like he thought. By the time she reached the school though, the student parking lot was nearly empty and the last bus had rolled away. For a moment, her skin prickled with unease.

The place looked deserted, the tall trees bare. Something rattled behind the bleachers. Maybe a couple making out. Or the smokers and pot heads gathering to get high.

Something caught her eye as she scanned the back exit and she thought she saw that black car again. But another sound drew her attention back to the fields and the bleachers. She had to catch Mitch.

She raced across the parking lot to the practice fields, which were empty due to the weather. A pine cone blew down from a tree and pinged off the metal stands, startling her. A shadow moved from the rear of the gym.

Mitch's car was in the parking lot so she propped her bike against a post and ducked under the stands to get out of the rain.

Footsteps sounded behind her, and she turned, expecting

Mitch. But a dark figure slipped from the shadows. A man? Black clothes. A back ski mask on his head and face.

She turned to run but he lunged at her and grabbed her. She tried to scream but he pressed a rag over her mouth and an odd taste filled her mouth. Her head spun and she gasped for a breath, pushing at his hands and kicking.

Seconds later, her head swam. Spots danced behind her eyes. The man's choppy breathing echoed in her ear as he dragged her into the woods.

Then the world faded.

ONE HUNDRED TWO

SOMEWHERE ON THE AT

He had to finish this. Homecoming was almost here. So fitting that it meant so much to Bianca. She'd put so much effort into it.

But now she wouldn't get to see the fruits of her labor.

Laughter exploded inside him, erupting like a balloon about to pop as he threw her inside the trunk of his car.

The pep rallies, football game, the dance... sneaking behind the bleachers for some touchy-feely fun. It had been the best time of his life.

Until it had become the worst.

Now it dredged up the pain and memories. His dreams and hopes... all shattered.

He'd loved Anna Marie so much. She was sweet and beautiful, her voice soft and angelic. She had dreams. So did he.

Like Kelsey, she used to strum the ukulele and make up funny words and wanted to be a songwriter. She was writing a love song when... it had all fallen apart.

Pain wrenched his insides every time he thought of her. She'd been innocent... until he'd learned the truth.

Kelsey and Ruby... virgins. They were so tempting, seductive in their innocence. Somewhere between a woman and a child.

But they'd made themselves targets with that pact.

Perspiration dotted his neck.

Bianca made no pretense at being innocent. At saving herself. She flirted with all the guys. Was chasing Mitch like her hair was on fire.

Now it was her turn to suffer the consequences.

The scratch she'd made on his arm stung like hell. The little bitch had drawn blood. She'd pay for that.

Grateful for the dark clouds and empty parking lot, he jumped in his vehicle and sped away.

Trees bent in the downpour as the rain intensified. The wind roared like an angry beast, twisting the branches, ripping off limbs and flinging them through the air like matchsticks. Rain pelted the windshield, beating it like a drum and his tires churned through mud, slinging gravel.

He pictured pretty Bianca lying side by side with Ruby, both sleeping, like angels, preserved in their innocence, saved from their unholy families.

A rhyme chimed in his mind.

The little girls lay sleeping, all nestled in bed, with dreams of sugarplums dancing in their heads. Then came the shadows, the prelude to the dead, the innocence destroyed as the seeds of desire spread.

"Soon it'll all be over," he whispered. Soon they would sleep forever.

And he would be free to visit Anna Marie any time he wanted.

ONE HUNDRED THREE

HOG HILL ROAD

Cord knew Ellie was beating herself up over losing Kelsey Tiller and was desperate to find Ruby Pruitt. Sometimes he was shocked at the violence and cruelty he'd seen, although he shouldn't be. He'd grown up enduring unimaginable horrors.

It didn't diminish the terror the families of those young girls were suffering now or the pain Kelsey and Ruby had endured.

A fierce protectiveness consumed him, eating at his calm and driving him as he searched the Landrums' old house again. The ERT was usually thorough and didn't miss much so he didn't know what Ellie expected him to find. But she'd asked him to come and he'd do anything he could to help her find Ruby and get justice for her and Kelsey.

If this was his own kid missing, he'd be crazy with the need to find him or her.

He studied each angle of the room where Anna Marie had died and where they'd found Kelsey's body, examining the windows, door and closet, then searched beneath the bed and mattress. He even lay on the floor and crawled under the bed to see if Anna Marie had hidden something beneath like a diary.

Nothing.

He went in and out of each room, focusing first on the girl's, then Digger's and Heath's, and last the parents'. No journals or evidence he could find. No goodbye note from the mother.

Frustration built like a pile of rocks in his chest.

Next, he searched the exterior of the house and property, then the woods again. About a quarter of a mile in, he noticed an old dilapidated treehouse near the creek. It was almost hidden by overgrown brush and weeds. They'd looked for Ruby and Darnell out here but ERT must have overlooked the tree-house. Curious, he walked to it and studied the rotting wood then slowly climbed the ladder, testing each rung with his weight as he did.

When he reached the top, he crawled onto the floor, brushing leaves and twigs from the fallen tree. He imagined Landrum and his sister and brother playing up here or meeting friends. Surveying the tree trunk, he found a carving of a heart with the initials AML & AJ.

AML—Anna Marie Landrum. AJ—who was that? Anna Marie's boyfriend?

Benji's bark made him look down and he saw his dog pawing at an overgrown area by the creek water. Curious, Cord climbed down and slogged through the weeds until he saw what Benji was barking at. He'd found something.

Ruby?

Moving closer he shined his flashlight into the brush and swallowed hard as Benji pawed at the dirt, digging until he uncovered a bone.

Not just a bone. A human skeleton.

Derrick escorted Gil Landrum to the interrogation room but
Ellie ordered Deputy Landrum to watch from another room.

She introduced herself to Heath's father as she entered.
The man was gruff-looking with graying hair, a scruffy beard
and scars on his hands that could have come from his job.

"I've been watching the news. Is Darnell here?" Landrum
asked, his tone icy.

"No, we're still looking for him. But Heath is here, too. He's
one of my deputies."

Gil jerked his head in shock. "What? Heath works for you?"

Ellie nodded. "You didn't know?"

He put one fist into the other palm. "No. We... haven't
spoken in a long time. Now, I know your agent said you're
looking for Digger, but I can't help you there."

"Are you aware he was released through the Innocence
Project?" Ellie asked.

Gil grunted. "Yeah, I saw it on the news. But I don't care
what that podcaster says. Digger killed Anna Marie. End of
story."

Ellie tapped her foot. "Actually Ms. O'Connor was

attacked, and we believe it was because she was helping Darnell. That someone didn't want him to go free."

His gray eyes flicked to Derrick, then her, his tone incredulous. "You think she found something to prove Digger's innocent? 'Cause let me tell you, I walked in and found him over her. I know he did it."

"We've reviewed his statement and the interrogation," Derrick interjected. "But we also have new information that could point to another suspect, something the original investigating officer overlooked."

Gil Landrum folded his arms, his flannel shirt stretched across his bulk. "You're wasting your time. That boy should be back in jail."

Ellie stiffened. Perhaps the motive for taking the teens was to incriminate Digger and do just that—put him back in prison. Then the actual killer could go free.

"You certainly seemed intent on convincing everyone of that years ago," Ellie said.

"Because I caught him red-handed," he snapped.

Ellie let his attitude float in the air and settle before she continued.

"As we said, we have uncovered new information. Anna Marie's autopsy and her medical records. We know she was diagnosed with a kidney disorder that would require a kidney transplant."

Landrum's jaw hardened. "Yeah."

"Were you and your wife tested to see if you were a donor match?"

He gave a quick nod, but pain laced his eyes. "We weren't. She was going to have to go on the transplant list."

Ellie and Derrick shared a look. "Transplant surgery can be expensive," Derrick said bluntly.

"Cost didn't matter. Somehow, we would have found a way, that is if Digger hadn't taken her from us."

"But your wife left the family before the murder," Ellie said. "Why would she desert her sick child when she needed her?"

He shook his head. "I guess she was just too freaked out," he said. "She left a note saying she couldn't handle things and had to get away."

"Do you still have that note?" Derrick asked.

He shook his head. "I was so pissed, I tore it in pieces and burned it in the fireplace."

Dammit. If they had the note they could analyze the handwriting and see if the wife had actually written it. She also had to consider that Gil lied about the note.

"Did you look for her?" Ellie asked.

"I called and called, but she didn't answer. She'd left a couple of times before but she always came back so I thought she would that time."

"But she didn't? Not even when Anna Marie died?"

Anguish streaked his face. "That really tore me up. I couldn't believe she didn't come to the funeral."

"Mr. Landrum." Agent Fox tapped the autopsy report. "Were you aware Anna Marie was not your biological daughter?"

Gil turned ashen. "What makes you think that?" he asked.

"The autopsy report and DNA prove she wasn't your child," Agent Fox said. "Perhaps you learned the truth when you were tested to see if you were a donor match."

His jaw clamped tight but he didn't respond.

"Do you know the name of Anna Marie's biological father?" Derrick asked.

Gil squeezed his eyes closed. "No, Mary refused to tell me. Now what the hell does this have to do with anything?"

"Because of your statement about Darnell, the police never looked for another suspect in Anna Marie's death. And Darnell told the prison counselor that he thought someone else was in the house the night Anna Marie died," Ellie said.

Landrum's eyes widened. "You think the biological father came to see her? That he might have been in the house?"

Ellie shrugged. "It's possible. In one of Darnell's interviews with the prison counselor, he said he heard a noise and thought someone else was in the house. That he moved the pillow and tried to do CPR."

"Good God, he's lying to get out of jail," Landrum said.

Although he wasn't backing down, for a second, she saw hesitation in the man's eyes as if he was considering the possibility that he'd been wrong about Darnell.

"Mr. Landrum," Derrick said. "Where were you three nights ago?"

He pinched the bridge of his nose. "Home."

"Can anyone vouch for that?" Derrick asked.

The man looked confused. "I live alone."

"How about two nights ago?"

"What the hell is this about?" Landrum snapped.

"It's about Kelsey Tiller and Ruby Pruitt," Ellie interjected. "Do you know who they are?"

"No. But I saw the news about them missing. Do you think Darnell killed them, too?"

"That's what we're trying to determine," Ellie said. "We actually think someone may be framing him to send him back to jail."

Derrick leaned forward. "You had reason to be upset when you learned Anna Marie wasn't your daughter. Is it possible you took out that anger on Anna Marie yourself?"

Landrum shot up from the chair, enraged. "What the hell? I loved that girl..."

"Maybe it was an accident," Ellie suggested. "And you already had trouble with Darnell, who wasn't your real son, so you blamed him."

Ellie's phone buzzed. Cord. "Excuse me, I need to take this."

She left Derrick with Gil Landrum and stepped outside the room and answered. "It's Ellie."

Cord's breath echoed back. "I found something at the old Landrum property."

Ellie's pulse jumped. "Ruby?"

"No, but it is a grave. Benji just dug up a skeleton. Judging from the size and decomp, it's been here a long time."

Ellie pressed her hand to her forehead. "Stay there. I'll send an ERT and Dr. Whitefeather out there." She hung up and strode back to the interrogation room, her patience wearing thin.

"Mr. Landrum," she spat. "We just searched your former homestead again and do you know what we found?"

He balled his hands into fists but said nothing.

She planted her palms on the table, and leaned forward, pinning him with a stare. "A body, that's what we found."

His sharp intake of breath rent the air.

"And you know what's been bothering me. The fact that your wife ran out a week before Anna Marie's death. Are you sure she ran off or did you kill her when you learned Anna Marie wasn't yours and bury her in your backyard?"

He shot daggers at Ellie, his voice cold and hard. "I want a lawyer. Now."

ONE HUNDRED FIVE

Heath watched the exchange between Detective Reeves, Agent Fox and his father with a sickening knot in his gut. The facts were pointing less and less toward Digger but to Heath's father, stirring doubts and suspicions he couldn't ignore.

His father claimed his mother left them, but Heath had never seen that note. And although she'd gone off on her own for a couple of days here and there, overall she'd been a good mother. Loving and kind. She used to curl up with him, Digger and Anna Marie, with popcorn and movies, and tell them stories at night.

He'd always felt abandoned and never understood why she'd actually leave. And now knowing Anna Marie had health issues, he couldn't believe she'd abandon her daughter.

His father had also shut down after she left, then disappeared deep into despair when Anna Marie died.

What if... He didn't want to even think it. But he had to face reality. A body was buried behind his old house. Anna Marie had died there.

He leaned on his elbows on his knees, dragging in a breath

as nausea built along with the realization that his own father might have murdered his mother and sister.

ONE HUNDRED SIX

While Ellie spoke with Deputy Landrum about this latest revelation, Derrick found the name of the specialist the family had consulted regarding Anna Marie's kidney condition, a nephrologist named Dr. Darren Pugh.

The doctor was now head of a nephrology practice affiliated with the Emory Healthcare Network in Atlanta. He called the number listed, spoke to the receptionist and explained his reason for calling. She agreed to have the doctor call when he finished with the patient he was currently seeing.

Derrick studied the whiteboard of information, adding Gil Landrum as a person of interest. He wrote "Anna Marie's biological father" beneath it. Both had motives for being upset with Landrum's mother and possibly reason to kill Anna Marie. And now Digger was out, her real killer might want to put him back in prison so he could remain unnoticed.

He studied Ruby's photo, willing it to present a clue as to where the killer had left Ruby, but there was nothing in the picture indicating a location.

His phone buzzed, and he connected. "Special Agent Fox."

"This is Dr. Darren Pugh. My receptionist said you needed to talk to me about a former patient."

"Yes. Fifteen years ago, you treated a teenage girl named Anna Marie Landrum who needed a kidney transplant."

"That's correct. What a sad story there. I was shocked when her brother murdered her."

Derrick measured his words. "Actually, new information has come to light that sheds doubt on his conviction. I have warrants that allowed me access to Anna Marie's medical records and autopsy, and learned the man believed to be her father was actually not her biological parent. I believe Mrs. Landrum may have contacted the biological father about being a donor and need to speak with him."

"You understand HIPAA laws, Agent Fox."

"I do, but this is a murder investigation and as I said, I have a warrant in hand. I'm faxing you a copy of it now."

The doctor breathed out. "Let me look at the warrant and then check my files."

"Thank you. I'll wait."

Piped music echoed over the phone and Derrick stared out the window as he waited. He'd seen the mountains during a freak snowstorm and rain but never the kind of stormy, dreary skies that had prevailed lately. At this point, it seemed like the bad weather would never end. The meteorologist had warned that the creeks and river might flood, which could cause more problems.

"The warrant looks to be in order," the doctor said as he returned. Derrick heard keys tapping over the line, then Dr. Pugh cleared his throat. "Yes, Mrs. Landrum had contacted the biological father. His name is listed as Jason Jones."

"Was he a donor match?"

"I have no record that he was tested," Dr. Pugh said.

"Do you have an address for Jones?"

"Yes." Dr. Pugh gave him the address of a house on Red

Clay Mountain, not far from Whispering Pines where Kelsey had lived.

Ellie burst back into the office, her breathing choppy. "Derrick, Captain Hale just got a call from the Copenhagens. Bianca is missing."

ONE HUNDRED SEVEN

GEORGIAN MANOR

While Ellie plowed through the rain to the Copenhagens'
house, Derrick issued an Amber Alert for Bianca. Tension
strained her muscles as the Jeep churned over the wet pavement, spewing water where it had collected on the street.

Tree limbs were boughed and sagging from the heavy
downpour, visibility hazy as she sped up the driveway. Guilt
and worry shadowed her mind but questions bled through the
fog. If Bianca had disappeared in the last two hours, Landrum's
father wasn't responsible.

Which meant the killer was still out there. How many more
girls would he take before Ellie tracked him down?

Tears of frustration threatened but she blinked them away
angrily. The girls needed her to get justice for them. And maybe
she could save Bianca.

The wind was blowing so hard, Ellie battled to keep
standing as she climbed from the Jeep and hurried to the front
door of the Copenhagens' house.

Mr. Copenhagen opened the door, looking harried, his tie
hanging askew, his hair mussed as if he'd been running his
hands through it. She and Derrick shook rain from their jackets

and raked their shoes on the outdoor mat, then removed their wet coats as they entered and hung them on the hall tree in the foyer.

Mr. Copenhagen pushed his phone toward Ellie, and she swallowed a gasp as she looked at the picture of Bianca, posed as the other girls had been. "Why would this maniac kidnap my daughter?" Mr. Copenhagen asked, his voice brittle.

Ellie tensed. Why would he take any of them? That was the question. And why not Bianca? Because her father had money?

"At this point, we're still in the dark," Ellie said. "But we hope we're getting closer to the truth."

"Mr. Copenhagen," Derrick said. "Let us come in and talk. Is your wife here?"

He spun on his polished loafers and led them through the massive formal foyer to a living room with expensive furniture and oriental vases. A fire glowed in the floor-to-ceiling fireplace, the only homey feature in the room.

Mrs. Copenhagen sat on the white couch, twisting her phone in her hands and staring at it. She glanced up quickly as they entered then returned her gaze to the phone and released a tiny whimper of despair.

Ellie and Derrick traded a look, silently deciding to divide up to question the couple.

Ellie joined the mother on the couch while Derrick and the father retreated to the kitchen.

"Mrs. Copenhagen, I'm so sorry Bianca is missing. Did you try calling Bianca's friends?"

"Yes, but none of them have seen her or talked to her since she left school today. Kelsey Tiller is dead and you still haven't found that other girl." She broke into a sob.

"We haven't given up," Ellie said, trying to soothe the woman. Although how could she blame this mother or the others for being angry and upset?

She was terrified herself. Ruby appeared to be dead and so did Bianca.

Stomach knotting as she studied the photograph, she knew the same person who'd taken the other girls was responsible. Bianca was posed exactly as they had been.

Get your mind focused on the case. Every second counts. "What time did you last see Bianca?"

"When we got home from the school about ten this morning," she said.

"You picked her up?"

"Yes." She wiped at her teary eyes. "The principal called us and s... said she was suspended."

Ellie wasn't surprised. "Then what happened?"

"We were all upset," she continued. "She went to her room." She licked her lips. "And my husband was going to look at boarding schools."

"He told Bianca that?"

She nodded. "Bianca ran to her room and slammed the door. That... that's the last time I saw her."

"When did you discover she was gone?"

"I had to go out for a while then looked in on her when I got back about two and she was upstairs so I rested for a while. When I got up about four, I checked again and she was gone. At first, I thought she might be outside but I looked and then called her friends but they hadn't heard from her." Her voice cracked. "Then this picture came through, and my husband called the police."

If the picture wasn't a replica of how the other girls were posed, Ellie might suspect the couple, the father, had done something to Bianca out of anger that she'd gotten suspended. But they hadn't shown the photograph to the press.

"Mrs. Copenhagen, can you please show me Bianca's room? We'll also need her phone and computer."

She stood on wobbly legs and led the way to the staircase.

Ellie held the rail as it spiraled up the two-story foyer, her feet slick on the marble floor. Wood floors gleamed on the second floor, and she surveyed Bianca's room as she entered. Nice brass bed. Plush bedding. The room resembled a designer showroom and the mother's taste, not a teen's room. Expensive art on the wall. No posters, trophies or personal photographs. Except for the backpack on the floor, the room was neat and sparse.

Mrs. Copenhagen walked to the bed and smoothed a wrinkle in the comforter.

"Does anything look out of place?" Ellie asked. "Or is anything missing?"

The mother glanced around the room then walked to the closet and looked inside. "No, not that I can see." She paused. "Wait, her raincoat is not here."

Ellie considered the missing jacket. If Bianca had gone out on her own, she would have taken it. And if the killer had been stalking her, he could have snatched her then.

ONE HUNDRED EIGHT

Derrick studied Mr. Copenhagen's body language as he relayed what had happened at school.

"Suspending Bianca was totally an overreaction and we will look into grounds for suing the school, but I'm sure they'll argue that they were protecting their reputation." He scoffed as if the school was subpar.

The temptation to put the man in his place bugged Derrick, but he bit back a retort. Kelsey and Ruby and their friends were working hard to earn scholarships and were excellent students who were total innocents in Bianca's bullying.

Still, he didn't want to see harm come to the girl. Although it might be too late.

He'd first sized the father up to being an arrogant rich prick who'd spoiled his daughter and shaped her into an entitled brat. The man's gut reaction after the trouble she'd caused was to send her to a boarding school so she'd be someone else's problem, or to rake her actions under the rug as if they hadn't triggered harm to come to two other girls.

"I can't believe some crazy person took her," he said, his face beginning to sweat. "What kind of psycho kidnaps teenage girls?"

Now his own child was missing, Derrick heard true fatherly worry in his voice.

Didn't matter. They had to find Bianca and stop this creep. Too many girls had already suffered. And Caitlin O'Connor, who fought to free innocents, was lying in the hospital fighting for her own life.

"Is it possible Bianca was angry and snuck out?" Derrick asked.

The man pressed his hands over his head. "Hell, I don't know. Maybe. She was really upset about that kid Mitch. She wanted them to go to Homecoming together and after being suspended, she may have called him."

"That's a good place to start," Derrick said. They'd questioned Mitch about Kelsey. Although if the person who'd killed Anna Marie, taken Kelsey and Ruby and assaulted the O'Connor woman were one and the same, Mitch was too young to be the perpetrator.

"I need a list of all of Bianca's friends so we can check in with them," Derrick said.

"We called them the minute we realized Bianca was gone," Mr. Copenhagen said. "No one had talked to her. In fact, they all sounded as if they were avoiding her and had dumped her as a friend the moment this all came out."

Fickle teens, Derrick thought.

"May I look at your security footage?"

He gave a clipped nod and led the way to his office. It took him no time to pull it up and they all watched as Bianca snuck out the back door and went to the garage. There she retrieved her bicycle and pedaled down the drive. They lost her when she hit the street and turned right.

"She snuck out," Mr. Copenhagen said in a raw whisper. "Where did she go?"

"Her phone is not upstairs," Ellie said as she and the mother returned.

"Is your phone set up to track Bianca?" Derrick asked.

Mr. Copenhagen looked sheepish but nodded. "She didn't know it, but yes. After the other girls disappeared, we got scared and enabled it." He quickly checked it and it showed that the last place Bianca was had been the school. From there, the phone didn't appear to be moving.

"We'll head to the school," Derrick said.

He and Ellie exchanged a look. What if the killer had left Bianca's body on the school grounds?

On the way to the high school, Derrick had phoned Mitch Drummond's house. If Bianca had a crush on him, maybe she'd convinced him to meet so they could hook up and he'd seen something. Or she might have told him if someone was watching her.

But Mitch hadn't seen or talked to her since she'd left school that morning.

The rain had dwindled as Ellie and Derrick parked at the high school. The parking lot was empty, teachers and students having left for the evening. They scanned in all directions for anyone on the premises.

Derrick had arranged for the principal to unlock the school, and the sheriff showed up with two deputies to search the interior of the building.

Around the side of the school near the football field, Ellie spotted a bike propped against the brick wall and pointed it out. "That looks like Bianca's bike."

"You're right. Park here and we'll check behind the bleachers." Derrick reached for the door handle. "Kids at my school used to meet there to make out."

Wind whipped Ellie's ponytail as she climbed out into the chilly air.

They pulled flashlights as they walked toward the bleachers, shining them all around along the wall and ground. The rain had muddied the dirt, but Ellie noted footprints and a muddy hand against the wall. It looked small enough to belong to Bianca.

"Something happened here," Ellie said, pointing to drag marks leading away from the building. She and Derrick followed them. Mud marred the concrete sidewalk and disappeared in the earth around the football field and then into the woods.

"I'm calling Cord and a search team," Ellie said.

"I'll get an ERT out here. Maybe he touched her bike or his prints are on the bleachers."

They made the calls, then Ellie phoned her captain and filled him in. "Issue an APB for Bianca Copenhagen and get her picture on the news. We have a third victim."

ONE HUNDRED TEN

Ruby saw monsters in the dark. Shadowy figures darting around the empty cold space. Her eyes felt gritty from blinking to search for a way to escape. In her mind, she saw Kelsey and June, the three of them hanging out, laughing at silly movies and whispering secrets.

It was hard to believe she might never see Kelsey again. That, if she was dead, Kelsey would never bop into her trailer, drag her outside, ignoring the clutter and filth where she lived and pretending Ruby's mother hadn't passed out on the couch. Never text her to ask if she was okay and if she needed to come over and spend the night.

Or that Ruby would never go home. Never see June again.

She thought she'd cried out all her tears, but another flood came, and they dripped down her face and chin. She raised her bound hands and swiped at them, choking back a sob.

You're going to be dead if you don't get out of here.

Suddenly her anger took root. No one was coming. She had to save herself. Do something while he was gone.

Because she had a bad feeling he would be back.

She thought she had no energy or fight left in her. But she managed to find it. She had to escape.

The pinging water grew louder. Stronger. As if rain was gushing in somewhere. She breathed in the icy chill as she rolled to her belly and began to drag herself across the room again. Feeling along the rough wall surface, she bit back a cry. She'd only made it halfway around before she'd passed out earlier.

Her arms strained as she pulled herself inch by inch along the floor. She felt for a window. A door. Crawled through a puddle of water streaming inside. Cold water seeped through her clothes. The sound of the wind wheezed from the right. If the wind was blowing through, there had to be an opening.

Hope fueled her determination, and she dragged her body toward it. Her limbs ached. Her head hurt. The rough floor scraped her hands.

Another foot and she spotted a thin stream of light in the distance. She clawed her way toward it. Grunting with frustration and exhaustion, she finally reached the light. A door.

She inhaled a deep breath as she crawled over the edge and to the outside. Rain splattered the ground. It was so dark outside she could barely see. She crawled forward and mud sucked at her. Eyes squinting through the fog, she saw trees bowing in the wind.

Then headlights.

Terror shot through her, and she struggled to move faster. Get into the woods. Hide somewhere. If only her hands and feet weren't bound, she could run.

She made it another foot. Heard the car door slam. A loud curse.

Footsteps. Shouting.

She tried to find the shadows and hide in the bushes, but he had a flashlight and shined it all around. The light blinded her. Then he was on her.

Grabbed her by the hair.

She screamed and kicked, but pain shot through her skull. Then he hauled her through the mud back to the building.

ONE HUNDRED ELEVEN

RED CLAY MOUNTAIN

Ellie made a quick call to her boss and updated him. "Bianca Copenhagen was taken from the high school. Ranger McClain found another grave at Landrum's childhood home. Dr. Whitefeather is at the old Landrum House with McClain and says the body looks as if it is an adult female," she said. "With the timing of the disappearance of Mary Landrum, my guess is it's her body, but Dr. Whitefeather will confirm with the autopsy."

"Do you think Woodruff killed her?" Captain Hale asked.

"I don't know. Landrum's father and Anna Marie's biological father both had motive."

Her boss must have popped a peppermint in his mouth, a substitute for a cigarette, because she heard him chomping on it. "By the way, Deputy Landrum burst into the room and confronted his father, asked him if he killed the mother."

Ellie cursed, watching as the ERT arrived and Derrick went to confer with them. "What happened?"

"I dragged the deputy from the room. But his father claimed innocence. Then he demanded his lawyer."

"Do you believe him?" Ellie asked.

"On the fence."

Ellie agreed. If Heath's father killed his wife and daughter and set up Darnell, she'd throw the book at him. "Even with the attorney, we can hold Gil Landrum for twenty-four hours. So make sure he stays put. And check his alibi for earlier today." If he was at work and now at the station while Bianca disappeared, that eliminated him as a suspect.

"Done."

"There's one other person with motive. Anna Marie's birth father. Jason Jones. We're on our way to see him now." They hadn't called because she and Derrick wanted the element of surprise on their side.

Another call beeped in, and Ellie transferred over. "Detective Reeves."

"It's Bryce," the sheriff said. "Ellie, they called from the hospital. Caitlin O'Connor has regained consciousness."

Finally, a break. "Get over there now and talk to her. Maybe she can identify her attacker."

ONE HUNDRED TWELVE

BLUFF COUNTY HOSPITAL

Digger knew it was risky, but he had to see Caitlin O'Connor. She was the only person in the world who'd ever believed in him.

Even if he went back to prison, at least he'd have that.

He'd waited until dark to come, hoping to get in and out without being noticed. He tugged his Braves cap on his head, pulled his dark rain jacket around him and entered the building. A few people sat in the waiting room, and he faced a nurse's station where a middle-aged woman with readers perched on her nose sat at a computer screen.

He glanced around quickly, but everyone seemed lost in their own business, cell phones glued to their hands, noses buried deep. A hospital staff member wheeled an elderly woman down the hall, an older man following along beside her.

Digger kept his head down as he reached the front desk.

"How can I help you, sir?"

"I need the room number for Caitlin O'Connor."

"And you are?"

"Her brother," he said, keeping his voice level. "I just got the call that she was here."

The woman peered at him for a moment, then consulted her computer and responded, "Room 634." She handed him a label with the word "Visitor" on it and he stuck it to his jacket and headed down the hall to the elevator. The hall was empty, and he rode the elevator up to the sixth floor, carefully keeping his face at an angle to avoid the security cameras.

The scent of medicine and cleaning supplies swirled through the corridors, voices sounded from the rooms, and a metal cart rattled as a staff member dispensed medication.

Crying echoed from another room and he saw a doctor talking to a couple, obviously delivering bad news.

He passed them, then swung around the corner and froze. An officer was stationed outside room 634.

He froze, breathing heavily. He should have foreseen that the police would guard her in case her attacker showed.

Footsteps sounded behind him, and he pivoted to head back to the elevator, but a uniformed man stood in front of him flashing his badge, one hand on his weapon. He pulled hand-cuffs from his belt, sparking déjà vu. How many times had those metal rings closed around his wrist? Just the sound made his skin crawl.

"Sheriff Waters," the man said brusquely. "Mr. Woodruff, put your hands behind your back. You're coming with me to the police station."

Darnell wanted to run, to escape the inevitable. More bars. Another cell. Accusations.

But the guard at Caitlin's door stood and walked toward him, and he was sandwiched between the cops. Dammit to hell. Running would only make him look guilty. Or get him shot.

So he ducked his head and let the sheriff cuff him.

"Watch him," the sheriff told the deputy at the door. "I need to talk to Ms. O'Connor for a minute."

The sheriff disappeared into the room and Digger held his

breath. If she was awake, maybe she'd tell the sheriff that he hadn't attacked her.

ONE HUNDRED THIRTEEN
LILY LAKE

Ellie sped up, her tires chugging around the winding road until they reached the Jones property, a large white farmhouse on several acres surrounded by nature and woods and a nice view of Lily Lake, which was known for the calla lilies growing in the fields nearby.

Derrick consulted his tablet where he'd been researching the couple. "Damn. Jason Jones is dead."

"What happened?" Ellie asked.

"A car crash not long before Anna Marie died."

"Then he's not the killer," Ellie said, shoulders knotting.

"He's married to a woman named Judy. Let's see what she has to say about the past."

As Ellie reached the house, she noticed a Ford SUV in the drive and a riding lawn mower parked beneath an open shed.

The rain finally eased up, and she and Derrick followed the walkway to the front door. The wraparound porch looked inviting with rocking chairs and a porch swing. Derrick rang the doorbell and Ellie watched rain drip from the awning as they waited.

"You know it's possible that even if Jason Jones learned Anna Marie was his, his wife might not know," Ellie said.

"True," Derrick agreed. "But it also gives her motive for murder."

The door opened, and a tall, thin, dark-haired woman who looked to be in her early fifties answered, a flowered apron around her waist.

"Judy Jones?" Ellie asked.

She wiped her hands on her apron. "Yes. How can I help you?"

Ellie identified herself and Derrick. "We need to ask you some questions about a current case we're working."

Frown lines fanned beside her eyes, and her knuckles reddened as she clenched the door jamb. "What case is that?"

"The murder of two teens who disappeared in Crooked Creek," Ellie explained. "We think they may be related to the murder of Anna Marie Landrum fifteen years ago."

The color drained from the woman's face, but she stepped aside and waved them in.

They followed her through a foyer to a cozy kitchen. The scent of cinnamon and sugar filled the room, and Ellie spotted the freshly baked cinnamon rolls that looked as if they'd just been pulled from the oven.

"You like to bake," she said, gesturing to the oven.

The woman nodded. "It's a hobby. Would you like one?"

Ellie's mouth was watering, but she declined. "Thank you, we just want to talk."

Judy sank into a kitchen chair, and they joined her. A second later, she looked up at them with disbelief. "I don't understand. I thought that girl's brother was in prison for killing her."

"You must not have seen the news," Derrick said. "He was

released through the Innocence Project and new evidence has come to light. He may be innocent."

Her hand trembled as she ran her fingers over the table edge. "What's this got to do with me?"

Ellie studied her, wondering if she knew the truth. The only way to find out was to ask. "Mrs. Jones, were you aware your husband was Anna Marie's biological father?"

Her eyes widened then she bit her lower lip and gave a small nod. "He found out a couple of weeks before she died. Mary Landrum came to see him. She said Anna Marie was sick and needed a kidney transplant. Jason was shocked. He never knew anything about the girl."

"How did he react?" Ellie asked.

Mrs. Jones twisted her apron between her fingers. "At first, he was angry that she'd kept his daughter from him. But then it settled in, and he wanted to get to know her."

"And he told you about her at the time?" Derrick asked.

She nodded. "Yes. We... had that kind of marriage. We didn't keep secrets."

"Are you sure about that?"

"Yes, and before you ask, he hadn't seen Mary in years. They had a one-night stand before we got together. She met her husband after they broke up and they hadn't communicated in years."

"How did you feel about the revelation?" Ellie asked.

Another rock of her head. "Naturally I was surprised. But Jason was hurting and the girl needed help. I told him if he wanted her in our lives, we'd make it work." She exhaled.

"How did he take the news that she needed the kidney transplant?" Ellie asked.

"He was upset at first, said he couldn't have just discovered he had a daughter only to lose her. So... he planned to donate if he was a match." She pulled a tissue from her apron pocket and dabbed at her eyes. "In fact, he was on his way to get tested when he had the accident that killed him." She sniffed. "My son was in the car with him. He was devastated over his father's death."

Ellie went still, considering the possibilities. What if this woman hadn't wanted the truth to be revealed? When she'd learned about Anna Marie, she could have confronted Mary Landrum and killed her to keep her from ruining her family.

And perhaps Anna Marie had been next.

"You weren't with your husband and son when he had the accident?" Ellie asked.

"No," Mrs. Jones said. "I was home."

"What caused the accident?"

"A deer ran out in front of the car and Jason swerved to the side of the road to avoid hitting it. He lost control, hit a tree and landed in a ravine."

"But your son survived?"

She stood, picked up a photo of her and her husband and a little boy. "Yes. Artie managed to jump from the vehicle just before it crashed." She pressed the picture to her heart. "Thank God, I couldn't have stood it if I'd lost both of them."

Ellie gave her a sympathetic smile. "And this happened before Anna Marie died?"

"Yes, a couple of weeks. I remember because it happened just before Homecoming."

The timing raised suspicions. Was Homecoming a trigger for this killer?

Derrick had walked over to the fireplace mantle and was

studying the family photographs. He indicated a photograph of the Jones family when the son was a teen.

"This is your son?" he asked.

"Yes," Mrs. Jones said quietly.

The woman's statement about the school echoed in Ellie's head, ringing alarm bells. "Your son attended the same high school as Anna Marie?"

Mrs. Jones nodded.

"Did he know her?" Ellie asked.

"He knew who she was, but they didn't hang out together."

More questions ticked through Ellie's mind. "Did he know Anna Marie was your husband's daughter?"

Mrs. Jones pressed a fist to her mouth. "No, we never told Artie. And after Anna Marie's brother killed her, I didn't see the need."

Ellie shifted as she remembered Cord's description of the treehouse he'd found on the Landrum property where Mrs. Landrum was buried. The initials AML and AJ had been carved in the tree.

"Where's your son now?" Ellie asked.

Mrs. Jones checked the clock. "Home, I imagine. He teaches computer science and technology at Red Clay Mountain High."

ONE HUNDRED FIFTEEN
RED CLAY MOUNTAIN

He spat curse words as he dragged Ruby back into the building. "Damn you, Ruby, I didn't want to kill you." He felt for her the most. But he should have finished her before. For some reason, he'd stopped himself.

Now she would have to die like Kelsey. And so would Bianca. Her parents had gotten the picture he'd sent and were probably already accepting that she was dead.

"Please let me go!" Ruby screamed. "Please, I won't tell."

She still didn't know who he was. If he let her live, she couldn't identify him. But that would be risky.

You've come too far to stop now.

She groaned and screamed as he hauled her down the steps toward the basement. This time, there would be no way out for her. She was already weak and tired and probably dehydrated. He could even leave her here and she'd die on her own and no one would ever find her. Then her body would lie in the place he and Anna Marie had used as their secret meeting spot.

Her sobs echoed off the concrete as he pulled her by her legs and they made it to the landing. The muscles in his arms bunched and strained as he hauled her down the hallway by her feet. The walls were dank and wet from where the rainwater was seeping in. The creek was predicted to flood and would soon drown her.

She groaned again as he shoved her into a corner and tied her to a pole.

His cell phone buzzed as he made it back up the steps. His mother. Gritting his teeth, he ran out to his car, ignoring her. He'd finish here then be back at home within the hour. Then he'd call her.

Pulse hammering, he ran outside to get Bianca from the trunk of his car.

He had no qualms about that girl dying.

ONE HUNDRED SIXTEEN
BOULDER CREEK

"Are you thinking the same thing I'm thinking?" Ellie asked as she entered Arthur Jones's address into her GPS. They'd already called the high school and he'd left for the day.

"That it's too coincidental that Artie was in the car with his father when he was on his way to get tested as a donor match for his illegitimate daughter? And that now he teaches high school at the same school where three of our missing girls are enrolled?"

Ellie nodded, switching on her wipers again as another cloud opened up.

"Some teachers confiscate their students' phones when they enter the classroom," Derrick said. "Jones had access to the girls' cell phones and could easily have gotten their parents' phone numbers."

Suddenly, the wind gusts picked up, ripped a thin pine from the damp ground and hurled it across the road. She hit the brakes and skidded, steering to the right to avoid the tree then screeched to a stop behind the eighteen-wheeler in front of her who lost control on the wet pavement. He swerved, brakes squealing as he jack-knifed, blocking her way.

Derrick grabbed his rain jacket and flashlight, jumped out and went to check on the driver.

Ellie flipped on her emergency flashers to warn approaching cars and turned her Jeep the opposite direction on the narrow road, knowing she'd have to find an alternative route to Jones's house.

Grabbing her phone from her belt, she called 9-1-1 for assistance.

"9-1-1, how can I help you?"

"This is Detective Ellie Reeves of the Crooked Creek Police Department. Accident on Deer Crest Road just south of Red Clay Mountain High near Boulder Creek. Request ambulance, tow truck and assistance."

In her headlights, she saw Derrick climbing onto the driver's side to open his door. She held her breath, praying it wasn't a fatality as the dispatch operator did her job. Rain began to pummel the windshield as Derrick pulled the driver through the window. They dropped to the ground and Derrick helped the man toward the bridge overhang.

Five minutes later, sirens wailed and the rescue teams appeared and took over.

Derrick ran back to the Jeep and jumped inside, water dripping from his soaked hair and jacket. "Driver's okay," he said. "Just banged up from the impact."

"We have to find an alternative route to Artie Jones's house," Ellie said, referring to her GPS for guidance.

She flipped on the radio for the news in case they detailed other areas that might cause potential traffic problems and heard there were downed trees everywhere. The weather report burst in, "This is Cara Soronto, your local meteorologist with a dismal report, folks. A heavy storm system is blowing in from the south and moving up the eastern coast of Georgia all the way north to Chattanooga. At this point, we're already inches above the average rainfall for this time of year and are expecting six more inches in the next twenty-four hours. There are flood warnings all over the state, including Crooked Creek, Stony Gap, Red River Rock and Red Clay Mountain. A wind and rain advisory is in effect, and we're cautioning everyone to please stay off the roads. There have been several reported accidents, including two fatalities."

The meteorologist paused for a beat and Ellie clenched the steering wheel as she pulled past the ambulance and tow truck and headed northeast toward the alternative route the GPS suggested.

"With the heavy accumulation of rain, grounds are saturated, trees are falling and there is a chance of a mudslide on Red Clay Mountain," Cara continued. "The mudslide five years ago destroyed half of the area and took over twenty lives. Again, folks, please stay home and be safe."

She signed off and Ellie cursed at the moonless night sky. An occasional streak of lightning lit the asphalt. The alternative route was all side roads, narrow and winding through the mountain. With visibility so poor, she had to drive at a snail's pace. Between the accident and weather, it took over an hour for them to reach the turnoff for the back road onto the street leading to Artie Jones's house.

Her headlights fought to add light through the downpour, but she plowed up the hill to an older ranch that was shrouded in trees.

"Good grief," she muttered. "That's Judy Jones's car."

"She beat us here to warn her son we were coming," Derrick said.

ONE HUNDRED SEVENTEEN
BOULDER CREEK

Ellie killed the headlights, pulled between a section of trees and parked, her instincts on alert.

She and Derrick checked their weapons in tandem, then slipped from the Jeep. Slowly, they eased past the bushes and up to the house, scanning the property and then the front windows. The force of the rain rattled the glass, the shutters nearly being ripped from the house, the sound of the storm drowning out their approach.

Derrick motioned that he'd go around back, and Ellie signaled her understanding then inched up the steps. When she reached the porch landing, she spotted Jones pacing the kitchen, his mother slinging her arms out and screaming at him.

Ellie texted Derrick.

Ellie: *Mother and son arguing. Going in.*

Derrick: *Coming in the rear.*

Easing closer, she tried the doorknob and the door

screeched open. Rain blew in as she tiptoed into the entrance, then she heard a clanging sound.

Not the wind. Jones kicked a chair.

"The police think you killed those girls," his mother cried. "You have to stop this insanity and talk to them."

"I'm not talking to the police," he snarled. "Everyone got what they deserved."

Was that a confession?

Ellie stepped forward, her hand over her holstered weapon hoping to persuade him to give himself up, not resort to more violence. "Anna Marie was only fifteen," Ellie said. "She didn't deserve to die. And Kelsey and Ruby and Bianca are only kids. They should be living their lives like normal teenagers."

Jones whirled on her, a .38 in his hand. "Anna Marie was going to ruin the family," he said, his voice shrill. "And those other girls are teases, Satan's temptation to the boys at school."

"How was Anna Marie going to ruin the family?" Ellie asked, fishing to see just how much he knew.

"She... she was my half sister," he wailed. "Everyone at school would know that Anna Marie and I were related."

His voice broke off and his mother reached toward him. "You knew about her?" she asked, surprise in her tone.

He nodded, his eyes wild with emotions. "I heard you and Dad the night he told you. Heard you arguing and then you were crying."

"Oh, Artie, I was upset at first," Mrs. Jones admitted. "But Anna Marie was sick and we agreed your father had to help her if he could."

Rage and other emotions Ellie couldn't quite define streaked his face, and the gun wobbled in his shaky hand. "Yeah, and he was going to. He even wanted me to get tested to be a donor."

Mrs. Jones gasped. "What? He asked you to do that?"

Jones's head bobbed up and down. "That's where we were going when we had the accident!"

"What happened then?" Ellie asked.

Jones shifted, running a hand over his eyes now, which looked wet with tears. "I told him no, I wouldn't do it. I couldn't."

"Why not?" Ellie asked.

"Because it was wrong," he screeched. "Everyone would *know*."

"Why would it be so bad if everyone knew you and she were related?" Mrs. Jones asked. "If you were a match and donated to her, you would have been a hero."

He shook his head wildly. "No, they'd think it was sick, that I was a perv."

"Because you and she were more than friends, weren't you?" Ellie asked. "You carved your and her initials in the tree behind her house."

His face crumpled with shame.

Mrs. Jones gasped, clutching her chest in shock.

Artie released a tortured sob. "I didn't know she was my half sister when we slept together," he protested. "I didn't know."

Mrs. Jones shook her head in denial. "Good God, Artie. What did you do?"

"Dad and I argued in the car and I tried to get him to turn around," Artie said in a trembling voice. "I didn't mean for us to crash. I just wanted him to stop and make it all go away."

Mrs. Jones stumbled backward, clenching the kitchen chair for support.

Ellie saw Derrick slowly easing down the hall toward them.

"What happened after that?" Ellie asked.

Jones sobbed out loud. "I was upset about losing Dad, and then Anna Marie's mother caught me outside her house one night at the treehouse." Tears clogged his voice. "She begged me to get tested to be a donor."

Mrs. Jones looked faint. "Please tell me you didn't kill Mary."

"I didn't mean to," he shouted. "She was going to tell Anna Marie and then she'd know what we'd done, and I had to stop her and I... pushed her and she hit her head on a rock..."

Anguish and desperation laced his voice. He loved Anna Marie, but what a shock to learn they'd had an incestual relationship. Compassion for the teenage boy mushroomed inside Ellie. Yet his shock and pain didn't justify taking lives.

"So you buried Mrs. Landrum in the woods beneath the treehouse where you used to meet Anna Marie."

He jerked his gaze to Ellie's. "I... didn't know what else to do," he shouted. "If I'd told the police, everything would have come out."

And the shame and humiliation would have been unbearable. "What about Anna Marie?" Ellie asked. "It sounds like she didn't know either, that she was just as innocent and in the dark as you."

"She was, and she loved me," he said, his voice thick.

"How did we not know about you and her?" his mother asked in a shaky voice.

"We wanted to keep it quiet," he said. "We used to meet in the basement at school after hours."

"When I thought you were at study hall," she said as if just realizing how blind she'd been to her son's actions.

"But Anna Marie discovered you were half siblings?"

His head bobbed up and down. "She called me, upset, and asked me to come over," he mumbled.

"Then what happened?" Ellie asked.

"Her father had told her she needed a donor and about my dad and me. She freaked out and started to scream while we were talking and I... felt sick inside and I... I only wanted her to be quiet."

"So you grabbed the pillow and pressed it over her face," Ellie filled in. "Just to shush her so you could talk."

He looked lost in the memory, the gun bobbing up and down. "She had to be quiet... so no one would know... but then..."

"She fought you," Ellie supplied.

He nodded, expression dazed as if he was reliving the moment. "I... loved her... I didn't mean to kill her. I didn't."

"But you framed Darnell for it? How did you do that?"

"I didn't plan to frame him. I heard footsteps and climbed out the window and he ran in. I thought he saw me but when I looked back, he was standing beside Anna Marie's bed with the pillow. I hid outside and I heard his father come in shouting."

"Darnell had taken Ambien and was confused and his father misread the situation," Ellie said.

His face crumpled. "I... guess so. They didn't get along and later, I heard Mr. Landrum told the police Digger did it."

And Artie hadn't bothered to come forward with the truth. "So you killed Kelsey and Ruby and Bianca to frame Digger and send him back to prison to safeguard your secrets."

He nodded, his eyes wild and glassy.

"But why take Ruby and Bianca? Wasn't one dead girl enough to set up Digger?"

"I had to make it look like he'd do it again and again," Artie said, as if his logic made perfect sense.

Ellie reached out her hand. "It's over now, Artie. Put down the gun and tell me where Ruby and Bianca are."

"Yes, son, it has to stop," his mother pleaded. "Please give her the gun so no one else gets hurt."

He paced the floor, waving the gun erratically. "You want me to go to jail?"

"Enough people have already died because of this," his mother said in a raw whisper.

The floor creaked as Derrick took a step forward. Jones whipped his head toward Derrick and saw Derrick's raised gun. "Put it down, Jones," Derrick ordered.

Jones grabbed his mother around the throat, yanked her in front of him and pressed the gun to her temple. "Come any closer and I'll shoot her."

Derrick lifted his gun hand in surrender. "You don't want to do that, man."

"Artie, please," his mother cried as he yanked her toward the front door.

"You don't want to hurt your mother," Ellie said softly. "She loves you."

"Tell them where the girls are," his mother pleaded. "Please, Artie, their families need to know."

"Cooperate and the DA will go easier on you," Ellie said softly.

Bellowing in rage, he shoved his mother to the floor. Ellie darted forward to help her while Derrick gave chase. A gunshot rang out just as Ellie herded the woman up against the wall for safety.

"Stay here," she hissed.

Mrs. Jones grabbed Ellie's hand. "Please don't kill him."

Ellie couldn't make promises she couldn't keep. She squeezed the woman's hand but said nothing, then pulled her weapon and crept to the front door.

Another shot rang out, and Derrick ducked behind a tree for cover, then fired at Jones, who was running for his truck.

Ellie eased onto the porch, crept down the steps and slipped to the opposite side, taking cover behind the rocks. Jones fired at Derrick again, and Ellie raised her gun and inched toward him until she was only a foot away. Then she ducked to the side of the man's car.

"It's over, Jones," she shouted. "Lower the gun and put your hands in the air!"

Instead, he fired at her but his bullet hit the ground. She had no choice. She fired back. A second later, he grunted and his body collapsed onto the muddy ground.

Ellie ran forward, gun still aimed. Blood was already pooling behind his head, his eyes staring wide in shock.

"Don't you die on me," she yelled as she started CPR. "Don't you dare die. Tell me where the girls are."

But his body convulsed, he coughed up blood and then he went limp.

ONE HUNDRED EIGHTEEN

A scream pierced the air and Ellie swung her head around to see Mrs. Jones running toward them. Derrick caught her before she could reach the body.

"You killed my son!" she screamed. "You killed him!"

Ellie wanted to bang her head against the rocks but shook Artie instead.

It was too late though. He was dead.

Emotions clogged her throat. Now he couldn't tell her where the girls were.

Derrick shielded Mrs. Jones from the sight of her son's bloody body while she cried hysterically. Ellie called the ME and an ambulance, then her boss to request an ERT. Hoping Ruby and Bianca were close by, she phoned Cord and asked him to bring a SAR team to the property.

Finally, as Mrs. Jones quieted, Derrick led her back to the front porch where she sat on the stoop, shivering and sobbing. Ellie braced herself for the woman's wrath and anguish, and walked over to her. She still had a job to do. The case wasn't over until she found Ruby and Bianca.

"You didn't have to kill him," Mrs. Jones said, her voice reeking of anger.

"Your son shot at Detective Reeves and myself," Derrick said. "I'm sorry but it was self-defense."

"He wasn't a bad boy," she whimpered. "He wasn't. He... just got..."

"Caught in a bad situation," Ellie said gently. "I realize he must have been devastated when he learned about his biological connection to Anna Marie. Bur Kelsey Tiller, Ruby Pruitt and Bianca Copenhagen had nothing to do with that."

"I... wish I'd known he heard us, or that he was seeing Anna Marie," she said, her voice tiny. "Only I didn't. I... thought he was just distraught over losing his father."

A heartbeat passed. "I understand this is difficult but think back to the last few weeks. Has he mentioned anything to you that might have triggered suspicion?"

Her brows wrinkled. "What do you mean?"

"Did he talk to you about the girls who went missing at his school?" Ellie asked.

Mrs. Jones sniffled then looked up at Ellie. "No. But he seemed more sullen than ever. He was just never the same after his father died. And now I understand the reason."

Sirens wailed and Derrick hurried to meet the ambulance and ME.

"I'm so sorry for your loss," Ellie said, earning an accusatory glare. "But if there's anything you can tell us that will indicate where he left the girls, please tell us."

"I don't. My God, I had no idea he had it in him to kill anybody," she cried.

Ellie rubbed the woman's shoulder to soothe her. "Did he have a second home anywhere or a special place he liked to go?"

She shook her head. "Not that I know of. He lived on a teacher's salary and was pretty much a homebody."

Except he'd preyed on the very students who'd trusted him. But Ellie wasn't cruel enough to say that to this grieving mother.

Derrick stepped over. "I'm going to search the exterior of the property."

"I'll take the inside." If there was a clue in the house indicating where he'd left the girls she'd turn the house upside down to find it.

ONE HUNDRED NINETEEN

While Derrick checked the outside of the property for a place where the girls might be and waited for the ERT, Cord, and the ME, Ellie rushed inside.

She quickly swept the interior of the house, looking for a place the man could have stashed the girls. "Ruby, Bianca! Are you here?"

Heart pounding, she shouted their names over and over as she checked the pantry, then the man's bedroom and office, which were empty. One by one, she searched the closets but nothing. The house had no basement, only a small attic.

Derrick met her inside. "Nothing in the crawl space or the old shed out back. ERT and McClain are here and starting to search the property. Deputy Eastwood is comforting Mrs. Jones and Dr. Whitefeather is with the body."

"Good, I was just about to go upstairs to the attic." Derrick followed her up the stairs, which creaked with every step they took.

The door was closed. Locked. Derrick slammed his shoulder against it, but it didn't budge so he raised his foot and kicked it until the wood splintered and he created a hole large enough to reach inside and open the door.

A musty scent assaulted Ellie, the space dark and unusually chilly. She and Derrick illuminated the room with their flashlights. At first look, it appeared empty. Cobwebs hung from the rafters and up the wall and she heard mice skittering across the wood floor.

She listened for the sound of one of the girls crying out for help but an eerie silence enveloped her.

An old wardrobe stood in one corner and an antique trunk sat against the wall. Both were big enough to hold a person. She moved toward the trunk while Derrick crossed to the wardrobe. He jiggled the door but it was stuck and he yanked at it until it opened.

Ellie held her breath as they looked inside.

Empty.

Inhaling sharply, she reached for the latch to the trunk.

ONE HUNDRED TWENTY

Relief whooshed through Ellie at the sight of old computer science magazines inside.

"Not here," Ellie murmured on a shaky breath.

"Where the hell are they?" Derrick muttered.

"If they're in the woods, Cord will find them."

Despair threatened but they'd keep looking.

Derrick led the way back down the stairs. "Let's search his office," Ellie said. "Maybe there's a clue in there or on his computer."

As Ellie entered the small office, she surveyed the space. Wall-to-wall oak bookshelves held textbooks and reference books for computer technology including coding. On his desk, she found a laptop and stacks of files filled with copies of student assignments.

Derrick claimed the desk chair, opened the laptop and began to comb through Jones's browsing history and files.

Ellie opened double wooden doors to a free-standing cabinet, her heart racing. Dozens of student pictures, which had been cut from the school yearbook, were tacked onto the interior. A photo of Anna Marie was placed in the center, a small heart-shaped locket hanging beside it. She opened the locket and found a picture of Anna Marie and Artie when they were teenagers. The two were gazing at each other as if in love.

She had been his world, Ellie realized. Then he'd learned they were related and his happy world had been shattered.

"Look at this, Derrick. I have a feeling he's been stalking these students for a while."

Derrick walked over and studied it. "He may not have been finished."

Ellie chest's tightened as Derrick returned to the computer. She dug in the drawer and found blueprints. Curious, she spread them out in front of her and studied them. At first, she didn't understand what she was looking at but then realized it was plans for a school. Another section held schematics for the building.

Ellie narrowed her eyes. The blueprints were yellowed slightly, indicating they were years old. Not the prints for the current school. They were blueprints for the original Red Clay Mountain High.

Her breath quickened.

"Derrick," Ellie said. "Look at this. What if he took the girls to the place where he and Anna Marie fell in love? He said they used to meet in the basement of the high school."

Derrick snapped his fingers. "That would make sense. Maybe that's the reason he got a job at the new school, to keep reliving his high school days."

Ellie shivered.

"Do you know where the old school is?" Derrick asked.

"Not exactly. But Cord could probably lead us there."

She quickly called him, then tucked the blueprints under her arm and they found Williams outside.

"Jones's laptop is in his office," Derrick told Williams. "Get someone to search it and look at his financials. See if he has another property where he may have left the girls he abducted."

"Copy that," Williams said.

"Also look at any social media posts for a place he repeatedly visited," Derrick said. "Some place that had meaning to him."

"Understood," Williams agreed.

"We're heading to the original high school," Derrick told him.

Ellie stepped to the door to meet Cord, who'd jogged back to the house.

"Leave your partner here searching the woods and come with us," Ellie said. "It would make sense that Jones carried the girls to a place that was special to him. A place that reminds him of Anna Marie. And one that now haunts him."

ONE HUNDRED TWENTY-ONE
RED CLAY MOUNTAIN HIGH

Thirty minutes later, Ellie drove toward the abandoned high school, which was set in a section of Red Clay Mountain, near a ridge overlooking a deep valley. Dark storm clouds had unleashed another deluge of rain that had slowed the drive and downed branches and limbs slowed her even more.

"Looks like the school was closed the year after Anna Marie's death," Derrick said as he looked up from his tablet. "The original high school was not only flooded but a tornado tore off the roof and demolished over seventy-five percent of the building. It wasn't the first time the school was hit so it was a good thing the new one was already underway."

Dread filled Ellie as she imagined the state of the building. There would be no electricity and judging from the damage Derrick described, if the girls had survived and tried to escape, they would have trouble finding their footing and could easily fall over a ridge. Although Jones had given no indication that he'd spared them or faked those pictures.

"It's about a mile east of here." Cord pointed out a narrow path that had once been a road and she followed it until she reached the abandoned building. They attached small mics to themselves to keep in communication, pulled their flashlights and climbed from the Jeep.

Each of them panned their lights around the overgrown brush and she and Derrick followed Cord as he led them toward the mud-coated concrete structure.

"The entire right side is gone," Derrick said. "Classrooms destroyed along with the offices and gym."

"I'll search the exterior of the property," Cord offered.

Ellie nodded, and she and Derrick battled the wind and rain to a doorway that led into a section of the building still standing. With the roof partially missing, rain dribbled inside, and at least an inch of water had accumulated on the floor. Wind whistled through the cracks, the interior dark and dank, the scent of mold so strong Ellie pulled a scarf from her pocket and covered her mouth.

Derrick took the lead as they combed the corridors and checked inside the empty rooms.

"Dammit, where would he put them?" Ellie muttered.

Derrick shined his light down another hall and they followed it into what might have been a cafeteria at one time. There were still a few tables scattered around, overturned and covered in water, grime, mold and mud.

A noise jerked Ellie's attention to the stainless steel doors. She opened one side then jumped back with a shriek when two giant rats floated out. Battling claustrophobia, she followed Derrick into a large room that must have been the pantry. He pointed to steps that led downward into a basement.

As they headed down the steps, they called the girls' names, using their flashlights to light the way. When they reached the landing, they stepped into four-inch-deep water that Ellie knew held germs and probably more rats, slimy creatures and snakes.

She cringed as the cold water seeped into her boots. She hated closed spaces, hated the dark.

"I know you don't like tight spaces," Derrick said. "You can go back if you want and I'll check it out."

"No, if the girls are down here, they need both of us."

Water swished around their feet as they walked, the musty odor nearly intoxicating. They followed the tunnel until it opened up to a basement then she came to a screeching halt.

Ruby and Bianca were lying on the floor, hands and feet bound, tied to a pole, not moving.

Heath, Digger and Heath's father had not all been in the same room for fifteen years and it was awkward as hell. His father sat ramrod straight, pissed at being held and now having to confront his stepson. Digger glared at the man, his hands clenched as the captain unhandcuffed him.

Heath's breathing eased as Captain Hale relayed what Ellie had learned about the Jones family and Anna Marie. He'd brought his father and Digger into the room to tell them both at once.

"Artie Jones lived two doors down," Heath said, his memory fuzzy. He turned to Digger and his father. "Do you remember him? Did you know Anne Marie had a boyfriend?"

Digger shook his head no.

"No," Gil said. "But I remember that kid. They worked on a school project together."

"How long had you known Anna Marie was not your daughter?" Heath asked.

His father tensed. "When the doctor told us Anna Marie needed a kidney transplant, Mary told me." A muscle jumped in his cheek. "Then she left."

"Except she didn't run off," the captain said. "Jones killed her because she wanted him to get tested to be a donor match."

"Dear God. I should have looked for her harder," Gil muttered.

Heath's stomach coiled into a knot. "So Artie didn't want the truth to be exposed."

"Can't blame him for being upset," Digger said. "Must have been a blow to realize he got in bed with his own sister."

"Yeah," Heath said in a muffled tone.

Digger's jaw tightened as he looked at his stepfather. "And you believed I killed her."

Heath's father hissed, "You were holding the damn pillow."

"I was trying to save her," Digger said, his voice hard.

"You didn't even give him the benefit of the doubt," Heath said angrily. If his father hadn't condemned Digger so quickly, maybe the police would have dug deeper, looked for other suspects. And if he'd searched harder for his mother and police realized she was dead and that she hadn't intentionally abandoned them, Anna Marie might not have been murdered.

Instead, Digger's life had been destroyed.

Jones was the one who should have been locked up.

Then none of this would be happening now.

"It'll take a couple of days to sort this matter out with a judge," the captain said. "But you'll be fully exonerated, Mr. Woodruff, and can get on with your life."

Digger ran a hand over his eyes. He was obviously relieved his name would be cleared. But he'd gotten a raw deal. He'd lost fifteen years, years when he could have built a career, had a family. Been part of Heath's.

Resentment ate at Heath. He couldn't imagine how Digger must feel. He would essentially be building a life from scratch at age thirty-one.

He vowed to help him any way he could.

Ellie and Derrick raced over to the girls, who were lying on white sheets on the ground, the white teddy bears tucked beside them. They looked so peaceful, as if they were sleeping, eyes closed, bodies still.

Cold fear washed through her as she and Derrick knelt to check for a pulse. She pressed two fingers to Ruby's neck and held her breath while she waited. Derrick stooped down beside Bianca and did the same.

Tense seconds passed. A minute. Two. It felt like a hundred.

Finally, Ellie felt a pulse. Faint and thready. "Ruby's alive," Ellie said, her throat thick with emotions. She noticed a rag on the ground and sniffed it. "He may have chloroformed them."

"Bianca's breathing, too," Derrick said.

The sound of rainwater trickling down the walls of the tunnel echoed in the cavern-like space. Then a gushing sound and Ellie looked over to see water pouring in through an opening above.

She shook Ruby, brushed her hair from her face and

straightened her glasses. "Hey, sweetie, it's the police. Wake up so we can get out of here."

"Come on, Bianca," Derrick said. "We need to move."

Ellie radioed Cord. Static rattled over the mic but his voice finally came through. "McClain."

"We found the girls. They're alive."

"Where are you?"

"There's a basement and tunnel below the school. We need ambulances."

Thunder popped over the line and Ellie heard the rain hammering down.

"Dammit, Ellie, we need to get them out of here," Derrick shouted. "This place is flooding."

Panic clawed at Ellie as she hurried to untie Ruby. He was right. Water was pouring in, accumulating. Suddenly a loud crash jerked her eyes back to the mouth of the tunnel and the ceiling crashed down. Mud and water filled the doorway. Oh, God, they were about to be trapped.

"It's flooding fast," Ellie told Cord. "We can't go back the way we came in. Look at the schematics for the building and see if there's another exit."

"Copy that," Cord said.

Ellie finished untying Ruby while Derrick freed Bianca. Then Ellie cupped water in her hand and trickled it over Ruby's forehead. "Wake up, honey. We need to hurry."

Derrick did the same with Bianca, the two of them repeating the ritual. Seconds bled into minutes. Water continued to flood the ground. It was cold and up to Ellie's knees now, soaking into her boots. Her feet were tingling, starting to feel numb.

Derrick examined the rocky wall and stared up at the hole where the water was pouring in.

Ruby started to stir, and Ellie squeezed her hand. "That's it, honey. Open your eyes for me."

Suddenly Ruby woke with a start. Her eyes widened, her mouth gaping open in a scream. Bianca came to a second later.

"Shh, it's okay," Ellie told them. "We're here to help."

ONE HUNDRED TWENTY-FOUR

Cord raced to the Jeep and studied the blueprints and schematics. Seconds later, he spotted the opening to the underground tunnel Ellie had mentioned.

Because the school had been built on Red Clay Mountain and the area was known for tornados, they'd built a safe zone for the students to shelter in case one struck. Unfortunately, sections of it had collapsed and were not accessible.

But the engineer had included an exit for emergency purposes. He spoke to Ellie through the mic. "El, there's an emergency exit at the south end of the tunnel. See if you can get to it. I'll find it and come in and help with the girls."

"Thanks. We'll head that way now."

Rain slashed the muddy ground and pummeled his face as he hurried toward the exit. Mud sucked at his feet as he jogged past the remains of the building, then hiked onto the trail behind the school, following the map.

When he reached the boulder marking the exit, frustration bolted through him. Brush, tree branches and mud blocked the opening.

Cursing, he pulled his phone and called Milo to help. "Ellie found the girls but they're trapped in an underground tunnel. Bring equipment. We have to dig them out."

ONE HUNDRED TWENTY-FIVE

"What happened?" Ruby asked as she gulped for a breath. "Where are we?"

Bianca looked around at the water with a horrified expression. "How did we get here?"

"You don't remember?" Ellie asked as she helped Ruby stand.

Ruby shook her head, shivering. "I... someone grabbed me behind my trailer."

"I went to the school to see Mitch," Bianca said in a haunted whisper. "But someone attacked me behind the bleachers."

Ellie glanced around, felt the cold as more water poured through. It was almost waist-high now.

"We'll explain everything later. But we have to get out of here now."

Cord's voice returned. "There's an exit south of where you are but it's blocked. Get to it and we'll be there with equipment to dig you out."

"I... I'm scared," Ruby screeched.

"Me, too," Bianca cried.

"I know," Ellie assured them, fighting her own terror. "But there's a rescue team here to help us."

"Lead the way, Derrick," Ellie said. "I'll bring up the rear with Bianca."

Ellie and Bianca fell in line behind Derrick as he helped Ruby, who seemed to be steadier than Bianca. The flooring was slippery with mud and rain and Bianca stumbled and went under, flailing. "Help me! I can't swim!"

"Keep going," Ellie shouted to Derrick and Ruby. "I'll get her."

She caught Bianca's arm and yanked her back to the surface, but the girl was screaming and hysterical, fighting her. "I don't want to drown!"

"You're not going to," Ellie said, trying to hold Bianca up. "But you have to stop fighting me and hang on to me."

The water was chest-deep now and rising, the walls closing around Ellie.

Derrick's shout echoed from ahead, his voice booming off the concrete walls. By the time she and Bianca reached him, he was staring at a blank wall.

"It's closed up with mud and debris," he said, his voice thick. "What do we do now?"

"Cord is here," Ellie said. "He'll get us out."

ONE HUNDRED TWENTY-SIX

Cord's pulse pounded with fear. Ellie was down there, trapped, and the place was flooding fast. If it kept pouring like this, there'd be a damn mudslide and everyone might die.

Milo and another SAR team member named Chase showed up along with Deputy Landrum and his brother, Digger.

"We're here to help," Landrum said.

Cord glanced at Digger and Landrum gave Cord a challenging look. "He's in the clear now. You need hands, we've got them."

He was right. They needed all the manpower they could get. "Then let's get to work. We have to clear the opening."

Milo and Chase handed out gloves and shovels and the men began digging. Sweat blended with rain, streaming down Cord's face as they worked.

"How many are there?" Milo asked.

"Detective Reeves, Agent Fox and the two teens. They're alive."

Relieved surprise flashed in Landrum's eyes and Digger's face, and they began to dig faster, pulling away brush, tree limbs and tossing them aside.

Thunder crackled and lightning struck a tree in the distance. The raging water washed debris and mud around them. They worked faster, sweating with their efforts as the storm intensified.

ONE HUNDRED TWENTY-SEVEN

Derrick frantically dug away mud from the opening. Bianca was so hysterical that Ruby consoled her, the two of them rocking back and forth as the water rose.

Keeping an eye on them, Ellie helped Derrick tear away mud with their fingers.

"I hear shouts," Derrick said. "Someone's coming for us."

"Tread water," Ellie told the girls.

Bianca cried out in fear. "We're going to die!"

Ellie slung mud away, her legs and arms aching. "Hold on to the wall," she yelled at Bianca.

Bianca reached for it but slipped under. Ellie started back to her but Ruby swam to her, grabbed her and dragged her up to the surface. "We're going to get out of here," Ruby told the terrified girl.

"Hang on, Bianca!" Ellie shouted.

"I see light!" Derrick shouted.

"Ellie?" Cord's voice. He was coming for them.

"Help's here," Ellie assured the girls.

Minutes passed as she heard the men digging outside. The

water was neck-deep now. The opening grew larger. Suddenly Cord was there.

"Come on," Derrick told the girls.

Ellie raced back to Bianca and grabbed her while Ruby swam to Derrick, and he helped her through the opening.

"Ruby's clear," Cord yelled. Ellie swam with Bianca to Derrick so he could lift her into the opening.

Muddy water swirled around Ellie. Something tangled around her leg tugging her under. A snake? Vines?

"Come on, Ellie!" Derrick yelled.

"My leg's caught on something." Ellie dove under and saw the vine wrapped around her ankle. The force of the water gushing in wrenched it tighter.

A second later, she felt Derrick under water, pushing her up. She yanked her leg to free herself but couldn't. Panic seized her. Her lungs begged for air. She held her breath, struggling to surface.

Derrick worked, using his knife to cut the vine, then he grabbed her arm and together they pushed to the surface. Panting for a breath, she wiped soggy debris from her face as Derrick dragged her to the exit.

Cord reached down and pulled her through the opening, then Derrick followed. Ruby and Bianca were hovering nearby, soaked and shaking.

Medics were already on scene and raced to help the girls into the ambulance and out of the downpour.

Cord hauled her into his arms. "You scared the hell out of me. Are you okay, El?"

She gasped for a breath as he wrapped his arms around her and ushered her to the medics.

ONE HUNDRED TWENTY-EIGHT
BLUFF COUNTY HOSPITAL

The girls were rushed to the hospital with Ellie by their sides. Ruby's mother arrived with Shondra by her side and the Copenhagens rushed in. Tears of joy flowed as the families were reunited. June ran in with her grandmother and dashed to Ruby, the two of them hugging and crying.

When June pulled away, Ruby's mother hugged her daughter hard. "I'm sorry for not being a better mother. I... I'm going to AA, honey. I promise to work the program."

"I love you, Mom," Ruby whispered.

Shondra leaned over and whispered to Ellie, "DFACS got involved. The social worker warned Billy Jean if she didn't get sober, they'd put Ruby in foster care. June's grandmother agreed to let Ruby live with her and June until Billy Jean finishes treatment and gets back on her feet."

Ellie hugged Shondra. "Thanks so much."

The Copenhagens looked shell-shocked as they stood by Bianca. "They... saved me," Bianca cried. "Ruby did... I don't know why, not after what I did."

"Thank you," Mrs. Copenhagen said to Ruby, her voice a pained whisper. "And thank you, Detective."

"I'm just glad they're safe now," Ellie said. She just wished she could have saved Kelsey.

"You need to be examined," Cord told Ellie.

Ellie shook her head. "I have a call to make first."

She walked over to a quiet spot in the waiting room and phoned the Tillers. Tension knotted every cell in her body as they put her on speaker. "I wanted to let you know that we found the man who murdered your daughter."

A heartbeat of silence passed, then Mrs. Tiller's shaky cries echoed back.

"Who did it and where is he?" Mr. Tiller asked.

"He was Kelsey's computer teacher, Arthur Jones," Ellie said. "And he's dead."

"Why would he kill Kelsey?" the man asked.

Ellie sank onto one of the chairs, her lungs screaming for air as she told them.

ONE HUNDRED TWENTY-NINE
CROOKED CREEK POLICE STATION

Tuesday

Ellie slept like the dead that night, grateful Ruby and Bianca and June were safe now.

But first thing the next morning, she drove to the station to meet Angelica and her cameraman for a press conference. The sheriff had texted her that he'd talked to Caitlin and she identified her attacker as Jones.

Deputy Landrum met her when she entered. "Digger went to see Caitlin last night to thank her for all she did for him."

"Good," Ellie said. "I hope you and he can work things out."

"I'll help him all I can," he said. "And thank you, Detective for helping to clear him."

Ellie sighed. "I was just doing my job." Under the circumstances she decided to let the fact that he'd withheld information from her go. In his place, she might have done the same thing.

Cord walked in looking tired and troubled. The night before he'd offered to drive her to her house, but she'd told him to go home to Lola. Derrick had left the hospital, quiet and almost sullen. She'd texted him about the press conference and expected him to arrive any minute.

"Are you okay?" Cord asked.

She averted her eyes, afraid he'd seen the pain and guilt overwhelming her. "I'm fine. I need to give the press conference. Thanks for your help, Cord. I don't know what we would have done without you."

"Glad I was there." He brushed his fingers over her cheek. "And that you're okay."

A shiver went through Ellie. She wanted him to hold her, for them to be together. But an image of Lola's baby bump flashed behind her eyes and she took a step away from him.

Touching Cord right now would be too dangerous.

Derrick walked in, his face clean shaven, his eyes dark. She sensed he was putting some distance between them.

"Angelica is here," he said stiffly.

Ellie nodded and Cord and Derrick followed her to the press room.

"You did it again, Ellie," Angelica said in greeting.

Mixed emotions clogged Ellie's throat. Yes, she was happy she found the girls alive. But they never should have been taken. And Kelsey was gone.

Angelica gave the cue for Tom to start filming. "This is Angelica Gomez, Channel Five News, with Detective Ellie Reeves with news on the latest developments in the current case." She tilted the mic toward Ellie.

"Detective?"

Ellie squared her shoulders. "I'm happy to report that the two missing teens, Ruby Pruitt and Bianca Copenhagen have been found alive. They have been reunited with their families and are undergoing medical evaluations now." She paused to gather her thoughts. "We now know that Arthur Jones, the computer science and technology teacher at Red Clay Mountain High, was behind the teen abductions, the death of Kelsey

Tiller and the attempted murder of Caitlin O'Connor, who identified him to Sheriff Waters. Thankfully, Ms. O'Connor should make a full recovery." She paused, grateful for that. "Ms. O'Connor works with the Innocence Project and coordinated the release of Darnell Woodruff, who was falsely accused of the murder of his sister Anna Marie Landrum fifteen years ago. Mr. Jones was responsible for Anna Marie's death as well and Darnell Woodruff is being exonerated."

"Can you share the motive behind these crimes?" Angelica asked.

Heath tensed as he stood watching, his anguished look making Ellie's gut twist. "I'm afraid I can't reveal details at this time." And maybe never would. Sometimes the public didn't need to know all the sordid details.

Although Caitlin would probably explain in her podcast series.

She gestured to Angelica that the interview was over. Exhausted and grateful that the families could sleep better tonight, she headed out the door. The rain had slacked off, but the dark gloomy sky mirrored her mood, and her despair over Kelsey's death felt like a heavy blanket smothering her.

Maybe it was the emotional letdown from working the case, but she felt very much alone. Guilt over her failures made her even more exhausted.

"I'm heading back to Atlanta for a few days," Derrick said.

Ellie nodded, knowing he had responsibilities there. Still, she felt as if she should say more. But at the moment she was too rung out to.

"I'll see you later," Cord said, his gaze lingering on her for an awkward second.

Another nod because she was too tired to talk, and Cord left.

"You look exhausted, Detective," Captain Hale said. "Why don't you take some time off?"

Ellie had been thinking she might do that. Take a hike in the woods to clear her head.

"Thanks. I think I will."

She grabbed her keys from her office and rushed outside to her Jeep.

She imagined Cord going home to Lola, the two of them on the verge of becoming a family. And for the first time in her life, she realized she wanted more than her badge.

But once she got some rest, she knew guilt over her failures would drive her to hunt down more killers instead.

ONE HUNDRED THIRTY
THE CORNER CAFÉ

Ellie drove back to her house to pack, but her stomach was growling so she turned into the Corner Café.

The parking lot was filled with the early morning crowd although she didn't see Cord's truck in the lot. Probably better she not see him again this morning when her feelings were raw. As she entered, Maude and her hens paused in their chatter to look at her, then quickly turned their heads away. Maude was obviously still smarting from Ellie's chastising.

Tourists and families gobbled down Lola's blueberry pancakes, waffles, omelets and pastries. Lola was behind the counter, bustling to speak to her customers, her hand fluttering to her belly as if guarding her unborn child.

Ellie lifted her chin and started toward the breakfast counter when she heard Lola talking to Shondra, who sat with her girlfriend, sharing mimosas.

"Congratulations on your engagement," Lola told Shondra and her fiancée.

"We're excited," Shondra said.

"That's fabulous," Lola chirped. "Cord and I are getting married, too!"

Ellie froze, her breath catching in her throat. Cord and Lola were getting married?

Of course they are. They want to create a stable family for their child.

Lola looked up and spotted her then she smiled. "Your usual, Ellie?"

Ellie nodded, although her appetite vanished and she didn't know if she could eat. But she slid onto the stool and waited, forcing herself to remain composed. Lola returned with coffee and a to-go bag and Ellie paid for it then took the bag and left.

Outside, she tossed the food into the trash, then walked blindly to her Jeep, started the engine and sped from the parking lot.

ONE HUNDRED THIRTY-ONE

Cord waited until the morning crowd died down before stopping at the café. Lola had left half a dozen messages the night before and two this morning, saying that she had something important to show him.

Guilt nagged at him. She wanted him to move in with her. He'd turned her down before. But now... the baby needed a father.

He had to learn how to be one. Even if his heart belonged to another woman.

When he entered, a few patrons were left but his bar stool was empty, so he crossed the room and sank onto it. Lola popped out from the back with a smile.

"Hey, it's about time you got here."

"It was a long night."

"I saw the news report. Y'all found the girls."

"Yeah, they should be home by now with their families."

"Speaking of families," Lola said. "Come back to my office."

Confused, Cord followed her into the small space, filled with recipe files and photographs of her dishes displayed on a bulletin board.

Lola removed something from a manila envelope then handed it to him. Cord narrowed his eyes. It looked like an X-ray.

Lola curled her fingers around his arm. "It's a sonogram of our baby."

Cord's breath stalled as he looked down at the small dark blob on the ultrasound. Except for the head, he could hardly distinguish any features.

His gaze met hers. "Is it a boy or girl?" he said, his voice thick.

"We won't know for a few more weeks." She took his hand and pressed it over her belly. "But seeing this makes it feel so real. And I got to hear the heartbeat."

Cord's throat closed. Lola cupped his face in her hands and kissed him. It was breathy and fast and the world blurred for a moment. When she released him, she accidentally knocked the envelope off her desk and it fluttered to the floor.

He stooped to pick it up and saw the label on the outside. Baby Parks. Due Date: May 1.

May 1?

He was going to have a May baby.

Excitement burst inside him. A beat later, he looked at the date again.

He mentally calculated the months. The last time he'd been with Lola was Memorial Day weekend. Nine months from that... would be February.

His fingers tightened on the envelope. This had to be some mistake. The timing didn't fit. "Lola, the due date is not till May?"

Her eyes widened and she snatched the envelope. For a moment she simply stared at it, biting her lip. Her hand began to shake and tears filled her eyes.

"The baby isn't mine, is it?" Anger sharpened his tone as he realized she'd lied to him.

Her lower lip quivered.

"Is it mine?" he asked.

Her hand trembled as she shoved the envelope onto the desk, and he took her by the arms and forced her to look at him.

"Tell me the truth."

"I... wanted it... to be yours," she said in a choked whisper.

"Do you think I'm so stupid I wouldn't figure it out?"

"No, of course not. But I wanted it so badly. I thought if we got married, I'd tell you and when you saw the baby, you wouldn't care."

Cord released her, anger churning through him. "Wanting it doesn't make it so, Lola."

Déjà vu struck him, a reminder of Melanie's biting words after she'd gotten rid of his baby. *I'd never raise a child with a man like you.*

But Lola... She wanted his child.

That should make him feel good. Instead, he felt betrayed and overcome by a deep sense of loss he hadn't expected.

Fool, he thought as he strode out the back door. Maybe it was for the better.

But he was tired of losing everything.

He had to see Ellie.

He jumped in his truck and called her. But her phone went straight to voicemail so he drove by the police station. Ellie's Jeep was not in the parking lot, but he rushed into the station and found Agent Fox talking to Captain Hale.

"Is Ellie here?" he asked.

Derrick glanced his way, an odd expression in his eyes. "No, she's gone."

"Did she say when she'd be back? Or where she was going?"

Derrick shook his head no.

"I told her to take some time off," Captain Hale replied.

Cord scrubbed his hand over his face. Dammit. He had to

find her. Tell her the truth about how he felt. He didn't know if it would make a difference to her.

But he'd almost lost her so many times. He couldn't lose her again. This time had to be different.

A LETTER FROM RITA

Thank you so much for diving into the world I've created with Detective Ellie Reeves in *The Sleeping Girls*! If you enjoyed *The Sleeping Girls* and would like to keep up with all of my latest releases, you can sign up at the following link. Your email address will never be shared, and you can unsubscribe at any time.

www.bookouture.com/ritaherron

I'm thrilled to bring you book nine in this series, which takes you to the neighboring small town of Red Clay Mountain.

One by one, three teenagers go missing in a case that is first thought related to cyberbullying, a growing problem that can cause devastating consequences for teenage victims. But when victim number one is found dead, posed on a bed of white sheets with a white teddy bear tucked in her arm, Ellie realizes the case is much more complicated.

She's facing another serial predator. In a race against time to save the other two girls from death, clues lead Ellie to a decades-old mystery. One connected to a convicted killer who has recently been released.

I hope you enjoyed *The Sleeping Girls* as much as I enjoyed writing it. If you did, I'd appreciate it if you left a short review. As a writer, it means the world to me that you share your feedback with other readers who might be interested in Ellie's world.

I love to hear from readers so you can contact me on social media or through my website.

Thanks so much for your support. Happy Reading!

Rita

www.ritaherron.com

 facebook.com/authorritaherron

 x.com/ritaherron

instagram.com/ritaherronauthor

ACKNOWLEDGMENTS

A special thanks to Christina Demosthenous for giving me a fabulous title for this story. I miss you!

Another big thank you to my new editor, Lydia Vassar-Smith for taking over the reins on this one. Her support, feedback and guidance were invaluable.

And again, thanks to the amazing Bookouture team for another spectacular cover!

PUBLISHING TEAM

Turning a manuscript into a book requires the efforts of many people. The publishing team at Bookouture would like to acknowledge everyone who contributed to this publication.

Audio
Alba Proko
Sinead O'Connor
Melissa Tran

Commercial
Lauren Morrissette
Jil Thielen
Imogen Allport

Data and analysis
Mark Alder
Mohamed Bussuri

Editorial
Lydia Vassar-Smith
Lizzie Brien

Proofreader
Elaini Caruso